Waking Her Bear

Weres & Witches of Silver Lake
Book 8

Vella Day

On a mission to secure medicine for a friend, witch Missy Berta encounters much more than she ever bargained for. Accidentally waking a sleeping werebear, the sexy stranger spins a wild tale that Missy can hardly believe. Struggling to fathom his story, she's inexplicably drawn to his charm, his unwavering desire to protect her, and of course, to his irresistible, mouth-watering body.

Zane Barons is completely out of his element. While his skills to survive are limited in this strange realm, he's delighted to have met such a delectable and curvaceous human. She might treat him with kindness, but she seems determined to avoid spending time with him.

Hell bent on proving that she is his fated mate, Zane will do anything to make her happy—except walk away.

Beneath the calm and shimmering surface lie intrigue, power, magic, and danger.
Welcome to Silver Lake—where appearances can be deceiving, and what you see isn't truly what lies below.

Chapter One

To learn about Vella Day's other new releases, contests, and find new authors, subscribe to her newsletter and get three free books!
http://smarturl.it/o4cz93?IQid=MLite

An Unexpected Diversion (book 1 of Hidden Hills Shifters)
Bare Instincts (book 2 of Hidden Hills Shifters)
Montana Desire (book 1 of Rock Hard, Montana)

MISSY BERTA WAS in a panic as she hurried to leave work. She was in need of some specific herbs to help heal her good friend, Anna Fairchild, who was expecting her first child next month. Anna had come down with the flu, and Missy knew what she needed to do in order to help her and her baby, but only one of the two ingredients was readily available. Natalie Fremont owned the local herb store that always carried the ginger root, but she was out of Reishi mushrooms. The only place to find any was south of town near the caves. Not wanting to waste any time, Missy gathered her herb bag and rushed out of the Crystal Winds Spa.

Thankfully her mom and her cousin Teagan had told her they would cover for her while she went in search of the needed medicine. No one would ever question the fact that Anna's health came first.

Once in the car, Missy rolled down the windows to breathe in the fresh May air, willing her pulse to slow. She was confident her magic would help Anna, but only if she could find the precise ingredients.

Normally, the late spring in Tennessee was Missy's favorite time of year, but her worry over Anna's condition tainted her joy. The sunshine, the chirping birds, and the scent of new blooms usually centered her, but not today. Something else besides Anna's illness was bothering her though Missy couldn't put her finger on what that was. For some reason, she felt a sense of impending doom. The odd part was that Missy rarely had premonitions. That honor belonged to Teagan.

Once Missy approached the entrance to the path that led to the caves, she cut the engine, grabbed her canvas bag, and jumped out. She probably should have stopped at home for her hiking boots, but she'd only be climbing the hill for a short distance, so she hoped her sandals would be sufficient for the short trek. Besides, time was of the essence.

With her herb kit slung over her shoulder, she began the journey up the rocky mountain trail. By the time she reached the large field that bordered the hillside, the sense of foreboding no longer had a tight grip on her emotions.

In the past, she'd often found these mushrooms in a cave that was only a short walk along the ridgeline toward the hillside. Between the ginger, the mushrooms, and her magic, Missy was certain she could reduce Anna's flu symptoms without harming the baby.

The vista of Silver Lake never failed to stun her with its beauty, but today she didn't have the luxury of admiring the view. Finding the mushrooms was her top priority.

Near the mouth of the caves, she spotted a clump of Reishi mushrooms, and Missy mentally pumped a fist. She picked them quickly, and relief at locating these few helped to settle her nerves. Unfortunately, she needed a lot more to make the right strength potion.

Hurrying on, Missy located the three-foot wide cave entrance without any problem, but as soon as she stepped inside, a strange vibration rattled her bones. Respecting her sixth sense, she stopped and looked around. Anticipation and unease battled for her attention. Her heart beat way too fast and that was never a good thing.

"Hello? Is anyone here?" she called, her voice a little shaky.

Missy had never encountered anyone in this cave before, but it wasn't out of the realm of possibility that someone might be there. In bad weather, campers often sought refuge inside, but perhaps this summer day had brought out lovers who wanted some privacy.

When no one answered, Missy figured it was her imagination. Retrieving the flashlight from her bag, she flicked it on, expecting the tightness in her body to ease, but it didn't. Most likely, she was just worried about finding enough medicine to help her friend.

Swinging the light around, she searched for her prize, but there didn't appear to be any in the main entrance area, which meant she'd have to continue deeper into the caves. While she doubted anything bad would happen, it was always possible a wild animal that'd decided to seek the coolness of the caves would attack if scared. Fortunately, part of Missy's Wendayan powers included exuding an aura of safety that seemed to calm even the most outraged beings.

Careful not to trip on any protruding rocks, Missy did a slow grid search to make sure she didn't miss any of the sorely-needed fungi.

About a hundred feet in, she spotted what she was searching for. Aha! Luck was on her side. Thrilled that her search had been short, she squatted down and carefully pinched off the caps then placed them in a plastic bag. She'd extracted about ten of them when a growl came from deep inside the cave. From the low tone, it was most likely a bear. Damn. While a bear shifter wasn't a threat, a real bear with cubs would be.

Holding her breath in order to distinguish her heartbeat from any wild animal sounds, Missy remained still, listening for movement. Even though she detected nothing more, she decided she had collected enough mushrooms to make the potion for Anna.

Careful not to make any noise, Missy rose. While she could

probably calm even a mother bear, she didn't want to test her theory. Turning off her light so as not to attract more attention, she twisted around and headed toward the entrance. In the dark cave, she stepped on a small rock that shot out to the side, causing it to ping against the wall, just loud enough to reverberate in the quiet cave. Crap. Her muscles locked, and her breath barely eked out.

Move.

Inhaling deeply, her muscles finally engaged, and Missy scurried forward with more care this time.

"Don't leave," a deep voice sounded from behind her before she'd even had the chance to take dozen steps.

Startled, she flicked on the flashlight, and when she spun on her heel, the light landed on the man's face. What skin she could see of his face behind his untrimmed beard appeared unlined. His dark tangled hair, which brushed his broad shoulders, implied he might have just shifted. That or he was some homeless man.

He instantly lifted his hands in front of his face. "Hey."

She backed up. Missy hadn't meant to blind him, but he had startled her. She lowered the light to his chest and noticed he wasn't carrying any weapons. While that was a good thing, the fact he was naked was not.

With effort, she kept the beam above his waist, not wanting to glance at his lower half. Fearing he might do something to her, she continued to move closer to the entrance.

"Where am I?" he asked, his words coming out thick as if he'd just awoken. When he reached up and dragged his hand across his neck, his shoulders slumped.

She'd have thought the answer was obvious: he was in a cave. The confused man stepped forward while she continued her backward movement a bit faster this time, all the while keeping her light on him.

"Wait. Don't go," he pleaded. Missy halted but said nothing, her heart pounding too hard. "This is a little bit embarrassing, but I need some clothes. If you could find something for me to wear and leave it outside the cave, I'd be eternally grateful."

Really? Did he think she'd have an extra set of clothes on her—ones that might fit his large body? She then recalled a few stories her sister had told her about some embarrassing situations her mate had found himself in after shifting. Perhaps this man was merely desperate and in need of some help. "What happened to your clothes?"

"I don't know."

"What about your wallet and keys? Are they gone too?"

He glanced to the side. "Yes."

It was decision time.

Trust him or run?

ZANEDAR BARONS HAD never met someone who wasn't a shifter, which meant one thing: he was in the Earth realm. Well damn. Right now he had two choices: one was to tell this delicate creature the truth about how he'd come to be there and chance her running away, or two, he could make up a story whereby she might help him. Mentioning he was a shifter was too risky since as far as he knew, humans weren't aware of his kind.

As much as he hated to deceive anyone, he had no weapons and no way to buy anything. Basically, he was at this woman's mercy. Without her aid, the next few hours would be harder than they needed to be. Stealing wasn't his thing.

Not wanting to scare her off, Zanedar stepped backward and his right leg buckled. Had he not reached out and grasped the rough cave wall, he might have fallen. Stupid injury. Hibernating must have triggered his bear's need to conserve energy and had shut down its ability to heal him.

"What are you doing here?" she asked, with a voice as strong as a steal blade, yet light and sweet as the finest wine.

Tell the truth or lie? "I don't know exactly. My best friend just died, and I remember deciding it might be a good idea to get stinking drunk. Apparently, I was mistaken. After that, it's all a blank." He swept his hand around. "Somehow I ended up in this cave." He was rather pleased that he'd come up with that story, though much of it was true.

"I'm sorry about your friend." She continued to edge backward, but he couldn't let her leave.

"Thank you. I'm Zane… Zane Barons."

Thankfully, she stopped. "I'm Missy Berta."

He liked the rhythm of the name. He liked a lot more than that about her, but he needed to focus. Figuring out how to deal with being on Earth had to be his first priority. "Nice to meet you, Missy Berta. So do you think you can help me find some clothes? I'd hate to have to live in this cave for the rest of my life." Zane smiled, hoping to disarm her.

She lowered the beam of light so that it lit the dirt at his feet. "I guess I could ask my sister. Her husband might have something you could wear."

While doubt filled her voice, he was thrilled she was considering helping him. He was also pleased that she hadn't said her husband might have something for him, though he wasn't sure why he should care.

She's your mate, his still sleepy bear chided.

You're wrong. If he were staying, however, he wouldn't mind enjoying someone as delightful as this woman.

"Zane, are you okay?" she asked, sounding worried.

He must have been staring. It was because his body had yet to fully wake. The last thing he needed was for her to doubt his sanity. "I'm still trying to get my bearings."

That wasn't a lie. Even his bear was grumbling, trying to rouse himself.

"I understand. I said I could try to get you some clothes."

"That would be great." He'd been led to believe that most of the men here were rather small. Wearing a shirt and pants made for the average man might prove difficult, but he couldn't be too picky.

"I need to go outside to make the call," Missy said, her words hesitant, almost as if she was considering running. "Cell reception inside the cave is non-existent."

He wanted to question her about what she meant by cell reception, but that might lead to her asking him things he wasn't ready to discuss. "Okay."

When his sweet smelling savior turned around and rushed toward the light, he followed her outside, remaining a good distance behind her. All of the women he knew could shift and fight if they were scared, but human women, he was told, had no such skills.

When she finally reached the forested area and turned toward him, he couldn't help but stare at her beauty. Her skin looked to be as soft as a doe's, and the color of her hair was a rich auburn, like the leaves of fall. Missy only came up to his chest, and while she wasn't slim hipped, he had no doubt he could have picked her up with one arm. Delicate women weren't something he often encountered, but he definitely found her shape highly stimulating.

I wonder why, his snarky bear retorted.

Zane needed his inner bear to go back to sleep. The long rest must have addled his brain. *Don't even start with that mate stuff again. I could never mate with a human.*

Don't be so sure.

Zane shut out his bear as the intriguing yet feisty woman pulled out something small and rectangular from her bag. Keeping her gaze on the item, she ran her finger across the surface and then placed it to her ear.

Her eyes lit up a moment later. "Izzy, I'm so glad I got a hold of you. I need a favor," she said. "I know you'll think I'm crazy, but I was picking mushrooms in one of the caves on the south side of town for a potion I need for Anna who has the flu, when I ran into a disoriented man hiding in the caves." She lowered her voice. "He's naked. He said he lost his clothes somehow." She turned her back to him, but her voice still traveled. "I don't know if he is. No, I don't think that would be a good idea. Just listen. All I need is for you to bring me some of Rye's old clothes. Or better yet, could you send Rye and maybe even Kalan?" She glanced over her shoulder at him and ran her gaze up and down his body. "I'd say he's about six feet eight." Her eyes stopped briefly at his cock. "Um…it's quite thick. I mean he's quite muscular. Thanks." She lowered her arm and faced him, still holding the odd device in her palm.

It must have been the lighting under the canopy of trees, but he swore blue sparks shot off one of her arms when she'd looked him over as she spoke into that little box.

"Did you find some clothes?" he asked, needing to take his mind off this alluring creature. His body was slowly waking up, which was why he had to keep himself covered with his hands or turn his body to prevent her from seeing his arousal.

"Yes. My sister said she was confident she could find something to fit you. It will take her at least half an hour to get here though." Missy lowered her gaze and sucked in a breath. "Your leg is cut. Do you need help?"

The unfamiliar sympathetic tone cut straight through him. Now that he was mostly awake, he could heal the gouge that sliced him from thigh to knee, as well as the injury to his joints, but if it meant she'd stay around longer, he'd let her look at it. "I'd like that."

She opened the bag slung over her shoulder, pulled out something, and then immediately stuffed it back inside. "On second thought, I probably should wait until my sister and her husband arrive."

Damn. Zane actually had to work hard not to let his chest cave. She was afraid, but he had no idea how to let her know he'd never harm her. To think he'd been so close to having her trust.

"No problem. It doesn't even hurt." To show her he was no threat, Zane slid down to the ground to wait for her sister to arrive.

Missy leaned forward, indecision crossing her face. It was if she thought he'd just collapsed. "Are you sure you're okay?"

Zane needed to keep his lying to a minimum. "I'll be fine."

She slipped off her sweater and handed it to him. "I don't want you to catch cold."

"Thanks." Zane smiled. Clearly, she was uncomfortable with him being naked as the temperature outside wasn't all that chilly. When he placed the sweater on his lap, her shoulders relaxed. "If you want to wait someplace else for your friends, I'll just rest here." Resting was the last thing he needed right now. He certainly wasn't sleep deprived.

"They'll find me, but I do need to call another friend. I was here collecting mushrooms for a healing potion for her, and I need to let her know I'll be delayed."

Collecting herbs, coupled with her nurturing nature implied Missy was a healer. "Go ahead."

Once more she swiped a finger across the rectangular box, tapped it, and then lifted it to her ear. Zane really wanted to understand how she was able to communicate with that box to another person without wires.

"Anna, it's Missy. How are you feeling?" She glanced off to the side almost as if she was trying to decide if she should leave. "That's good. I'm calling because I got a little caught up at the caves, but I'll be there as soon as I can. Please rest. I'll see you soon."

His gaze lowered to the torch in her hand. Even though he understood its purpose, the size and shape wasn't anything he'd ever seen before. More proof kept coming his way that the life he knew was about to change.

Between the light emitting device and her fascinating communicator, he needed answers in order to decide his next course of action. Unfortunately, he had to keep his secret a little longer.

After walking about fifteen strides, Missy leaned against a tree and studied him. As long as he was in acting mode, he decided to carry his ruse a little further, mostly to see how she'd react. Zane leaned over, rubbed his scalp, and let out a slight groan, pretending as though the blow from the fight still affected him. "I think I might have hit my head before I passed out."

Missy straightened. "How long were you out for?"

He had no idea. That was the problem. "I'm unsure. Right now, everything is a bit fuzzy. I know this sounds crazy to ask, but what year is it?" She'd used the same *crazy* comment as an excuse for asking something out of the ordinary, so he thought it might work for him.

"It's 2017. What year do you think it is?"

Zane's heart nearly stopped. She had to be wrong, but to question her again would ruin things. "The same year."

Well damn. His situation was worse than he could have ever imagined.

Chapter Two

M ISSY KEPT CHECKING the time on her phone to see what was keeping Rye and Kalan. In case this man wasn't on the up and up, having the Clan's Alpha and his Beta join her would prevent a bad incident from occurring. And if he were some fugitive or criminal from another town, Kalan should be able to figure it out.

She probably should ask this newcomer if he was a shifter, but if he weren't, no telling what havoc might result. Questions would abound, and she wasn't prepared to answer them without a lot of thought. Rye and Kalan would know for sure if Zane were one of them.

She tried to get a look at his back to check for a paw print, but the man managed to keep that part of his body out of sight. It wasn't a big deal. At the moment, he didn't seem to pose any threat.

With her sweater across his lap, he was leaning back on his elbows, looking up at the sky, seemingly disinterested in her. The trees, the clouds, and the small animals had captivated him. She should be happy he was ignoring her, but his actions still seemed suspect.

It wasn't as if she was interested in the scruffy man who had drunk himself into a stupor. She was staying only because he was in need of some clothes. Once Rye provided him with some, she'd go on her way and not give him a second thought.

Liar.

Fine. Zane intrigued her. Missy glanced his way once more. His abs were flat, and his upper thighs were bodybuilder large. She let her gaze drift downward. Damn sweater blocked her view of his cock. She never should have given it to him.

Shame on me! While Missy wasn't a prude by any means, she wasn't in the habit of taking a quick peek just for a thrill—or to indulge in a one-night stand. Before she did anything risky like that, she'd have to learn a lot more about him.

In all honesty, she'd given up hope of finding that someone special. Her sister Izzy, her cousin Teagan, and many of her friends were mated. She, however, hadn't even had a date in quite some time. At a few parties she'd attended recently, Missy had overheard words like spinster, too sweet for her own good, and focused on helping people. She didn't think the last two descriptions were particularly bad, but she probably should be more aggressive when it came to men. Somehow it just wasn't in her nature to be that way.

Missy returned her attention back to the enigmatic man. "Zane, where did you say you were from?"

He shot to a sitting position. "I didn't. But I'm from..."

She waited a beat for his answer, but then his face changed from cheerful to confused. "From where?" she asked again. Oh crap. "Did you lose your memory when you hit your head?"

"I must have." He almost sounded happy.

"What is the last thing you remember?"

He glanced off to the side. "Sitting in a pub and having a drink."

"Where?"

"I can't say."

This poor man really was a lost soul, and her need to help him resurfaced. "I should see what's taking my friends so long. I'm going to the ridge to make sure they can find us. Wait here."

It wasn't so much that she feared this man, she just didn't want Rye and Kalan to have to search for them. Not only did Zane need some clothes—and soon—but he needed medical help.

As she headed back along the ridge, she wondered if Zane had arrived at the caves naked or if someone had stolen his clothes while he'd been passed out. It was possible that he'd shifted at some point, and his clothes had shredded.

Missy picked up her pace until she spotted one man, not two, coming up the path toward her. It was Rye. She waved, and when he waved back, she stopped to wait for him. Two minutes later, he reached her with an armful of clothes.

"Are you okay?" he asked. "You look a little spooked."

"I'm fine."

"I was worried about you, Missy. You shouldn't have stayed around a stranger. You don't know if he is dangerous or not."

She shook her head. "I would have sensed it if he meant me any harm."

Rye cocked a brow. "Since when does your magic extend to reading people's minds?"

She blew out a breath, not needing him to be so overprotective. "You're here now. That's all that matters."

Rye nodded. "Next time, run and get help first."

"Hopefully, there won't be a next time."

"What do you know about him?"

"Not much. He told me he was drowning his sorrows with a few drinks because his best friend had died, and the next thing he knew he'd woken up in a cave naked."

"I trust he's a shifter?"

She shrugged. "I didn't ask him."

He studied her. "Something is bothering you, or you wouldn't have suggested I come with Kalan. I did ask him by the way, but he was busy with a case and couldn't come."

"I wanted to be cautious."

"If that's true, why didn't you move to safety and then call me?"

She didn't like the grilling. "Like I said, I don't think he's a threat. He just seems to need some clothes and medical attention."

Rye's brows rose. "Where is he from?" he asked as he motioned they walk and talk.

"He doesn't remember."

"So our mystery man is a naked amnesiac?" She could hear the censure in his voice.

"Seems so." All the more reason why she shouldn't have reacted to him physically.

With a pile of clothes snug in his arms, Rye walked alongside her toward the cave. When they arrived, Zane was still sitting on the ground studying the sky. As soon as he noticed them, he jumped up, but then winced, careful not to let her sweater drop.

Missy wanted to help him, but she refrained. Rye would have a fit. "Zane, this is my sister's husband, Rye."

With some hesitation on Rye's part, the men shook hands. Rye then handed Zane some clothes. "Not sure these will fit, but it's the best I could do on such short notice." Rye smiled, but the cheer didn't reach his eyes. "I've been in this kind of situation a time or two after I was forced to shift."

Zane chuckled. "So you understand. I didn't want to mention anything about shifters to Missy since she's human."

He turned his back and pulled on the black pants that were a good two inches too short. He then rotated back around and slipped on the T-shirt that had Silver Lake Fire Department blazoned on the front. My, but it fit him well—too well in fact.

"She's more than a human," Rye said. "Missy's a Wendayan."

"Good to know," Zane said, but something about the way he hesitated told her he'd never heard of her kind.

Zane then slipped his feet into the sneakers, which looked like they barely fit. Considering Rye's feet were huge, she thought for sure there would be room to spare.

"How about coming back to town with us? I'm our Clan's Alpha. I'd like to have one of our doctors check you out to see if he can do something about that memory of yours."

Zane held up a hand. "I'm good. Really. Once I shift again, I'll heal quickly. My bear can help with my memory issues as well."

Missy stepped closer. "How can you be sure? Has this happened before?"

"I haven't lost my memory in the past, but I have been injured. I'm not sure why my bear didn't do his job this time. If I can't remember anything by tomorrow, I'll let the doc have at me."

If she'd been in Zane's position, Missy would probably do the same thing.

Rye placed a hand on Zane's shoulder. "Sounds good. How about we go to the fire station where I work? You can grab a meal and a hot shower. Maybe the food will help jar your memory."

"I'd like that. I am definitely hungry."

Rye smiled. "Great. Are you looking for a job by any chance?"

Zane stared at Rye for a moment, as if he were crazy. "I have a job. Only problem is that I don't know where it is."

"Amnesia does have that effect on a person. I'm sorry. I shouldn't have asked. I just thought you could use a helping hand while you figure things out. We have a janitorial opening. I need to ask my boss first if he'd consider you for the vacancy, but I'm pretty sure he'll say yes."

"I could use the help, but even though your offer is really kind, especially since you don't know me, I couldn't impose."

"You wouldn't be. You'd be doing us a favor. Our janitor, Victor, is in the hospital and will be out of commission for an unknown length of time. We could really use your help. Pay's not great though."

Zane grinned, and Missy's stomach fluttered.

"Then thank you. I promise I won't disappoint you."

"I'll tell him it's just until your memory returns."

Damn. She didn't need Zane hanging around longer than necessary. He was sending out a vibe that had her off kilter.

"That would be great," Zane said.

"Come on," Rye said. "Let's get you that shower."

His jaw tightened. "Sure thing."

He couldn't have forgotten what a shower was, could he? Missy's sympathy surfaced once more at the possibility.

Together, the three of them headed back down the mountain. At the bottom of the hill, Rye motioned for Zane to slide into the front seat. Instead of hopping in, Zane just stared at the truck.

"Something wrong?" Rye asked.

"No."

Was it possible he'd forgotten how to open a car door? If so, then he was worse off than she had first thought. Trying not to embarrass him, she stepped in front of him and opened it. "Climb in."

Only after Rye hopped into his side did Zane enter. He looked up at her. "Thanks for everything. Will I see you again?"

The intensity of his tone had heat racing up her face once more. "I'm sure we'll run into each other. Silver Lake is a small town." She smiled. "Take care."

Missy closed his door, and as quickly as she could, rushed off to her car. Even though the man needed a shave and a shower, she had a good feeling about him. Zane seemed like a gentle soul, and she liked that. Sure, he was a bit odd, but that could be explained by the amnesia.

Be honest. Being near him had amped up her blue sparks to the point that she had to slap them away. Fortunately, Zane hadn't seemed to notice. If he had, he probably didn't know what they represented.

Ready to help reduce Anna's flu symptoms, Missy continued down the hill. The herbs alone would do wonders, but when Missy added in her magic, she was sure to succeed.

By the time she arrived at Anna's house, Missy had been gone far longer than she'd intended. Before she rushed inside to help her friend, Missy called her mom and briefly explained what happened.

Her mother sighed. "Just so you know, my sweet girl, we will be having a conversation on the potential dangers of friending a stranger. You need to think twice about going off on your own from now on."

She restrained from telling her mom she knew what she was doing. "I could sense he wasn't a threat."

"This time, maybe. Go take care of Anna. If you have time later, come back to the store. I love you."

Missy rolled her eyes. "I love you too, Mom." Grabbing her bag with the mushrooms she'd collected and the ginger from Natalie, Missy pushed open her car door. When she reached Anna's door and knocked, her friend answered a few seconds later.

"You made it!" she said, rubbing her stomach.

Missy stepped inside. "I'm sorry I'm late. You won't believe what happened."

"Do tell." The fact Anna was animated implied she was feeling better.

"Let me fix this concoction first and then I'll tell you a strange tale."

"You have me intrigued."

"I have to admit even I'm intrigued."

Anna motioned her to the kitchen. "Go ahead and do your magic. I'll just sit on the sofa. If you can mix and talk at the same time, I'll listen."

Missy smiled. "That works."

ZANE WASN'T SURE he could pull off this ruse. The way Missy was able to communicate with her sister while being so far away from her had his mind spinning. Next was her portable light, and now Rye's transportation that was so sleek, it couldn't possibly be safe. Zane's cover would surely be blown, as he had serious doubts about his ability to adapt to this new-to-him world.

He'd almost ruined things already when he couldn't figure out how to get into the damned huge vehicle. The cars he'd seen on rare occasion had levered handles not pullout ones. Thankfully, Missy had stepped in front of him and tugged on the long slit of metal to open it. He was even more convinced it was going to take all of his concentration to remember what to do and how to do it.

When Missy hurried away, it was clear she wanted nothing more to do with him, further taking him aback. Women in his world did not reject Zanedar Barons, but apparently his lack of knowledge didn't sit well with this one.

Pushing the slight aside, he sat back and studied the vehicle's interior. Zane was struck by all the dials and displays. As much as he wanted to reach out and touch everything to see how they worked, he refrained.

Without a doubt these next few days were going to be highly challenging. Zane's main concern right now was avoiding any doctors since he could only claim amnesia for so long. The only way to pull off this deception would be with a lot of nodding and not asking too many questions.

One thing in his favor was that Zane was built more or less like a human, or rather like a shifter who looked like a human. Blending in would be easy—or so he hoped.

Rye's truck engine roared to life, and he headed down the mountain following in Missy's wake of dust. Zane worked hard not to grasp the seat. *Holy shit*, but the man was driving fast.

"Put on your seatbelt. It's the law," Rye said.

Shit. To him, a belt went around the waist, and Rye hadn't provided him with one. *Don't ask any questions.* Zane checked out Rye, noticing he had a black strap across his chest. Not wanting to run into trouble with the law, Zane studied what was hanging over his right shoulder, recognizing that it matched what was on Rye's side. Zane tugged on the strap, and to his delight, it moved. Some kind of thin metal clip was at the end. He drew it across his body and when the metal hit the second clip, it slid right in and held. Pleased with his success, Zane leaned forward to test it. Because it constrained his movement, his first instinct was to fight the pressure, but since Rye seemed so calm, Zane leaned back and tried to go with the flow.

The vehicle hit a small rut in the road and to his delight, the truck barely dipped.

"So you have no inkling where you are from?" Rye asked, sounding a bit skeptical.

"No. I keep picturing lots of trees and rocks though." That much was true, but they had cities too.

"I'm sure things will slowly come back to you. You mentioned you had a job. What did you do for a living?"

"I was a blacksmith and an artist. I love to combine iron with either wood or glass to create works of art, such as swords, wall art, or whatever someone commissions me to make." He hoped that true admission didn't make Rye wonder how he could know what he did for a living, but not where he lived or how to open a car door.

"That's cool. A fellow bear shifter owns a woodworking studio in our compound. I bet you two would have a lot in common. Brian can make anything."

"I'd like to meet him." Zane owned a great work place back home too that he was going to miss. No matter how much he wanted to return, he doubted he could. Assuming it really was 2017, he bet the building had probably been sold or torn down. His gut churned at the thought of how things would have changed in one hundred years. "Your friend is lucky."

"He is that."

The road turned from dirt to smooth, but was unlike anything Zane had ever seen. The surface was black pitch, and as soon as the rubber wheels touched the surface, the noise dropped to almost zero. At the same time, the speed of the car increased, and Zane became intrigued about how that was even possible. He refused to admit that he was a bit uncomfortable moving so swiftly.

"How do you know Missy?" Zane asked this Alpha man.

"She's my mate's sister."

Missy had told him that. Damn. Perhaps he had a brain injury after all. "She seems really nice and caring."

"Missy is the best.

Zane wanted to know more since it might give him a leg up in being able to court her. "She was picking mushrooms when I met her. I take it she's some kind of healer?"

"She is, but she's more than just someone who waves candles and gives you potions to drink. Missy uses her magical skills to heal people. She can't do surgery or anything, but when I was stabbed, even though I managed to shift, my injuries were extensive. Had it not been for her, I might not be alive today."

So this human was more than what he'd first believed. In his world, most of the witches were evil. There was no way in hell that Missy was. He would have sensed it if she had been.

For the rest of the drive, Zane said nothing as he absorbed the oddities of this town. Vehicles like Missy's and Rye's littered the sides of the street. He'd never seen so many at one time!

Another thing was that the names of the storefronts were written in colorful lights. He'd seen light bulbs, but nothing as elaborate as these. Had he really been asleep for what seemed like an eternity?

When Rye finally pulled to a stop in front of the fire station, Zane let out a breath that the truck had stopped moving. In a flash, Rye released his bondage strap and was out of the truck. Zane tugged on his, but it wouldn't budge. Damn.

A second later, Rye opened the passenger side door. "Push the button on the side to release it," Rye said.

Heat raced up Zane's face. In his world, there wasn't anything he couldn't do. He was a master at not only riding horses, but caring for them as well. His ironwork graced many homes and stores, and his fellow shifters often relied on his strength and agility to help them. Incompetence was foreign to him.

Zane looked up at Rye and smiled, hoping his expression hid his anxiety. Doing what Rye suggested, Zane pressed the red button, and instantly, the strap released. Hmm. That wasn't so hard after all.

"Thanks. I admit I'm a little scared to find out what other things I might not remember."

"Don't worry about it. In time, everything will come back to you. Come on in and I'll introduce you to the guys."

Zane already remembered everything. His problem was that he'd never been exposed to this new way of life.

"I'll speak to the Captain about that job. First though, I'll give you a quick tour." Rye entered the building and Zane followed.

As he walked in, Zane stopped in his tracks, stunned by the size and quality of the equipment. The fire trucks he remembered were red, like this one was, but the driver's seat was in the open on top of the engine, and the ladder was attached to the side. This vehicle was totally enclosed, like Rye's truck. And the ladder? Yes, it sat on top, but it was bigger than anything he'd ever seen.

"I'll show you where we eat," Rye said, interrupting his perusal.

As much as Zane wanted to check it out, he needed to go with Rye. "Great."

He followed his new friend into a huge kitchen area that contained about seven tables, implying the station must have a huge staff. The icebox against the wall was silver and very large.

"You can shower through here." Zane followed, trying to take it all in. "We have a weight room if you want to work out, though from the looks of you, you won't need to do much of that."

Zane chose to take that as a compliment. "Thanks."

"Go on in. I'll try to find something else for you to change into when you're finished with your shower. We can't have you sweeping floors in clothes that don't fit." Rye chuckled, and Zane did the same.

While people were nice where he lived—except for the demons, of course—those who lived here were more than friendly. Instantly, the image of the lovely Missy appeared. She'd been willing to take time from her chores to help him. As for Rye, never did he expect anyone to offer him a job. It was truly outstanding.

The door closed behind him, and Zane was left to himself. Storage units sat off to one side of the room, probably to keep one's clothes in. Through an open doorway sat the shower room. Finally, there was something that hadn't changed too much. Tall metal poles with showerheads filled the space. It was time to look presentable and then figure out a way to seek out Missy Berta.

Chapter Three

"WOW, THAT'S SOME story," Anna said. "This Zane guy is quite the character."

That was a good word for him. "He is odd, but remember he suffered a head trauma. I can't imagine what it would be like not to even remember where you live."

"That would be tough. Not knowing who my birth parents were was enough to drive me crazy, let alone if I'd lost all my memories."

"It is sad." Missy took over the broth she'd made with the mushrooms and ginger. "I need you to drink all of this. I've been told it tastes rather good, and the ginger will settle your stomach pretty quickly and help reduce your other flu symptoms."

Missy handed the bowl to Anna and then lit some candles and incense to help calm her. She then walked behind the sofa and placed her hands on Anna's shoulders, sending her magic through her. Once Anna finished drinking the warm broth, she placed it on the coffee table and then closed her eyes.

Waiting for sleep to overtake Anna, Missy moved across from her and sat down. Between the flu and the baby, Anna looked as if she needed a few hours rest to start the recovery process.

While Anna dozed, Missy replayed this morning's event. Anna had also commented that Missy probably shouldn't have gone to the caves alone because she wasn't a shifter who could defend herself. That wasn't quite true. Missy's ability to calm even the most ferocious beast would have given her enough time to get away—or at least given her a head start. Of course, the last time she'd encountered any kind of hostile animal had been about six years ago. And that had been a mama deer defending her newborns. Truth be told, the doe had seemed more afraid of her than Missy had been of the deer.

Anna's body slumped, and her breathing slowed. Good. The magic and the potion were taking hold. Only then did Missy allow herself to relax. She closed her eyes and pictured Zane. While she loved big, burly men, she wasn't a fan of beards or long shaggy hair. If Rye was able to get Zane the janitor's job, the chief might suggest he clean up, as image was important.

Missy debated heading back into the caves to see if Zane had left behind a wallet or a set of car keys. While he claimed nothing was there, he had been disoriented and the interior had been dark. Without a flashlight, he might have missed finding them. If he'd shifted, she should find evidence of tattered clothes. This time if she went, she'd be more aware of her surroundings.

Missy replayed the event in her mind once more, looking for inconsistencies. How had Zane ended up at the caves? No vehicle was parked at the base of the mountain, which implied he might have hiked in. But if he'd been as drunk as he claimed, scaling the mountain would have been next to impossible—unless he'd been in his bear form. Most likely someone had driven him there and then helped him to the cave, thinking he could sleep it off there. Somewhere along the way, Zane had hit his head.

In the end, she decided it would be best if she let Rye deal with him. Hopefully, in a few days when Zane's memory returned, he'd go home, and she wouldn't have to worry about him anymore.

Missy expected a shot of relief to surge through her at the thought of him leaving, but instead, a bit of sadness edged its way inside. What was that about? Sure, he had a great body and seemed to possess a rather calm demeanor, but it wasn't as if he was her fated mate. Granted, only shifters could be positive, but as a Wendayan she should have some indication. And no, it wasn't the presence of those blue sparks. Missy dismissed them as nothing more than being lonely.

Before she could dwell on her dilemma any further, Anna's front door opened, and Missy's heart hitched. It was Dalton. He rushed in, looking handsome in his sheriff's uniform. One glance at his mate and he smiled. Missy stood and motioned him toward the kitchen.

"How is she?" Dalton whispered.

"She's sleeping peacefully now. I expect the flu will be gone by tonight. She should feel like her old self by morning."

Dalton stabbed a hand over his thick hair. "I can't thank you enough, especially with all that you've been through today. Kalan told me Rye had to rescue some werebear with amnesia that you stumbled across."

There were no secrets in Silver Lake. "That's true. Other than his name, he remembers almost nothing."

"Are you sure he isn't faking it?" Dalton asked.

How could anyone forget how to open a car door? "I wondered that, but I don't think so. He seemed rather frustrated with his inability to remember and how to do things."

"I'm sure Rye will get to the bottom of it."

"I hope so—for Zane's sake."

Dalton glanced over at Anna. "I told Kalan I'd be taking off the next few hours to stay with her."

In other words, he wanted to be alone with his mate. "Let me know if Anna needs anything else."

Dalton smiled. "Will do."

Missy was pleased that the time she spent helping Zane hadn't caused any bad effects for Anna. As for her, the only side effect was that Missy was now starving.

Feeling bad that Teagan and her mom hadn't been able to have lunch out, Missy called in an order to the Silver Lake Café. By the time she arrived, the three pieces of chocolate cake were ready for pick up, along with a sandwich for herself. With the special treat in tow, she headed down Maple Avenue and hung a left on Robin's

Ridge. When she passed the fire station, she couldn't help but glance at it, wondering how Zane was faring. She didn't picture him as the janitor type, but he did seem like a person willing to do whatever it took to achieve a goal. Right now, he needed money in order to reach home.

Once she returned to the Crystal Winds Spa, Missy parked in the alley behind the store and headed inside. Thankfully, there wasn't a line of customers waiting for service. Teagan was helping one lady while Missy's mom was in the office probably doing her usual accounting.

Missy knocked softly so as not to startle her and then stepped inside. Her mom looked up and slipped off her glasses. "How did it go?"

"Good." Missy gave her a more thorough explanation about how she'd come across Zane.

"You're telling me that while you were searching for the mushrooms, a naked man stumbled out from the back of a cave claiming to have forgotten everything?"

She wished her mom didn't sound so skeptical. "Yes. He hit his head, which explains why he remembers very little."

Her mom frowned at her. "You do realize how lucky you are that he wasn't dangerous? You were all alone up there where anything could have happened."

Missy sighed. She didn't need another lecture. "Mom, I am a grown woman, and I had my cell phone with me. Trust me; if I felt he was dangerous I would have called for help. Plus, I did contact Izzy for the clothes and asked that she send Rye and Kalan to bring them. So you see, I was being smart and cautious."

Her mother raised her eyebrows, reminding her to watch her tone but then gave her a little smirk. "Was he hot?"

"Mo-om. Why would you ask that?" Sometimes Missy swore her mom's focus in life was finding someone for her to marry.

She shrugged. "It's not every day that you run into a naked man. Now that I know he isn't dangerous and that you are safe, we can talk about the good stuff."

"He's a shifter, albeit an unprepared one, who didn't have any spare clothes nearby. I think after he passed out, his bear needed him to shift in order to heal, though he didn't do a very good job since he still has a cut on his leg. I would have thought his healing animal would have helped with his memory, but apparently he failed at that too. And yes, from what I could tell under his beard, he is a good looking man." Missy got lost in remembering Zane. "I will say he has quite a body: muscular biceps, defined abs, toned thighs, and he was…" Uh, oh. She'd just spoken out loud. "Um, he had very kind eyes."

Her mom grinned, catching the slip. "So, he was completely naked when you discovered him. Was he…?"

"Oh my gosh, Mother!" Missy just stared at her wide-eyed.

"What? From the way your voice sounds, you noticed everything about him, and you're interested in him."

"Not in the least."

"Really? You just described him using words like muscular and toned."

Zane's image jumped into her mind's eye once more. "All I could see was his straggly hair and really full beard. Heck, his mustache covered most of his lips." Even with all that, he was sexy as hell, but she wouldn't tell her mom that. It made Missy wonder what he would look like all cleaned up.

"Fine. Just be careful."

"I will. I brought you a little treat since I know you wouldn't go out and leave Teagan alone." She placed the bag with her mom's dessert on her desk and left, not wanting to continue this conversation. Missy entered the main room where the customer was just leaving.

"How's Anna?" Teagan asked.

"She'll be fine with some rest. Dalton is watching her." Missy handed her the bag from the café. "I bought you some dessert as a thank you for covering for me."

"Really? That's so sweet of you." Teagan smiled as she opened the bag and withdrew the box. "I'm glad Anna will be okay. So what took you so long?"

For the third time today, Missy began with her search for the mushrooms. With each telling, a few more details surfaced that made her a bit more suspicious of the man. Perhaps it was time to do a little Internet research on amnesia.

"GOOD NEWS," RYE said as he entered the locker area carrying more clothes.

Zane had a towel wrapped around his waist and was studying how things were constructed, from the locks to the metal locker doors. He spun around to face his only friend. "Tell me."

Rye handed him another Silver Lake Fire Department T-shirt, along with a pair of pants and boots. "Try these on. They should be a better fit. My Beta, Kalan Murdoch, dropped off the pants and boots. He is a rather large bear shifter, closer to your size."

Zane tugged them on, and to his delight everything fit. "How do I look?"

"Like you could be a fireman."

Zane chuckled. "Other than dousing a campfire or two, I don't remember putting out a blaze."

"Then your new job as janitor will suit you just fine."

"So your boss gave his okay?"

"Yes. Pays only eight bucks an hour, but on short notice it might be the best you can get."

"I'm just happy to have a job."

Rye nodded. "I also called my parents. They have a guesthouse at the back of their property that's not being used right now. You can bunk there until you get on your feet. Even if you regain your memory, you'll need time to earn enough money to travel."

Zane wasn't usually one to question a person's motive, but he did wonder why Rye was being so accommodating. Zane shook his head. Right now he needed to concentrate on the present. "I can never thank you enough."

"Doing a good job will be sufficient. Once I show you what to do, look in the fridge for a bag with your name on it. I know you haven't eaten since yesterday."

Try a hundred years. "Thanks."

"Let me show you what we need you to do. How are you with a broom?"

Zane laughed. "I'm pretty damn good."

"Then you'll do just fine. Come with me."

To Zane's surprise, he was actually looking forward to being useful, even if it was only cleaning. Hard work had been his constant companion, and he wasn't happy unless he put in a full day of labor.

When they passed the kitchen, Zane was confused. "Don't you need to show me what to do in there?"

"No, the men take care of cooking and cleaning. There's a lot of downtime built into their stay, and Chief doesn't want us sitting on our asses. Most work seventy-two hours straight and then have four days off. I've negotiated more regular hours."

Perhaps being the Alpha of his Clan gave him some benefits, assuming their chief was a shifter. He had to say their boss seemed like a good guy. While Zane had never worked for anyone before, he'd want a boss who didn't tolerate slacking off.

Rye opened a door, and when he tapped the wall, the room flooded with light. How cool was that?

"I see you like our supply closet," Rye said with a chuckle.

It was the sudden infusion of light that delighted him, but he wouldn't let on. The massive amount of supplies likewise impressed him. "I am."

"Your biggest area of concern will be the bathroom. You'll have to constantly work on keeping the mold at bay. Bleach will be your best friend." Rye tapped a large white bottle.

Zane picked up a can called Pledge. "What's this for?"

"Dusting and all purpose cleaning." Rye's brows furrowed. "Are you sure you're up for the job?"

Fuck. Zane needed to remember to keep his mouth shut. "I'll have this place sparkling in no time."

"I hope so." He glanced down at his watch. "Your shift ends at six today, as does mine. I can drive you over to my parents' house and introduce you."

If more shifters from his world knew about all these things in the Earth realm, Zane bet they'd be clamoring to come. "I appreciate it."

Rye nodded and left. His comment about the Pledge had almost caused him a problem with his new job. Damn. Zane couldn't let that happen again. Cans came with instructions, and since he could read, he'd be okay.

Before he started, he found the bag with his name on it in the icebox and wolfed it down. Zane wasn't sure exactly what he was eating, but it sure tasted good. Once he finished and cleaned up, he headed back to the closet to study.

For the next half hour, he sorted the cans and bottles according to their purpose. By the time he finished, Zane was quite confident he could do this job. With a mop, bucket, and a bottle of Pine Sol, he headed to the bathroom.

From the moment he'd awoken from his long slumber, his goal had been to find food and shelter. With those two things accomplished, his new focus was to keep this job, and then figure out a way to reach out to Missy.

Missy.

During the last few minutes of his hibernation, he'd sensed something had changed in his surroundings, causing his body to react. His heart rate had increased, and then his blood began to surge through his body. Even before he awoke, his bones had cracked, and his mind had sharpened. Seconds before he regained consciousness, his bear shifted into his human form.

When he'd come to, Zane had no idea where he was or why he was in such a dark place. Only after Missy's scent permeated his body did his memory of the fight return.

Voices sounded outside the bathroom, jarring him out of his reverie. It was time to do his job. He started with the floors and then moved onto the other areas. The rhythmic movement of the mop reminded him of hammering iron, and his mind once more returned to his savior. The more he thought about it, the more he was convinced it was her presence that had caused him to wake.

Mate, mate, his inner bear urged.

Zane shook his head. *No way. I told you she's human.*

So?

All of his friends had mates who were shifters. Of course, only shifters, gods, goddesses, demons, and witches lived in his realm, and they only mated with their own kind. Given how long Zane had been hibernating, his fated mate must have already been born and was now long gone.

Damn. Zane had enough to worry about without considering the depressing concept of being alone for the rest of his life.

"Hey, are you the new janitor?" someone asked.

Zane spun around, pleased to see a rather youthful face. "I am, or at least I will be until Victor returns."

The fireman, wearing the same T-shirt as the one he wore, held out his hand. "Welcome. I'm Tanner March. I'm the new kid on the block."

New kid on the block? Zane wouldn't ask what that meant, but from his youthful appearance, he could guess. "Zane Barons."

"Zane, if you need help figuring anything out, just ask, but I can't promise I'll know the answer."

Zane smiled, but his heart was pounding. Had Rye sent this guy here because he figured something out about his secret? "I just might do that."

Chapter Four

I T HAD BEEN five days since Zane had stumbled out of his hiding place in the cave, yet Missy had not heard a word from Izzy about how he was doing. Not that Missy wanted to see him, but she was curious if his memory had returned.

Two days ago, she'd gone back to the caves and searched for something he might have left behind. Zane had been right. There weren't any torn clothes, a wallet, or keys. It was almost as if the man had dropped down from the sky. She had however found a beautifully polished burnt orange stone with a hole through it, but she figured some poor camper must have dropped it—or maybe it had belonged to the person who'd stolen Zane's clothes and possessions.

The front door to the spa opened and who should walk in but Izzy. "Hey," Missy said. "I was just thinking about you."

Her sister smiled. "I hope good thoughts."

"Always." Missy closed the cash register and rushed over to her. Even though she was six months pregnant, Izzy had barely gained any weight. Had it not been for the basketball size bump in her belly, no one would know she was carrying a little male shifter. They hugged, and the warmth seeped straight to her soul.

"I wanted to pick up some soap," Izzy said. "My skin seems to crave moisture these days."

That was probably an excuse to stop by, but Missy was thrilled to see her. "We have a new shipment of chamomile soap."

"That would be perfect."

Even though Izzy had worked in the store when she first returned from her studies in Scotland, once she started teaching, Izzy hadn't kept up with the new products.

"Here's my favorite," Missy said, picking up the package painted with lilacs. She handed it to her sister.

"I'll take it."

That was quick. "How's Logan?"

Izzy patted her stomach. "I think he waits for me to fall asleep and then starts kicking hard." She laughed. "Other than that, it's wonderful, but I am ready to have this baby. And speaking of good things happening, Rye says that Zane is doing a great job."

Missy straightened the soap display. "Good to know."

Izzy placed a hand on her shoulder. "I've stopped in a few times, but you've been with a client. How about coming over for dinner tonight so we can catch up?"

Something in her voice sounded a bit too cheerful, but Missy did enjoy spending time with her and Rye. Soon she'd be visiting the three of them, and Missy suspected her sister's attention would be on the baby. "Sure. What can I bring?"

"Nothing. I'm just making spaghetti and meatballs. It's what Logan likes to eat."

Missy chuckled. She never thought that an unborn child would care, but maybe he did. "What time?"

"How about seven? Rye gets off work at six and needs time to shower."

"I'll be there."

IT WAS JUST dinner with her sister and her mate, but for some reason, Missy felt like getting more dressed up than usual. She put on a turquoise T-shirt that had some sequins sewn on the front that was casual yet festive at the same time. To prevent her sister from razzing her for being so dolled up, she went with khaki capris and sandals.

For makeup, she brushed on a pretty shade of pale lavender eye shadow. As she picked up the eyeliner, she halted. What was she doing?

I'm hoping Zane is there.

True, but why? She was definitely not interested in such a troubled man, yet Missy had to fight her draw to him. Zane was so big and strong, however seemed so gentle and kind. She refused to allow herself to be attracted to this man, especially since his goal was to return home soon.

Missy tossed down the eyeliner and then swiped on clear lipgloss. As for her hair, she let it hang. Not even glancing in the full-length mirror attached to the back of her bedroom door, she stepped into the living room of her small two-bedroom house.

Snatching her purse and keys from the dining room table, she left. Her place might only be three streets away from her parents' home, but it still gave her the freedom a thirty-year old desired.

The scenic drive over to Rye's compound took about ten minutes. The sun was only now setting, causing light to bathe the area in pinks and yellows, and she sighed at the beauty. Before Missy had the chance to daydream about anything or anyone, she arrived at Izzy and Rye's place.

She knocked on the front door then let herself in. The moment she stepped foot into the living room, she spotted Zane, causing her heart to flutter. Then her muscles froze as she fought to compose herself. She was a bit pissed at being tricked, but it was possible Rye had brought him home after work without knowing Izzy had already invited her.

"There she is," Rye said. "Have a seat. I was just telling Zane about how you healed me after Izzy's stalker stabbed me."

She didn't want anyone to think she was some hero. "Your wolf did most of the work."

Rye waved a hand. "Not true. Sit."

Conveniently, the only seat available was on the sofa—next to Zane—which made it look more and more like a set up. While Zane had pulled his hair back with a leather thong, his beard remained ragged, hiding what she believed to be a handsome face. The best part of his attire was the snug black firemen's T-shirt that outlined his upper body well.

Missy sat down then twisted toward him. "How's your memory coming?" she asked, not sure what else to talk about.

"I'm remembering more each day."

"Great. Do you remember where you're from?" That might give her a clue as to why he appeared a bit backward.

He shook his head. "That's still a mystery, but I remember what my house looks like and who my parents and siblings are."

"You remember their names?"

"Yes."

"That's great." In the last few days, she'd researched amnesia. He'd known his name, which meant he might only be suffering from transient global amnesia. With that kind of condition, his memory should have returned within a day. Apparently, it had in part. Zane must have been able to follow instructions, like how to clean a firehouse, so why didn't he know more? "Have you seen a doctor yet?"

His smile didn't match the slight tic around his eye or his clenched fists. "No. I don't need to. I'm doing great." He faced Rye. "Right?"

Rye lifted his glass and tossed back half of it. "I have to say the firehouse has never looked so good. Zane is a hard worker; he never stops."

She liked that about a person, but she had the sense there was something in his background he was covering up. *Give the guy a break.* Most people have secrets. Missy wished she knew why it bothered her that Zane did. "I'm happy to hear it."

Izzy stood. "I forgot to get you some wine. Red or white?"

That was Izzy's way of forcing a change in subject. "Red's good."

Izzy returned a moment later with a glass for her, and Missy drank half of it. "So, Zane, where are you staying?" Missy asked, curious if he was imposing on her sister.

Once more he grinned, and her pulse rate increased. There was no reason for that reaction.

"At an amazing place. Rye's parents have a guesthouse, and they're letting me stay there."

Missy glanced over at Rye whose face remained blank. She'd been to that guesthouse. While nice, it was rather small, which made her wonder where he'd lived before his accident. The kitchen, she recalled, hadn't been updated in years. "That's terrific."

Rye set down his glass. "Zane tells me he's quite the horseman. Since you used to ride, I thought you might be willing to take him on an outing." She leveled him with a stare, but he seemed oblivious to her concern. "The Renfords have a stable of horses. I'm sure they'd be happy if their animals received some exercise."

Being around Zane unsettled her, but if Rye needed her to entertain Zane, she would. "Sure."

"Great. When is your next day off?" Zane asked.

"I have Fridays off."

"Fantastic. So do I!" He glanced over at Rye. "Can you make the arrangements?"

"I sure can. How does noon sound?"

"It's good," Zane said.

Rye nodded then turned back to her. "Maybe you can show Zane where the river meets the mountain and then head on down to the lake."

Silver Lake was only the most romantic spot in the whole town. What was he trying to do? Missy wouldn't be surprised if Mom hadn't suggested this meeting to Izzy. The two of them would have to talk.

"Sure."

A timer dinged and Izzy stood. "That will be the bread."

Missy jumped up. "I'll help."

Because the kitchen opened onto the dining room, she couldn't hide if she wanted to. Whispering wouldn't help since shifters had great hearing.

Nonetheless, she needed to find out a few things. "What can I do?" Missy asked as they both stepped into the kitchen.

"Nothing. I just need to put the spaghetti into the boiling water and dinner will be ready shortly," Izzy said.

"I'll stir the tomato sauce." It didn't matter it was simmering slowly on its own. The men began to chat about some of Rye's more spectacular fires, giving her a chance to speak with her sister. "Did you know Zane would be coming to dinner when you asked me this afternoon?"

"That's why I asked you. I didn't know what to talk to him about, but I thought you might. Besides, I think he likes you."

Missy's shoulders sank. "He's nice and all, but he's not exactly my type."

Izzy dumped the spaghetti into the boiling water and set the timer. "I'm not asking you to sleep with him—just keep him company until he gets back on his feet."

"Why me?"

"Well, I can't go horseback riding."

Izzy was being silly. "How about Blair or Molly or Chelsea?"

"Blair's slammed at work at the rehabilitation center and has little free time. Remember Molly not only waitresses at McKinnon's Pub and Pool, she attends school full time. As for Chelsea, I doubt Rye would consider fixing his little sister up with anyone. If he had his way, he'd lock her in her room for the rest of her life."

"Having an overprotective brother would suck, but if this is just a platonic date, why not Chelsea and Zane?"

Izzy laughed. "Maybe Chelsea doesn't ride."

"She's a vet tech. Of course she rides."

Izzy leaned against the counter and shrugged. "You've met Zane. Chelsea hasn't. Listen. Rye thinks Zane is a good guy, albeit a little confused about some things. Rye trusts your sixth sense about people. He figured if you didn't think Zane was on the up and up, you wouldn't have called and tried to help the guy."

Missy's mind spun. Helping someone did not mean she believed he was some kind of lost saint. "Since when did I develop a sixth sense?"

Izzy let out a sigh. "You're an empath. It's partly how you can heal people so easily. I never believed that your talent was strictly due to your ability to use your healing magic on people."

"Fine. But just this one time, okay?"

Her sister hugged her. "I promise. Just this one time. Now, how about taking the bread over to the table?"

"Will do." Missy walked into the living room. "Come sit down. Dinner's almost ready."

Zane kept his gaze on her as he stood. A bit self-conscious, Missy turned around and rushed to the table. While it sat six, she had no doubt that Izzy and Rye had conspired for her and Zane to sit next to each other. That was okay with her since she wouldn't have to watch him.

Izzy pointed to the chair across from Missy. "How about sitting here, Zane?"

Seriously? Her sister would pay. Or did she know something about this man that Missy didn't? It didn't matter. She'd try to keep an open mind.

Rye faced Izzy, and Zane sat across from Missy. Rye passed the spaghetti to Izzy first. After she served herself, she gave the bowl to Zane who took the same amount as his host. It was almost as if he wasn't sure how much he should take.

Once the food was served, everyone dug in. "So Zane, tell us about your family," Izzy said.

Missy was thankful she didn't have to keep the conversation going.

"I have two older brothers and an older sister. I had a younger brother, but he passed away recently." He cleared his throat. "My older brothers run a small general store in town."

"General store?" Missy asked. "Do you live in a rural area?"

"Yes. Besides the mountains and oceans, we have a lot of farms and ranches."

She leaned back. "Ranches mean horses, and horses need some-one to shoe them. Is that how you became a blacksmith?" Izzy had mentioned that was what Zane told Rye he did for a living.

"It is, though it's not a full time job by any means. It was why I began playing around with metal. I found that not only did I enjoy bending iron to make beautiful pieces of art, I was really good at it." He held up his hand. "But I can build shelves, metal tables, or anything else that a customer needs. Hell, recently, I made a shovel for a man."

"I've never known anyone who made shovels. I thought people went to hardware stores for them."

He smiled. "Mine are made to order."

Missy did like the fact that Zane was proud of his profession. Liking what he did for a living made a man content.

Okay, maybe there was more to this man than Missy first thought. Tomorrow, when she rode with him, she'd find out just what he was made of.

Chapter Five

ZANE WAS DYING. Okay, that might have been a slight exaggeration, but it sure felt like it. His gut was churning something fierce, and he feared he might not be able to control his shift. It didn't matter that both Rye and Izzy were shifters and that Missy knew about them, shifting during a meal at his benefactor's house would not only break furniture, he would get fur all over the food. Rye and Izzy would not be pleased. He didn't want to think about Missy's poor reaction. Zane debated excusing himself, but he couldn't come up with a good reason. Saying that being around Missy distracted him too much was not an option.

Messing up now was the last thing he needed. Zane liked his new job and wanted to keep it. Cleaning and sweeping floors in a cool environment was a total delight since most of his life had been spent heating iron over hot coals. If asked, he might have to say the best invention in the last one hundred years was air conditioning. The fast cars and wireless phones were remarkable too, but it was the cool air that really excited him.

So why was he so out of sorts tonight? It was sitting across from Missy, inhaling her scent, and not being able to touch her that was driving him crazy. At first, he thought it was her beauty that had him at a loss for words. Her soft-looking skin had the faintest hint of freckles, and her fiery hair did something to his insides. Where he came from, women were a lot taller and beefier, and most had dark brown hair. He liked that Missy was tiny, and her coloring was exciting. But that wasn't the basis for his concern. It was her alluring scent—sweet like a rose—that was driving his bear wild. If he could stop breathing, it might solve his problem.

She's your mate, his bear insisted. *Why can't you just admit that?*

Zane huffed out a laugh at that thought. His bear hadn't been able to hunt or fish in years. That had to be what caused his animal to scream for his freedom—not this charming, sexy woman.

"Why is that funny?" Missy asked.

Had she read his mind? *Holy hell.* "I don't know why I chuckled."

Her brows pinched and her eyes narrowed. Now she must think he was crazy. "You were talking about your shovels."

He'd totally forgotten. "Oh, yes. I was thinking about one request a few years back. The customer wanted the metal to look like lace. I remember laughing, saying it wouldn't be a shovel if I punched holes in the metal."

Her eyes softened. "I bet that would be beautiful."

Much of his artwork was beautiful, but this piece wouldn't have been. "What good would a shovel be if you couldn't dig with it?" he asked, curious to hear her response.

"You said you're an artist. Surely you can see that something like a lacy shovel is the definition of art. You take an ordinary object— one that is meant to do menial work—and turn it into something delicate. It's the contradiction that makes it so divine."

Missy looked up at him with such hope that he wanted to give her the world. "I've never heard anyone describe art in that manner. Thank you."

A pretty pink tinged her cheeks, and Zane decided at that moment that he had to find a way to pursue her no matter what. His body might be urging him to claim her for his own, but he could tell that Missy was not the type to accept such an advance. He needed to make her see who he really was as a man and how well he could protect her. While she seemed to respond to him on a physical level, clearly she wasn't impressed with his lack of awareness to the world around him. If he told her the truth about where he'd come from, she was sure to run. Damn. There had to be something he could do.

As much as he wanted to ask about what she liked to do, he'd save those questions for tomorrow. Having Rye suggest horseback riding had been a stroke of luck. Once she realized what an accomplished horseman he was, she might give him a chance.

WHY HAD RYE told Zane that she liked to ride? Missy couldn't remember the last time she'd even been on a horse. Sure, she'd loved to go riding as a kid, but one needed to practice in order to be able stay on the horse. Zane was supposedly this super equestrian while she was a total novice. Not that she wanted to impress him, but she didn't need Zane telling Rye that his mate's sister was a total klutz.

Missy stood in front of the mirror and shook her head. Damn. Her riding habit was way too tight. The moment she swung her leg up onto the horse, her pants would probably split. Oh, hell. Who was she trying to fool? She wasn't fifteen anymore with slim hips and no chest.

Missy tore off the old outfit, deciding that comfort was more important than style. Besides, this wasn't a date. It was an obligation to a man she respected. Missy might not be a shifter, but Rye was the Alpha of his Clan, and as such, deserved a lot of respect. The fact he treated Izzy like a queen was enough to endear him to her for life.

Already late, Missy tugged on a pair of baggy jeans along with worn sneakers. Not wanting to chance being sunburned, she tossed on a long sleeved, white stretchy top. To keep her hair out of her face, she tied it back with a green ribbon. Without checking her appearance, she dashed out of her house.

Her six-year old Saturn started on the first try and off she went. While she didn't visit Rye's parents often, she knew exactly where they lived. She would feel a little funny driving past their home to the guesthouse in back and not stop in, but if she said hi, Mrs. McKinnon would insist on fixing a cup of tea and chatting. That would make her even later for her date with Zane, and Missy prided herself on being on time. Unfortunately, her wardrobe malfunction had already caused a delay.

As she pulled past the McKinnon home, Missy debated whether she should honk to let Zane know she was there and then wait for him to come out of the house, or walk up to his door and knock. If he asked her in, it would be rude to say no, but she wasn't all that comfortable being alone with him. At least horseback riding took place outside.

Thankfully, when Missy arrived, Zane was sitting on the porch. He stood and came toward her. Uncertain if he would be able to open the car door, she jumped out and nodded to his backpack. "Hey. Whatcha got there?"

He froze for a moment as if he had to figure out what she'd said. "Mrs. McKinnon made us some lunch."

What was up with everyone trying to fix them up? Didn't they realize Zane would be gone soon? Just her luck, he'd win over her heart, and then she'd be heartbroken when he left. No, today had to be her last exposure to him. "That was really nice of her."

"She's the best."

Just as she was about to open the car door for him, he yanked it open and slid in. Before she'd even settled into her seat, he had his seatbelt fastened and was holding the backpack containing their picnic lunch on his lap. Apparently, his memory was coming back if he could do those movements, though she still wasn't convinced part of his actions weren't an act for some reason. She hoped he wasn't hiding out in Silver Lake, trying to avoid detection from the law. Knowing Rye though, he would have already had Kalan check him out.

"How often do you ride?" Zane asked as she drove down the McKinnon's drive.

"The truth? I haven't ridden in probably fifteen years." She glanced over at him to see if he'd be disappointed, never expecting a grin.

"Then I can help you. I ride more than I drive."

Missy glanced over at him. "Even when it's raining?"

"The rain washes away the dirt." Zane laughed, but she had no desire to live that primitively.

"Don't tell me you avoid running water."

He huffed out a breath. "I can see we've gotten off to a bad start. I use a shower just like everyone else."

That was good to know. "I bet at home you don't have a dishwasher though."

His eyes sparkled. "You're very astute. I don't have one. Washing for one doesn't make me need one. Besides, appliances cost money."

So he was frugal. She liked that. Given his desire to ride a horse rather than drive a car, she bet he would live off the grid if he could. Missy had run out of questions. Even if she hadn't, it would be better to keep who he was a mystery. The less she knew, the less likely she'd fall for him. His gentle ways were already dissolving her resolve to keep her distance.

Once they arrived at Renford's Farm, she cut the engine and pocketed the keys. "Ready?" she asked, trying to keep the jitters at bay.

Her big hope for the day was that she didn't make a fool of herself. If she fell, Missy would be mortified.

"I'm more than ready." Zane pushed open the door and hopped out, acting like a man in charge.

Together, they walked over to the barn where Chris Renford, the owner, was inside, brushing one of the animals. "Hey, Chris," she said.

Chris was a couple of years older than she was and a werewolf. His parents had died a few years back, and he was now in charge of running the farm.

"Hey, Missy. Haven't seen you in a while." His gaze shot to Zane. "You must be the new guy in town. I'm Chris Renford. Welcome."

Zane shook his hand. "Thanks." He nodded to the horse Chris

was brushing. "She's beautiful."

"This is Dasher. She's my favorite. This filly is fast yet gentle."

Missy liked the gentle but not the fast part. She spotted a pinto horse that looked like she might be slow. "What horses do you have for us?"

A horse whinnied in one of the stalls, and Zane immediately strode over to him. From his pocket he dug out an apple and let the animal feast on it.

"That one's a bit wild," Chris said nodding to the one Zane had taken a fancy to. "You'd be best with a mare. One that's older and gentler."

"Perfect," Missy said, pleased he didn't pressure her to ride a more temperamental horse.

The animal with Zane backed up and whinnied. "May I try him?" Zane asked.

"That stallion is a handful."

Missy wanted to have a better look at the animal. As she approached, the stallion calmed, and she smiled. She still had the touch.

Chris came over and stood next to Zane. "Rye said you were quite the equestrian. If you think you can handle him, I'd be happy for you to take Storm out. He can always use the exercise."

"I'd like that."

Chris opened the stall and led the animal out. Storm nudged Zane, and then whinnied at Missy. "I think he likes you," Zane said.

"It's my magic. I have a calming effect on beasts." Zane let out big guffaw, and heat raced up her face. "What? You don't believe me?"

He held up his hands. "Oh, I believe you all right. You just proved it to me. I need to make sure we ride side by side so the horse doesn't act up and throw me."

She smiled. "Funny."

Chris brought over a horse for Missy. "Here's Grandma."

Seriously? "I have ridden before."

"Good, because Grandma can be feisty if provoked."

She stroked the mare's flank. "She's lovely. We'll get along just fine."

Chris held Grandma's head. "Do you need help getting on?"

Even if she did, she wouldn't admit it. "I'm good."

Missy placed her left foot in the stirrup and pulled herself up. She must have misjudged her own strength, for when she swung her leg up and over, her momentum carried her too far. Hanging on, she stopped her forward progress, but then couldn't right herself immediately.

Before she managed, strong hands gently guided her onto her saddle. Embarrassed, she cleared her throat. "Thank you."

"Are you okay?" Zane acted as if she'd taken a tumble.

Missy forced a smile. "I'm good."

He patted her leg then helped Chris saddle his stallion. A minute later, Zane swung onto his horse's back with little effort. "We'll take it slow."

She nodded and walked her horse outside to a day that was sunny with just a slight breeze. Perfect. As soon as Missy smelled the loam of the earth and the fresh air, she calmed. She and Zane were just two acquaintances going for a ride. Nothing more. Rye had suggested she take the path along the river to the mountain before heading back to the lake, and that was what she planned to do.

They rode side by side at a nice pace. Had he been her typical date, he'd be trying to show off, but not Zane. The man seemed content merely to be out for a lovely outing. When they reached the riverbank about twenty minutes later, they let their horses drink their fill before heading toward the mountain. The flowers were in bloom and the trees lush.

Happy to enjoy the fresh air, they continued to where the river flowed down the mountain. Missy was totally lulled into complacency by the slow pace and beautiful scenery when suddenly her horse reared up and pawed the air. Shocked at the unexpected movement, she didn't have a chance to send out her calming thoughts to the spooked animal. Hard as she tried to hold on, Missy lost her grip and flew through the air. Her feet hit first then her butt, and finally the back of her head slammed against the ground. Stars spun and adrenaline coursed through her.

"Don't move," Zane said, holding out a palm.

How had he dismounted so quickly? "I don't think I could if I wanted to," she panted out.

Damn. This was certainly not how she wanted the day to end.

Chapter Six

Z ANE KNELT IN front of Missy and lifted her hand. To her surprise, her pulse calmed at his touch.

"You hit your head. Did you pass out at all—even for a few seconds?"

Missy tried to recreate the fall. "Everything happened so quickly, but I don't think so. I'm just shaken."

Grandma whinnied then took off at a fast trot, heading back toward the farm. "Wait! Come back here," Missy called after her.

The horse did not stop, and Missy didn't want to think about what that meant. Storm, on the other hand, seemed content to wait for the trauma to be over.

"We don't need you losing your memory too." Zane winked then ran his hands up both arms before checking out her legs. "Nothing appears to be broken. How's your head?"

Missy rubbed her neck then touched the back of her skull. Other than some dust and sticks stuck in her ponytail, she seemed to have come out okay. "I'm good. Can you help me up?"

She didn't want to chance trying to rise on her own and failing. Zane grabbed her hands, and slowly helped her to her feet. When he didn't let go, a flush raced up her face. She eased her hands from his and then brushed off the dirt from her butt. "Did you see what happened?"

"A snake crossed your path and spooked Grandma."

Just her luck. "I thought Storm would be the wild one."

"Oh, he bucked all right and actually kicked the thing. Fortunately, the snake wanted nothing to do with that fight."

Missy actually chuckled. "Smart snake."

Zane reached out and plucked something from her hair. She must have flinched because he held it out. "It's just a stick."

Normally, Missy wasn't skittish, but there was something about Zane that had her on edge. She smoothed her hair once more. "I must be a mess."

His eyes changed from dark brown to a soft hazel. "No. You're perfect."

The way he said those words had her pulse spiking again. Missy glanced away, embarrassed by the incident and his words. Needing to take a step back to put more distance between them, she tested her limbs. Thankfully, nothing was broken or severely injured. A slight headache had surfaced, but hopefully it would disappear soon.

Her stomach grumbled, and Missy pressed a hand to her gut. Not ready to deal with walking back to the farm or riding double, she pointed to a three-foot tall boulder that could seat two. "What do you say we have some lunch while we wait for Chris to bring us another horse?"

"You think he will?"

"Sure. Once Grandma trots home, he'll realize something happened."

"That would be great. How about you sit, and I'll get the food?" When Zane rubbed her arm and smiled, a blue spark shot off her hand. Damn.

Why were her sparks appearing now? It wasn't like she was sexually excited—or so she wanted to believe. Sure, he'd been helpful and even kind, but that didn't mean she was attracted to him. Blue spark indeed. Most likely she was overjoyed that her fall hadn't been worse.

Zane led his horse over to a copse of trees and tied the reins to a limb. They didn't need his horse to take off too and leave them to have to fend for themselves. An image of them stranded for a few hours came to mind. Knowing Zane, he'd wrap the picnic blanket around her shoulders and hold her tight. She quickly pushed that ridiculous thought aside. They weren't more than two miles from Chris's farm. They could walk back in less than an hour.

"Need help getting onto the rock?" Zane asked. His backpack was slung over his shoulder, and she had to say the Paul Bunyan look had its appeal.

"I'll try it myself." She liked to believe she was self-reliant. To her dismay, when Missy planted her foot on a small outcropping, her leg gave way and she slid back down.

Zane set the backpack on top, lifted her in his arms and deposited her on the slab. "If you hurt yourself anymore, I'll feel really bad." Even though there was a hint of humor in his tone, Missy believed him.

"Thanks." Zane's legs were so long, he only had to bend his knees to sit on the rock. "I'm not usually so clumsy," she said.

"You weren't clumsy at all. You didn't ask for the snake to jump out in front of your horse and spook her."

His comment made her feel a little better. Zane opened his backpack and pulled out a bag that smelled divine. "What do you have there?" she asked, craning her neck for a sneak peak.

He shrugged. "I don't know. About a half hour before you stopped over, Mrs. McKinnon knocked on my door and said she'd fixed us a picnic lunch, but she didn't say what she'd made."

Missy wouldn't be surprised if her mom hadn't made the meal and asked Rye's mother to drop it off. He pulled out a few plastic containers. One held strawberries, but she couldn't tell what was in the other ones.

Missy opened one. "Mmm, fried chicken. My favorite."

Zane smiled. "Mine too."

He set the food out along with two paper plates, plastic silverware, and a bottle of water. "I need to thank Rye's mom for this," Missy said.

"Me too." Zane was about to pick up the chicken with his fingers but then stopped. It was as if he wanted to see how she planned to handle the food.

"Fingers are okay to use," she said as she grabbed a piece of fried chicken. When she followed her comment with a smile, the tension around his eyes disappeared. Whether it was because she wasn't being totally proper or something else Missy couldn't tell. All she knew was that Zane appeared truly relaxed for the first time.

Once she took her first bite, he grabbed a chicken thigh and munched on it. Being outside, coupled with narrowly escaping a severe injury, made Missy almost high with relief. While she was enjoying the food, she didn't miss how Zane would wait for her to serve herself first before he sampled his. Perhaps he was being a gentleman, but he seemed unsure how to proceed.

"So you get a chance to ride a lot?" Missy asked.

"I do since I live in the country. Sometimes, when I want to go to the store I get on my horse and head on out."

She didn't dare ask where he tied up his horse. Parking lots didn't have hitching posts. "Does that mean you remember where you're from?"

He tossed back half the bottle of water. "Yes. I'm from a small town in North Carolina."

She refused to address the wave of disappointment. He'd be leaving soon. "Great! I bet your parents and siblings are relieved that you're okay. They must have been frantic when they didn't hear from you for a few days."

A flash of melancholy crossed his face. "Yes, they were."

"Now that your memory has returned, will you be leaving soon?" she asked. North Carolina was only one state away.

Zane leaned back on his elbows. "I'm not so sure. I like Tennessee."

That answer surprised her. "I do too. The terrain is pretty much the same as North Carolina."

He looked off to the side, as if he was trying to come up with a good reason why he wanted to stay. "That's part of it, but I told Rye that I would stay until their janitor, Victor Muñez, returns."

Zane did seem like the type of guy to honor a commitment. "That's very nice of you."

He shrugged. "Rye did me a great service when I was down and out, and I want to pay him back in kind."

It seemed like she had misjudged the man. "What about your job back home? I thought you shoed horses and made art from iron."

He smiled. "You were listening."

Well, of course she listened. "I'm interested in people."

"I like that about you."

He was good at changing the subject, but she wasn't going to let him off the hook. "Won't your clients need your services?"

His brows rose. "Are you trying to get rid of me?"

"No!" Damn. She shouldn't have been so emphatic. "I just like to consider all aspects of the situation."

Zane sat up and opened the container of strawberries. "That's smart."

"So tell me, do you have any theories about how you ended up in a cave hundreds of miles from home?"

He held up his hands. "Do you want the truth?"

"I do." The sudden crinkles around his eyes implied he would be making something up, but that was okay. "I'm game."

"Game? What are we playing?" he asked in a serious tone.

She chuckled. "I meant that I'm willing to listen to your new theory."

His mouth slowly opened. "Ah. Okay. Well, I'm not really from North Carolina. I live in a realm similar to your Earth called Cargonia. It's just a portal jump away."

She hadn't seen that coming. "Really? When I checked out the cave the other day, I didn't see a space ship."

He waved a hand. "I didn't need one. All anyone has to do is to step into the portal and a short while later, you're here!"

She was beginning to enjoy this fun side of Zane Barons. "Why would you come without any money or clothes for that matter?"

"I entered the portal without meaning to. If I had planned it, I would have been more prepared."

She laughed. "You have an answer for everything, don't you?"

"You act like you don't believe me."

"No, I do. Do you know I also came from a different realm?"

His eyes widened. "Really? Where?"

"It's called Witcheron—where only women live, and where we don't need money because we all live on a commune and share our goods."

"Witcheron? That's good. There's one problem with your scenario."

She sat up straighter. "What's that?"

"You need men to procreate."

"Well, smarty pants, it just so happens that on this realm, women can reproduce without their help. We breathe different air, and over the years have developed the ability to reproduce. It's called asexual reproduction."

Zane dropped back his head. "Well, that doesn't sound like very much fun, but I do love your imagination."

Perhaps she had been too silly, but his made up realm wasn't any better. "Tell me this. Is your portal two-way?"

His brows pinched. "What do you mean?"

"If you came here via a portal, can you go back the same way?"

He snapped his fingers. "Now why didn't I think of that? Actually, that's not how it usually works. You see, I don't have the clearance level to use the portal. It's mostly reserved for those beings who have a higher purpose—like gods."

"But you said you came through one. Don't tell me you're a god, or did you lie about that?"

"On the contrary, I'm not a god. I was sent through without my consent. You see, I was in an altercation with a very bad being who decided to shove me through one." He opened his arms. "And here I am!"

Admittedly, Zane was one of the best storytellers she'd ever met. "Do you ever write down your sci-fi ideas?"

"Sci-fi?"

Missy couldn't fathom why he pretended not to understand. "Science Fiction."

"You think my ideas are fiction, do you?"

His faked outrage was enjoyable, and she saw no reason to halt this fun. "You have to admit, your ideas are rather unique. I bet others would enjoy hearing about your homeland."

Zane shook his head. "It's probably better if you don't let on to anyone that I'm not of this world."

"Not even to Rye?"

"Especially to Rye. He might think I'm a threat to his Clan."

She'd play along. "Mum's the word."

As if that conversation had closed, he plucked a strawberry from the container, and stuck it in his mouth. "Mmm. Good." Juice dribbled out of his mouth, and he dragged the back of his hand across his lips.

Missy stuffed one in her mouth and immediately enjoyed the burst of flavor. With his gaze still on her, Zane popped a second one in his mouth, only this time he slipped it between his lips then slowly sucked it into his mouth. She had to look away. The man was trying to seduce her.

Horses' hooves broke the erotic spell, and Zane looked up. "Looks like Grandma arrived home rather quickly and brought the cavalry."

Missy didn't know whether to be happy she wouldn't have to walk the two miles to the farm or be disappointed her date was about to end.

Chris pulled to a stop. "Are you two okay?" he asked as he dismounted.

Zane slid off the rock then reached up to help her down. "We're fine. Grandma spooked when a snake darted out in front of her. Missy took a little tumble, that's all."

That was all? Hell, she could have broken her neck. To be fair, she had acted as if it wasn't a biggie. "My pride was damaged and my butt will be bruised, but other than that, I'll be okay."

"I'm glad to hear it. The old mare promises to behave, don't you Grandma?" Chris let go of her reins, and the horse lowered her head as if she was embarrassed for having thrown her.

"I appreciate you bringing her back."

"No problem. I was really worried when I saw her. Stay out as long as you like." He looked up at the sky that had turned gray. "But it looks like we're in for an afternoon shower, so be careful." With that he mounted his horse and trotted off.

Getting rained on would ruin the pleasant time they'd had after her fall. Missy moved toward Grandma and moaned.

"Are you in pain?" Zane asked.

"My muscles have tightened up, that's all." No doubt she'd be sore tomorrow. As much as she enjoyed his humor, her senses were already on overload. "If you don't mind, I'd like to head back. I could use a hot bath."

"I understand. We can return another time."

Missy managed to smile, but it was a chore. Zane Barons was a nice guy, but spending more time with him might cause problems in the future. He'd charm her, just like he had today, and then leave. After all, he had a life in North Carolina.

Zane insisted he clean up while she rested. In less than a minute, he'd packed up, filling the backpack with their leftover food. "Need help getting onto the horse?" he asked.

"Let me try mounting her myself." Not only was her pride at stake, having his hands on her again might cause unwanted lust to shoot off sparks. Stupid Wendayan body.

Missy slipped her foot in the stirrup, but when she swung her leg over, many of her muscles rebelled, shooting pain up her spine. With effort, she was able to hold in her moan. Once seated, she twisted toward him. "I'm ready."

He gave her a thumbs up. While riding would be painful, she focused on getting home and soaking in the tub. Hopefully, when she dropped Zane off, he'd have forgotten all about them going out again.

Chapter Seven

W HAT HAD ZANE been thinking telling Missy about his home world of Cargonia? One benefit was that he now had a clear conscience. He'd told her the truth. It wasn't his fault she didn't believe him. However, he had chuckled at her fictitious story about her being from Witcheron. Clearly that was make-believe.

Side by side, they rode back to Chris Renford's farm. Every few minutes, he'd study her, trying to detect if she was in pain. Missy was probably uncomfortable, but with the way she was looking around with a small smile on her lips, she seemed to be doing okay.

Zane too was enjoying the outside. He also loved the feel of the beast under him. Storm was headstrong, yet controlled at the same time—kind of like Missy. She wasn't looking for a man to take care of her, and that attitude was refreshing. While the women in his realm could shift and fight, they preferred a male's protection and rightfully so. The demons often targeted the female werewolves who didn't stand a chance against one. That wasn't to say he wasn't at the mercy of the demons either. He'd gotten lucky on his last encounter—or rather his second to last encounter. When he'd killed the demon Janoc, Zane had been carrying a sword of the finest steel. His one hefty strike had caught the animal off guard, and that mental lapse had given Zane the chance to cut off his head.

"What are you doing for transportation?" Missy asked as both horses entered the barn.

"Right now, Rye drives me to work." Yes, it made him sound

needy, but Rye had insisted.

"How long will Victor Muñez be out of work?" Missy dismounted, and when both feet hit the ground, she swayed.

In a flash he was off his horse and helping to steady her. "Are you sure you're okay? Maybe we should take you to a hospital to get checked out." Zane was quite good with animals, but he had no experience with humans.

She waved a hand. "I'll be fine, I promise. I just need a hot bath and some rest."

She sounded like him—in denial. Zane took pride in being self reliant, but sometimes, one had to accept a helping hand.

Chris was in the barn brushing one of his horses. When he spotted them, he came over and took Storm's reins. "How did you like him?" Chris asked.

"He's special. We mostly walked, but someday I'd like to see what he can do going full out."

Chris smiled. "I'm sure Storm would like to be given a free rein. Let me know if you're interested in him. He's for sale."

His heart jacked up. What he wouldn't give to own such a fine animal as this stallion. "I'll start saving."

Chris smiled. "I hear ya."

"Do you want me to brush him down?" Zane asked. As far as he knew, Missy hadn't paid for borrowing the horses. It was the least they could do.

"Nope. I owe Rye a ton, and this is my small way of helping. You two head on out."

They both thanked him again. As Missy walked toward her car, she rubbed her neck and that worried him. Zane placed a hand on her back. "I know I keep asking, but you don't seem okay."

She stopped and faced him. "I appreciate your concern, but I'll be fine. Trust me."

He knew better than to argue with a woman, especially one that kept him off balance. Most likely, she just needed some alone time. As much as he wanted to tell her everything about who he was and why he was there, if he were too convincing, she'd really freak out, and he couldn't let that happen. His goal was to earn her respect and then try to win her heart. After today, he had no doubt that Missy Berta was his mate. Convincing her would be another matter—especially once she believed that he really was from another realm.

When they reached her car, he tossed the backpack in the back. Instead of her walking over to the driver's side, she held out her keys. "Would you mind driving? I'm not feeling one hundred percent." He moved closer, but she held up a hand. "Don't ask. I'm good. I figured you'd want to drive. Most men do."

He wanted to learn how, but getting behind the wheel could lead to disaster. Telling her the truth however might be worse. Sure, he'd driven something that resembled a model T—twice in his life—and Zane had been watching Rye every time they were in the truck together, but that didn't make him an expert. "Sure."

Crap. His ego had gotten the best of him. But hell, driving couldn't be that hard. The roads were super wide, so staying in his lane would be easy. He was used to maneuvering a cart down a canyon that wasn't more than four feet wide.

Missy dropped the keys in his palm, and he inhaled deeply. *You can do this.*

Pretending he was Rye McKinnon, Zane strode over the driver's side and slid in. Missy smiled and eased into the passenger seat.

Trying to mimic Rye, Zane put on his seat belt then shoved the key in the ignition. At first, he had the key upside down, but Missy didn't seem to notice. "I have to admit, I didn't pay a lot of attention to how we got here."

"It's really easy. Just follow this road until you come to a T-intersection then hang a right. The McKinnon's estate is about a half mile on the left."

That sounded easy enough. "Lean back and close your eyes. We'll be there in no time."

She smiled, and Zane wanted to reach out and hug her tight. He might be from another realm, but he had enough sense to know

Missy was skittish around him, which meant touching her wouldn't help his cause. Most likely his size scared her—or the fact he'd been in a cave when she found him.

Zane looked at the gearshift, and once he started the engine, he carefully put the car in reverse. Now came for the difficult part. He had no idea how much pressure to exert on the pedal, but he figured driving was like riding a horse. Kick the animal too hard and he'd go flying. It was all a matter of finesse.

Zane pressed on the pedal, and the car lurched backward. Missy jerked to a sitting position. "What happened?"

"Nothing. I'm used to driving a much larger truck and using more pressure."

"Oh." She leaned her head back and closed her eyes once more.

That was close. This time Zane wasn't so heavy-footed, and he successfully backed up the car. Maybe driving wasn't so hard after all. Once in drive, he eased over the bumpy dirt road that led to the farm. After he arrived at the paved road, driving became easier and a lot smoother. Because this was shifter territory, the roads were private, and as such, didn't have that handy white stripe down the middle to help guide him.

To make sure he didn't wreck, Zane kept his speed right around twenty-five miles per hour. While it seemed as if he were flying, it was as fast as he dared to go given this was his first time behind the wheel.

When he spotted the McKinnon estate a few minutes later he let out a breath. "Are you okay to drive home or do you want me to drop you off at your house?" he asked. Not knowing where she lived, the walk back could be several miles.

She opened her eyes, sat up, and looked around. "I really am good to drive."

Zane hadn't wanted to lie to her again, but since she didn't seem to believe him when he told the truth, his hands were kind of tied. "I have missed it."

Maybe because men liked driving, Zane decided to show off a

little, hoping to impress her. He took the turn into the driveway too fast and overshot the entrance. A second later, the front end of the car ran into the bush. His excellent reflexes engaged, and he shot out an arm to stop her forward momentum while he pressed on the brake. Her chest and his forearm collided, but at least she didn't hit the dash. "Shit!"

"It's okay, it's okay," she said, her voice almost an octave higher.

Damn. Any hope of her thinking of him as a hero just disappeared. "I'm sorry. I took the turn too fast. Are you okay?"

"Yes." Now she sounded pissed—and she had every right to be.

He backed up to get out of the bush and then pulled to a stop, hoping he hadn't damaged the car. The bush would grow back, but the metal would not. Zane jumped out and rushed to the front. Kneeling down, he ran a hand over the bumper, but he didn't detect any damage.

Missy eased out of the seat and stood over him. "It's okay," Missy said without any anger in her voice. "It could happen to anyone."

"I need to stick to horses. They're smarter."

When Missy chuckled, his muscles relaxed. No one was hurt, and that was all that mattered.

Zane stood and handed her the keys. "I can walk to the guesthouse from here."

"Thanks again for the picnic." The shine in her eyes spoke of sincerity.

"It was my pleasure." Zane opened the door to the backseat and retrieved his pack. "I'd like to pay you back for taking me riding. How about dinner tomorrow night? My treat."

Rye said he'd be paid tomorrow.

Her glance to the side spoke of heartbreak—his. "Listen, Zane. You're a really nice guy, but why start something when you'll be leaving soon?"

"Who says I have to leave? I promised to stay until Victor returns to work." That didn't come out with as much assurance as he'd planned.

"You have a family and a job one state over."

He couldn't let her go. "It's just dinner."

Missy moved to the driver's side and opened the door. "Maybe some other time."

"Sure."

He didn't move until her car disappeared from sight. Well, damn.

"WHY DID YOU turn him down?" Izzy asked.

With the phone cradled between her ear and her neck, Missy poured a glass of wine then propped her feet up on the coffee table. "Eventually, he has to go back home."

"So? Men have been known to move."

Perhaps that wasn't the real reason why she'd decided not to go out with him. "There's just something that seems off about him."

"He has amnesia," Izzy said.

"Zane is remembering a lot." She chuckled. "In fact, he told me he's from another realm. I have to say the man has quite an imagination."

"Another realm? That's a new one."

"I know. I did enjoy the tale he wove though."

"Is he too forward then?" Izzy sounded concerned.

"No, Zane was a real gentleman."

"Is it his looks?"

Missy didn't want to consider she could be so prejudiced. "I hope not, though the straggly hair and untrimmed beard just aren't my thing." The rest of him looked good. The image of Zane standing in front of her naked with his cock erect surfaced, and heat raced up her face. "Look. I know Rye likes him, but I need some time."

"Sure. I just want you to be as happy as I am."

Missy smiled. She loved her sister. "I will be. My time has yet to come."

"If you change your mind, I'm sure we can arrange for the two of you to bump into each other."

Missy polished off the rest of her wine. "Let's just let nature take its course."

"Understood."

Somehow she doubted her sister would refrain from interfering.

Chapter Eight

ZANE HAD A very restless night reviewing what had gone wrong with his date. Yes, Missy's horse had bucked her off, but his little magic girl had popped right up, ready to get back on—or she would have had Grandma not run away.

As for his grand reveal, he thought it had gone well. He had told the truth, but she seemed to think his tale belonged in some science fiction book. Zane had learned that it was impossible to control another person's thoughts, which meant if she wasn't going to believe him, she'd never accept what he said as truth. It wasn't like he could prove to her another realm existed—short of taking her there, which was impossible.

She seemed to enjoy what she thought was his humor. During lunch, Missy had told him a tale of her own, and he'd enjoyed their banter. So why had she turned him down for a date? Who knows? He hadn't really understood women all that well on Cargonia, so why should this realm be any different? Right now, he had a job to do. Daydreaming would only get him fired.

When he reached the supply closet, he grabbed the mop, bucket, and a few cleaning solutions, ready to start his chores. Just as he walked into the bathroom, Tanner March, the new kid on the block, was coming out from the showers with a towel wrapped around his waist.

"Hiya, Zane. How's it going?"

Zane smiled. He enjoyed this young man's enthusiasm. "It's

going well. You? Have you had to put out any fires yet?"

He shook his head. "Not yet. For now, I'm studying to be a paramedic. I prefer the after care than fighting the blaze."

Zane could respect that. "Can I ask you something?"

"Shoot."

In the last week, Zane had been thrown off by all the colloquial expressions, especially from the younger guys, but he was slowly learning their meaning. "There's a girl I like, but I can't convince her to go out with me."

"Seriously?"

"Yes." Zane puffed out his chest at the man's comment.

"Well, if you're asking, I'd get a shave and hair cut."

Zane had worn his hair shorter, but his hair had grown during his hibernation. "You might be right."

Tanner ran a hand over his shorn hair. "I think women dig the short look nowadays. Long hair kind of went out with the seventies."

Zane wouldn't know as he'd slept through that time, but Tanner hadn't even been born yet. "Can you recommend a barber?"

"I cut my own hair, but my brother goes to Carmen DeLong over on High Point and Oak. He's really good. And cheap."

"Thanks. I'll give him a try."

As soon as Tanner headed to the locker room to change, Zane returned to work. If Missy hated the new look, it wouldn't take long to grow it back.

In the middle of mopping the floor, the siren sounded and Zane stopped, enjoying the pounding of feet and the intense hustle to save someone in need. He'd thought about learning to be a fireman, but he enjoyed creating art with his iron too much to change.

"Is SOMETHING WRONG?" Teagan asked.

Missy had been standing in front of the register at the Crystal Winds Spa for a good two minutes and had yet to count the cash. "I think I hurt Zane's feelings when I turned him down for dinner."

The invitation had been four days ago, and she was still dwelling over it. That wasn't a good sign.

"It's an easy dilemma to solve." Teagan straightened the business cards on the counter.

Her cousin was no help. "What's that? Go out with him? If I did, I'd be leading him on."

Teagan placed her hands on the counter and leaned forward. "If you don't like him then you were right to say no. But if you do like him, then it's not raising his hopes."

"I do kind of like him. I mean he's sweet and funny."

Teagan stood up straighter and crossed her arms over her chest. "That sounds like a deadly boring combination. Listen, if he doesn't get your blue sparks shooting, then you shouldn't go out with him. You need to move on."

"Yeah, well, actually, a few did escape."

Teagan's face lit up. "That's wonderful. Then what's the problem?"

"I don't know. He's hiding something. I can feel it."

Her brows pinched. "Have you asked him about it?"

"Yes, and you won't believe what he told me." Missy detailed the story of him being from another realm. "He doesn't seem to want to tell me any details about where he is from. He's secretive."

"About what though?"

"I don't know. He is really good at telling a story. If I didn't know better, I would've almost thought he believed his own tale."

Teagan chuckled. "Personally, I'd give him a shot. Rye seems to like him, at least according to Izzy."

So now her own sister was talking behind her back? "I could tell." An idea popped into her head, and Missy pointed a finger at Teagan. "You can see into the future. How about concentrating on Zane and tell me where he'll be in a few months."

Teagan cocked her head to the side. "You know that's not how it works. My visions are spontaneous. I can't force them."

"That was in the past. Ever since you and Kip mated, I thought things had changed." In actuality, Teagan's visions had almost halted—at least the bad ones had.

"It changed in the sense that now I can predict good events too, instead of everything being so dark. It's not like I'm a fortune teller who can predict things at command."

It had been worth the shot to ask. "Well, if you ever see anything about him or me, let me know."

"Will do." Just then Teagan's cell rang, and she slipped it from her pocket. "It's Ainsley. Hey there. What's up?" Teagan turned around and wandered toward the front of the store. "Yes, I remembered. Seven tonight. I'll be there. Thanks."

"Is everything okay?" Missy asked when her cousin returned to the counter.

"Yes. When our men are working on a case, the three of us often grab a drink. You should come."

Missy shook her head. "I'm not the party-hardy type."

Teagan smiled. "We only have a drink or two over some girl talk. Come and join us. You need to get out of your shell."

Okay, that stung. "I get out plenty."

"I didn't mean hiking outdoors to pick mushrooms. I mean getting out there and meeting people. Your future mate isn't going to drop on your doorstep."

An image of Zane popping out of the cave surfaced, but she pushed it aside. Missy often shunned going out with the girls because she never had anything interesting to say. Maybe it was time to change things up, if only to stop the tongues from wagging. "Fine. I'd love to come."

Teagan smiled. "That's great." She ran her gaze from Missy's head to her waist. "Just be sure to wear something sexy."

"I thought this was a girl chat evening."

"It is. We're all mated, but you're not. It won't hurt to have some interest thrown your way."

Great. Why was everyone trying to fix her up? They all believed in fated mates, so it wasn't like they thought some stranger would whisk her away, though she supposed getting more experience wouldn't hurt when the right man did show up. "I don't think I own anything sexy." That really sounded lame.

"Then buy something!"

Diana's Dress Shop on Pine and Maple always carried some cute things. It might be time to change her look anyway. "Where and when are you meeting?"

"McKinnon's Pub at seven."

"Fine. I'll see you there."

As much as she wanted to wipe the victorious grin off her cousin's face, it would be good to enjoy some different scenery. It might even help take her mind off Zane.

Promising herself she'd keep an open mind about the evening, Missy went back to work. When five o'clock rolled around, Teagan insisted that she close. "You need to get ready."

"Wait a minute. Is there something you aren't telling me? Did you invite Zane to the bar?"

Teagan's mouth dropped. "No! I'm not sneaky like your sister. I've never met the man."

"That better be the truth." Thankfully, it had been Mrs. McKinnon who'd made their picnic lunch and not Mom.

Once she said goodbye to her mom who was working in the back, Missy headed off to Diana's Dress Shop. If she had any hope of stopping her relatives from meddling, she needed to show she wasn't the recluse they thought her to be. This couldn't be a half-hearted attempt either. Missy inhaled, trying to ready herself for being pushed out of her comfort zone.

When the shop owner heard what she needed, she was excited to help. "Greens and turquoise look good with your skin tone and hair color," Diana said. "I have just the thing.

By the time the shop owner was done, Missy had spent a week's salary. Even she had to admit it was fun to do something so daring, even if it was only for one night. Once home, she tried on the outfit and was pleased with the result. The low cut emerald green top was a shock for her system, but the short leather boots with the two-inch heels really looked good with the skinny jeans. The wow factor was the amber necklace she'd purchased. Ever since she found the burnt orange stone in the cave, she'd been thinking about that color. Not much of a makeup person, all she did was dab on a light pink lipstick and a bit of blush.

The timer she'd set on her phone rang. It was time to go. After taking one more look in the mirror, Missy headed out. The late spring still smelled sweet as the sun began to set, creating a colorful pallet across the sky.

Missy had targeted arriving five minutes late, but when she entered the bar neither Teagan or Ainsley nor Lexi were there yet. For a minute she thought she had the time or day wrong, but when Ainsley walked in a minute later with Lexi, relief washed through her.

"Missy," Ainsley said right before hugging her. "I'm so glad Teagan could convince you to come."

She shrugged. "Sitting home alone can get old."

Lexi laughed. "Tell me about it. That was my life before I arrived in Silver Lake."

Ainsley nodded to one of the tables. "Teagan called a minute ago and said she'd be here shortly. By the way, I love your top and necklace."

Missy fingered the smooth stone. "Thanks."

She slid into the booth, and Ainsley sat next to her. She too looked good in her pretty white tank top. Lexi took the seat across from her. Thankfully, her top was more revealing than Missy's, making her feel less self-conscious.

"So Teagan tells me you met someone," Ainsley said without any preamble.

Her cousin and her big mouth. "Let's say I ran into someone." Missy proceeded to regale them with her story of how she and Zane met.

"And this Zane guy doesn't remember anything?" Lexi asked. "I find that hard to believe."

"I know!" Missy said. "I can understand not remembering names or places, but not knowing how to open a car door?"

Lexi laughed, but Ainsley didn't. Before Missy could ask why the sudden serious expression, Teagan arrived.

"Sorry, I'm late." She sat down and waved at Molly, Rye's cousin, who rushed over.

"Hey, ladies. What can I get you all?" Molly asked.

"How about a pitcher of Sangria?" Lexi looked around and everyone nodded.

"You got it. I'll be right back." Molly trotted off.

"Missy has been telling us about Zane," Lexi told Teagan.

"He does sound interesting. I can't wait to meet him," Teagan chimed in.

Oh, boy. She didn't need her cousin working on her too. "I'm sure he'll show up at some event," Missy said.

Ainsley held up a finger. "Where did he say he was from?"

"Some small town in North Carolina." Missy should have paid better attention.

"I thought you said that he told you he was from some other realm?" Teagan said.

Missy laughed. "That was make believe."

Ainsley shook her head. "Another realm? Zane might have been telling you the truth. Tell me exactly what he said."

Had she not sounded so serious, Missy would have laughed it off. What had he said the name of the realm was? "I think he said it was called Cargonia. To be honest, I was enjoying his story so much that I didn't pay attention to the details."

"This realm is like Earth, right?" Ainsley asked.

"Seems to be, but he was just making that up."

The pitcher arrived, and Molly poured each of them a drink. Missy needed to end this crazy discussion and held up her glass. "To fantasy."

They all tapped their glasses and drank.

For the next hour they chatted about what they were up to, leaving Zane out of the conversation for which she was glad. "Are you planning on staying at McKinnon and Associates?" Missy asked Lexi, hoping to keep the spotlight off of her.

"Sam and I have had long talks about that. I want to, but he fears something bad will happen to me if I do because of what he does for a living. I keep telling him that I'd rather work in a safe environment all day than teach school where anyone can find me."

Missy sighed. Her cousin was so protective. "Do you like answering the phone? I mean, aren't you bored?"

Lexi laughed. "Trust me, every day I find more ways to get involved in the business. I love hearing about their cases, and I often offer suggestions—but only to Sam. I've created spreadsheets and databases that cross reference their cases. Already, it has come in handy."

Missy smiled. "McKinnon and Associates is lucky to have you. I'm thrilled things have worked out so well for you."

"They sure have. From almost being sold to finding my mate, life can't be any better."

Missy turned to Ainsley. "Any more run ins with the men from the hill?" She didn't want to mention the Changelings by name.

"So far, they've been quiet, but I'm sure they're still on the lookout for their sardonyx."

"Shh," Missy said. "What if they hear you?"

Ainsley held up a hand. "I can assure you none of them are here."

Missy was slipping. She'd forgotten about Ainsley's special talent. "Good to know."

"Missy?" The deep voice startled her, and she twisted in her seat to face the source.

At the end of the table stood two men. One was about six feet with military-short, sandy blond hair. He was the classic military type—broad shoulders and a powerful chest. While he was good looking, he was nothing compared to the man next to him. That man was a giant. Clean-shaven, his brown hair was short on the side while thick and full on top. She couldn't stop looking at him. His rich brown eyes drew her in.

"Yes?"

"It's me!"

As soon as he grinned she recognized him. "Zane?" Oh my goddess. The man sure did clean up well.

"It is. I thought it was about time to get rid of the shaggy beard and hair."

"You look…great!" That was an understatement.

The shorter man held out his hand. "I'm Tanner March, paramedic in training."

It made sense that Zane would befriend someone he worked with. "Nice to meet you. I haven't seen you around. Have you been in town long?"

"No. I just moved here."

No wonder Missy didn't recognize him. Once she introduced everyone at the table, they all welcomed Zane and Tanner to Silver Lake.

"If you'll excuse us, ladies, I promised to show Zane a thing or two about playing pool."

Zane shook his head, leaned over, and winked. "The youngster doesn't stand a chance."

Everyone at the table laughed. A second later the two of them disappeared into the poolroom.

Ainsley grabbed Missy's arm. "That's the man you turned down for a date? He sure as hell didn't look odd to me."

Even Missy was having second thoughts. Maybe she had judged him by his looks and ill-fitting clothes—ones that were hand-me-downs. "I have to say, he's not looking odd now."

The women all seemed to agree. "Go talk to him," Teagan urged.

That wasn't Missy's style. "Let him have fun with his friend." She studied her cousin. "You didn't call Izzy and tell her where I'd be tonight, did you?"

"No. You told me you weren't interested, so I let it be, though now that I've seen him, I think I should have called her."

Missy polished off her glass of Sangria, more confused than ever. Before she did anything rash, she reminded herself that once Victor Muñez returned to work, Zane would head home to North Carolina. Not that they'd be all that far apart, but even a few hours separation would make dating difficult—and potentially heartbreaking.

Nope. It would be best to let him go before she became too attached.

Chapter Nine

T ANNER NUDGED ZANE as soon as they entered the poolroom.
"I think you impressed her," Tanner said with a big grin.

"You think?" Zane's heart had yet to calm. His bear was stomping and huffing, wanting to run free.

"Shit man. She couldn't keep her eyes off you."

It was Zane who couldn't get Missy's image out of his head. She'd never looked more beautiful. Her V-neck top showed off just enough of her cleavage for him to picture what her perfect breasts would look like, and that color green made her hair glow even redder. Maybe it had been the amber pendant that had his heart pumping way too fast. Zane ran a hand across his neck, forgetting that he'd lost his Clan's stone—a stone he'd never been without. The burnt orange talisman had been his last connection to his world, and all he could think of was that it had to be in the cave, probably buried under an inch of silt. He refused to believe it had been lost when he'd tumbled through the portal.

Tanner touched his arm. "You okay?"

His friend stared at him, waiting for a response. "Ah sure. Do you think I should go back out there and talk to her?" Zane had never been at a loss about how to win over a woman. Now, when it counted, he was acting like a fumbling teenager.

"No. Don't chase her."

Zane wasn't sure that was sound advice, but he didn't want to interrupt her fun with her friends. For now, he'd have to be content to learn as much as he could about this type of pool and forget the distracting Missy Berta.

Good luck. I sure plan on focusing on her, his bear told him.

Shut up.

Zane used to play quite a lot of pool, but the number of balls and size of the table were different than where he lived. "Let's rack 'em up."

For the next ninety minutes, Tanner March showed him the finer points of playing pool. Making the transition to this type of play was rather easy, and Zane actually won the last game.

Tanner leaned his cue stick across the table. "I say that victory calls for a beer."

"I'm game," Zane said, happy he'd learned that idiom from Missy.

When they finally made it to the bar, Missy and her friends had left, dropping him into a funk. One positive note was that Missy did seem to find him attractive—or so Tanner claimed. While that was good, looks alone did not make a relationship.

After two beers, Zane said he wanted to head home, mostly because his bear needed to run.

"We'll have to do this again," Tanner said. "You're a fast learner. You sure you don't want me to give you a lift home? It's not a problem."

"I appreciate it, but I rode my bike." Zane had borrowed a bicycle from Mr. McKinnon—a bike that used to belong to Rye when he was a kid. While it wasn't as fast as a car, it beat walking.

Maybe he should ask Tanner to teach him to drive. On second thought, if twenty-four year olds on Earth were anything like those on Cargonia, Tanner would be hell behind the wheel.

All during the bike ride home, Zane questioned whether he should have tried to speak with Missy. Had he not been with his friend, he would have asked to have a word with her.

Before he'd figured out his next move, he was back on the McKinnon estate. Needing some release, Zane undressed then took off outside, not caring which direction he went.

While his bear seemed to enjoy the freedom of loping across fields, the run didn't provide Zane with any answers to his current dilemma. Not paying attention to where he was going, he burst through the forested area and found himself at Silver Lake. Streams were more his style, but he'd take any kind of water tonight. Even though the evening was cool, a good swim might clear his head, especially since the rays of the full moon shimmered off the surface, making it rather magical.

Just as he was about to dive in, he sensed a presence nearby and stilled. It couldn't be Raymolt, could it? Zane spun around and searched the nearby woods, but he didn't detect anyone. The couple of beers he'd had must have messed with his head, because he refused to believe it could be someone from his world. The aura definitely didn't belong to a shifter—that much he was certain—but it was highly improbable that it belonged to a demon either.

Convinced his imagination had run amuck, Zane dove into the refreshing lake. On Cargonia, the rivers were warm, and finding something this cool was a delight.

By the time he'd had his fill and climbed out, the odd sensation emanating from near the rocks was gone. Maybe it had been a sign that he should figure something out soon—or chance being killed.

TEAGAN HAD PICKED up an extra sandwich from the deli for Missy because Mom was out on a call and someone needed to mind the store. While Teagan took her turn manning the front, Missy ate her lunch in the break room. Halfway through her sandwich, a knock sounded on the door and then it opened.

She looked up. "Jackson! What are you doing here?" Missy didn't remember Ainsley's mate ever stepping foot in the store before.

Jackson came around and gave her a peck on the cheek. "Hey, sweetie". He pulled up a chair at the small table. "Ainsley told me about Zane being from Cargonia."

She laughed. "It was pure fiction, I can assure you."

"I'm not so sure he wasn't telling you the truth." Jackson placed his backpack on the table and extracted a much worn looking book.

Missy chuckled. "Really?"

Jackson Murdoch was a fun loving guy, but when it came to history and research, he was deadly serious. She remembered the time when no one believed him about some treasure being buried under where their new office was now located. Jackson had insisted something was there—and he'd been right, but just because he'd been right once didn't mean he was right a second time.

"Yes." He flipped open to a marked page. "I know this claims to be part mythology and part folklore, and that scientists will say it is pure fiction, but I'm convinced it has merit. It makes a lot of sense."

Missy was kind of nervous, but at the same time very interested in what Jackson had discovered. "What makes sense?"

"According to this ancient story in our shifter history, we came from another realm that originally was a separate world—if you will—from Earth."

"A separate world?" Her pulse sped up.

"Yes. The gods and goddesses were at odds about how to protect the shifter secrets from the humans who inhabited Earth."

Jackson acted too excited. "Where did you find this book? In a thrift store?" she asked.

"No. It was in my father's library. I asked him where it came from, but he doesn't remember, or maybe he's afraid to reveal its origin."

She supposed it didn't matter where it came from. "Go on."

He ran a finger across a well-worn page. "The gods fell into one of two camps about how to protect shifters. One group wanted to let the shifters and witches live on Earth, interacting with the humans as they saw fit, while the others wanted more control. This second group insisted the shifters be protected from the humans. That meant they wanted the shifters, witches, and demons to live in a completely different realm."

Jackson had lost it. Having met the goddess Naliana, Missy believed in many deities, but she wasn't buying into the idea that they would fight over what happened on Earth. "I'm confused. Are you saying there is a second realm?"

"Yes. The gods couldn't decide which way was best—total control or merely overseeing the shifter world—so they broke it into two realms connected by a portal. It goes on to say that this portal can be accessed on either side by the gods and goddesses or by someone of higher lineage that has been bestowed that power. This restricted access was designed to protect the shifters and demons from humans who accidentally entered."

"Do you have any other proof of this? I have to say this sounds more fanciful than even Zane's tale."

"No additional proof, but it sounds logical. Think about it. We have Wendayans, shifters, Changelings, as well as immortals and gods. You believe in them, don't you?"

He was being silly. "You know I do."

"So why not add one more thing? A second realm."

"I'll bite. Go on about this other realm."

Jackson smiled then refocused. "Naliana, and those she answers to, pretty much let the shifters and witches live among the humans as they see fit without too much interference—unless of course there is a serious danger to life. If the gods' help is sought, they may offer guidance. They want to encourage the shifters and Wendayans to learn on their own."

"It's the way it's always been."

"Right, but this other realm runs on a stricter premise and must follow more of the ancient rules. Even though the shifters and witches are in a protected world, there are still dangers to them that come in many forms like demons and dark magic. Shifters and witches—many of whom are like our Wendayans—have to answer to and obey the gods and goddesses in their realm. There are many levels of hierarchy. Anyway, guess what their realm is called?"

"Don't tell me it's Cargonia?"

Jackson leaned back and smiled. "Yes. The place does exist."

Jackson Murdoch was an extremely intelligent man. He could hack into anything and had even been able to figure out where Anna was being held captive by looking at a video a few seconds long. Despite his brilliance, she wanted to believe he was wrong. "Did it occur to you that Zane might have read the same book? You said it was folklore. Wouldn't most shifters have heard the stories passed down by their ancestors?"

"Maybe, but you should ask Zane for more details."

"He'll think I'm a fool if I question him about being from a realm closely linked to Earth."

Jackson closed the book. "Suit yourself. Oh, one last question. Do you know how he ended up here?"

"Besides arriving by portal?" She didn't wait for his answer. "I have to assume he took a bus or hitched a ride."

"And then what? He walked to the caves and shifted knowing his clothes would be destroyed, leaving him naked?"

Her theory sounded better than his though. "It's possible, though not very practical. Someone could have knocked him unconscious and dumped him in the cave."

Jackson snapped his fingers. "Or he was pushed through the portal unwillingly. He wouldn't be able to get back without help from someone who held the power to access the portal from his realm. He would need to find shelter in order to survive. His best protection would be in his shifted bear form, which was why he went into hibernation. Find out what you can and let me know. I'm totally fascinated by this." His escalated voice proved it.

"I'd rather have you ask him."

"No, this is your story to learn."

Figures he'd say that. "Did you show this to Rye?"

"Not yet."

That was probably because Rye would have laughed at him. "You need to."

Jackson stood and jammed the book back into his pack. "Just be open-minded," he said. "It's how I've solved a lot of crimes. As I always say, things are not always what they seem."

Missy stood too. "What aren't you telling me?"

"Nothing." He grinned, gave her a wink, and left.

Well damn.

For the rest of the afternoon, Missy tried to ignore everything Jackson had told her, but she couldn't. She replayed the folklore many times, but each time, it seemed to line up with what Zane had told her. Had she found the story online, she might have dismissed it as total fiction, but two things did seem to be true: one was the name Cargonia. Sure, Zane could have been aware of this book, but the probability of having read the same chapter seemed unlikely. The second was why there were two realms in the first place.

When Missy reentered the main room, Teagan was saying good-bye to a customer. Once Mrs. Adams left, Teagan strode up to her. "I saw Jackson leave. What did he want? Is Ainsley okay?"

"Yes. She's fine." Missy wasn't sure she should bother telling her cousin the outrageous story, but since no one was in the store, it would help pass the time. "He told me Zane might really be from Cargonia."

Teagan laughed as expected. "How did he figure that out?"

"Ainsley must have mentioned it to Jackson." Missy explained his book's claim. "If it is in their shifter history books like Jackson says, then maybe…"

"Just stop right there. Clearly, there's only one thing to do," Teagan said with a sparkle in her eyes.

Missy glanced to the ceiling then returned her gaze to Teagan. "What's that? Ask Zane about it?"

"Yes! This is your chance to go out with him again."

Missy smiled, but she had no such intention of doing any such thing. This was all so surreal. "I'll think about it."

"That's a start."

As soon as Teagan disappeared into the back for more soap,

Missy let out a breath. Jackson's visit had proved to her that something odd was going on with Zane, and she wanted nothing to do with him. Gods breaking the Earth into two realms was a far-fetched theory, but not an impossible one. Because scientists had extensive research to show how the Earth had been formed, and there never had been any mention of two sets of deities fighting over how it should be run, she tended to dismiss the double realm theory. On the other hand, scientists didn't know about shifters, Wendayans or Changelings. So maybe another realm wasn't so crazy after all.

Why am I even trying to make sense of this? This was probably a ploy by her sister to create more interest in Zane. But why would Izzy be so focused on a man she hardly knew? On rare occasions, Naliana spoke with Izzy, but if the goddess had contacted her sister, Izzy would have told her.

Trying to make sense out of all this was starting to give Missy a tension headache. She needed to clear her mind and not think about it for awhile.

Focusing on work for the next few hours helped ease her tension, and she made it to five o'clock without going crazy. Once the store closed, Missy wanted to go to the library. Mostly, she was hoping to find some other source that either proved or disproved these two realms of Earth theory so she could know for sure if Zane Barons came from the good ole US of A or from some similar realm.

Missy often did research on herbs and how they could heal a person, but she'd never spent time looking around the library to see what else it had to offer. Not wanting to take too much time searching, she asked the librarian where she might find the lore behind gods, magic, and shifters. "I read somewhere about the possibility of other realms."

The librarian smiled. "That would be in the myths and folklore section. You'll find tons of stuff on the gods. Come with me and I'll show you that section."

"Thanks."

For the next two hours, Missy poured over the books on the

Norse gods, but there wasn't a mention of another realm being formed away from Earth, but that didn't prove Cargonia didn't exist. When her stomach growled, Missy decided to pack it in. While the information had been fun to read, it wouldn't prove or disprove what Jackson had found.

Tonight she might have to crack open the laptop since it would be easier to search the topic that way. With better keywords, she might find what she was looking for.

As Missy headed home, the irony of her thoughts hit her once more. If she'd read on the Internet or in one of the books that someone could part water, make a vine grow ten feet in a few seconds, and create a storm of epic proportions—like her sister could—Missy would have tossed down the book and called the information a load of crock. So why was she so skeptical that gods would fight over how the shifters should be ruled?

Hell if she knew. Right now, Missy wasn't sure what to believe—or who to believe. What she did know was that she needed to find out more about the mysterious Zane Barons and what kind of game he was playing with her.

Chapter Ten

V INEA WASN'T IN the mood to talk to anyone. Her fellow gods and goddesses from the dark realm never shut up about their amazing feats, and of late, she had nothing to toss back at them. Prestige in the Ebony realm was gained by doing terrible deeds, and after her stupid sister decided to show off and blast her with light, Vinea's ability to do evil was slowly waning.

Carnella's voice drifted over the clouds, and her tinny tone set Vinea on edge. Oh how she hated that woman. Her newest brag was about how she'd seduced some poor human male right before he was to be mated to a werewolf. Apparently, Carnella had been able to transform herself to look like his sweet mate right before she bit him. Now, that was worthy of living well in the dark realm, because when the werewolf learned of her cheating mate-to-be, she ran off. Breaking up mates—particularly those arranged by Naliana—earned a god or goddess a lot of power down here.

What Vinea wouldn't give to have the talent of transforming into another person and then performing unspeakable acts? But alas, so many of her abilities had been stripped when she'd been booted from the light realm. Through sheer determination though, Vinea had been able to hold her own, but she wasn't convinced she could last much longer.

"Vinea!" The command made her whip around so fast she almost tore a muscle in her neck. Okay, that wasn't possible, but something appeared to have snapped—her patience most likely.

"What do you want?" Being interrupted when she was in the middle of a pity party really pissed her off.

"Androf wants to see you now." The messenger spun on his heels and floated off.

The god, Androf, was in charge of their area of the realm and controlled her destiny. He was a total ass, but let's face it, no one was nice where she lived.

"Coming," she mumbled to herself.

As Vinea floated toward the large dark empty space, devoid of all happiness, she wondered why she'd been summoned. The last time she'd been called in, it was because she'd requested an audience with him. Androf had reluctantly agreed to let her try to steal Sam Pompley's powers. The fact she'd failed had lowered her status to a dangerous level.

"You called?" she asked.

"Vinea, I am going to give you one more chance to redeem yourself."

His sneering words had her standing taller. She still couldn't believe he blamed her for not succeeding in taking Sam's powers. Given her limited abilities, she had done the best she could. It was why she had wanted Sam's powers in the first place.

"You don't expect me to give you a bow for that, do you?"

Androf floated off his golden throne and moved closer to her. She would not cower. "Show some respect or I'll toss you out of the dark realm right now."

He wouldn't dare. For hundreds of years, she'd done his dirty work and done it well. She reluctantly bowed her head and with a bit of snark said, "What do you need me to do, my Dark Lord?"

"Watch it! I could make your existence very painful. We have a possible incident brewing in Silver Lake."

At the mere mention of that town, conflicting emotions swamped her. It was where her sister visited every white moon. It also was where Devon McKinnon went periodically. Had he not distracted her the last time, she might have succeeded with her mission.

"What exactly would you like me to do?" *Kill Devon?*

"One of our demon spies in the Cargonia realm got carried away. He foolishly shoved a werebear down the portal and straight to Earth. This Zanedar fellow is a threat to not only shifters but to our existence. Should he tell anyone how he ended up in the Earth realm, we'd be in trouble. We can't let that happen."

"Why would that be so bad?"

By the time Vinea became of age, the realms of Earth and Cargonia had already been distinctly different for a long time. Then the dark realm was formed for banished gods and goddesses. Over time, the most senior of those banished formed a small council called the Elders of Ebony. They now ruled the dark realm, which had become either a place where all of those with dark powers resided or a sanctuary to those who needed to hone their evil skills.

"If any humans find out that Cargonia exists, the gods will have to remove that information from their minds and will most likely close all portals forever—including the one from here to Earth. Then we'd be exiled permanently with no chance for us to take over and rule either of the realms."

Vinea actually shuddered. "That would definitely not be good. What are my instructions?"

ONCE MISSY RETURNED home from the library, she tossed some chicken in the oven. Despite promising herself to put this issue to rest, she couldn't help but question a few things. To ensure she'd be able to sleep tonight, she booted up her computer. The first thing she typed in was *the realm of Cargonia.*

The name Cargonia showed up multiple times but the sites were for some video game. One article on fables and folklore did say there was supposed to be a realm much like our own that occupied the same space as Earth. Really? Two Earths occupying the same space? How was that even possible? Even Jackson hadn't made that claim.

VELLA DAY

She wouldn't discount it yet as there were a lot of mysteries she had yet to solve—such as where did the gods really live? Certainly, they wouldn't live in houses in the sky, but did they float around all day? Ugh. Not knowing was so frustrating.

Missy was about to hit the back button on the story she was reading when she spotted a cartoon drawing of a large man wearing a leather necklace. Attached to the leather strap was an orange stone. Her mind instantly shot to the stone she'd found in the cave. The caption read: The many different clans on Cargonia live in harmony.

Her mind must be on overdrive, but she swore he looked kind of like Zane.

Missy closed her laptop, disgusted that she'd spent so many hours trying to figure out who Zane Barons really was and whether he was from some other realm. Even after all of her searching, she was no closer to the truth.

At a loss for what to do next about Zane and Jackson's disturbing claim, and not wanting to involve Rye yet, she decided there was really only one thing to do—go to the source and ask Zane more questions.

Sure, she'd turned him down for another date, but Jackson hadn't revealed the myth of Cargonia to her then. Once she learned more about Zane, she could put this nonsense to rest. The question was how to contact him besides going through Rye. As far as she knew, Zane didn't own a phone, and most likely he didn't have access to a computer. Everything he owned seemed to be back at his home—make that his home in North Carolina!

She glanced over at the orange stone she'd set on the entrance-way table. Checking it out again, she noticed that the hole in the stone appeared to be rather primitive and not smooth. This implied it might have been manmade. Was it possible this belonged to Zane? He had woken up in that vicinity. She shivered just thinking what that might mean—that he might really be a clan member from Cargonia.

Stop it. Her imagination was out of control.

Running her thumb over the smooth surface, the stone seemed to flicker. Okay, that was really strange. Now she was seeing things. Hopefully, Anna would be able to get a reading off it. Teagan had mentioned that Anna's talents were developing in new ways. Sure, her friend often saw unresolved tragic events in a person's past when she touched that person, but she might be able to detect something from an object, especially if the person had worn it.

As much as Missy didn't want to disturb her friend, especially since she had just recovered from the flu, Missy needed to find out as much as she could before speaking with Zane. After locating her phone, she called Anna.

"Hey, Missy."

"How are you feeling?" By now the elixir should have worked its magic.

"I'm good as new. Better even. I can't thank you enough."

Oh, yes you can. "I have a small favor to ask."

"Sure. What is it?"

Missy explained about finding a stone in the cave where Zane had been. "I think it belongs to him. Before I return it, do you think you might get a reading off it?"

Anna said nothing for a second. "I can try. Dalton is still at work if you want to stop over now."

Missy smiled for the first time today. "I'll be right there."

Once she disconnected, she pocketed the stone and rushed over to Anna's house. As soon as Missy parked, Anna opened the door, looking healthy. Even though she was due in a month, all of her weight was in her stomach. Her cheeks had a healthy color, and her eyes were clear—all signs that the illness had indeed gone.

"Come on in," Anna said.

On the table sat a set of house plans. "Is that for the house you and Dalton plan to build?"

"It is. He says I can design it any way I want, but every time I show him my crazy ideas, he gets this weird look in his eyes."

Missy laughed. "I think all men say you can have what you want.

What they mean is that it's good as long as he approves."

"You got that right. Now show me this stone you think may belong to Zane."

Missy retrieved it from her pocket and handed it to Anna who stepped over to the sofa and sat down. "Give me a minute."

"Take all the time you need."

Anna clasped the stone in her right hand and closed her eyes. Her brows furrowed, and her lips thinned. A few seconds later, she clutched the sofa with her left hand and groaned. While Missy wanted Anna to learn as much as she could about Zane, she didn't want Anna to experience any pain.

Just as Missy was about to tell her to stop, her friend opened her eyes and placed the stone next to her on the cushion. "That was intense. I can't be sure who owned this, but whoever it was experienced a lot of turmoil. Someone close to this person died, sending him into a rage."

Zane's words came back to her about his best friend dying. "That makes sense. Did the owner see this death and has yet to deal with it? Is that why you got the reading?"

Anna nodded. She picked up the stone and handed it back to Missy. "I suggest you ask Zane if it belongs to him. It's okay if you tell him that I saw the vision."

"I'm not sure I want to."

"Why?"

That was a good question. "It will bring back bad memories. The poor guy has enough on his plate."

Anna nodded. "It's probably best to let him tell you about the tragedy on his own."

"I agree."

They spent another half hour chatting about the baby and how excited Dalton was to be having a girl. Anna always thought men wanted boys so they could teach them to throw a ball or play football, but Dalton just wanted a child. For a moment, Missy allowed herself the luxury of thinking about what Zane would want.

Most likely, he'd be happy with a ton of children to dote on, not caring about the sex.

What the hell was she doing? She had no right thinking about having babies with the man. She needed to get a grip.

Missy stood. "I don't want to tire you. When is Dalton coming home?"

She grinned. "He's here now."

The door opened, and Dalton Garner strode in wearing his sheriff's outfit. "I thought that was your car, Missy." He rushed over to Anna. "Are you okay?"

She grinned. "Yes. Missy was just keeping me company."

Missy leaned over and gave Anna a hug. "Thanks for helping. I'll let you know what happens."

It wasn't until she was in her car and halfway back home that she realized she'd be seeing Zane again. The big question was whether she had the courage to tell him that Jackson believed Cargonia existed. Once she spoke about the portals between the two realms, Zane would wonder just what she'd been up to.

Perhaps the best thing would be to say she'd gone back in the cave to look for some of his belongings and she'd found a polished stone that looked as if it had been a necklace. Did it belong to him? It would be best to leave Jackson out of it.

If Zane said it was his necklace, she might admit that in trying to find the owner's identity, she'd asked Anna to give a reading of the stone. One thing would hopefully lead to another, and she'd find out the real reason why Zane was in Silver Lake. Because prying was not her style, she'd have to play it by ear.

Her current dilemma was in figuring out how and when to reach out to him. Missy basically spent her life at the store or going to people's houses to help them heal. Hoping to run into Zane just wouldn't work. He did have Friday off and would probably be home. Knocking on his door might be the only way to see him.

Missy pulled into her drive and headed inside. While she thought about researching other folklores that referred to different realms, given she had a very active imagination, it might keep her up all night. It would be best to forget about everything until she spoke with the mysterious Zane.

Chapter Eleven

ZANE HAD SPENT the last few days trying to figure out what he could do to convince Missy to go out with him again. She'd had fun with him on the horseback riding adventure—not including her fall. It must have been his tale of Cargonia that put her off, but lying to her wasn't his style.

Zane stepped out of the shower and towel dried. The run this morning had been good for his bear, but it had caused more unwanted yearnings to surface. Every time he thought about Missy, his bear reminded him that the two of them belonged together. Zane tried to tell the feisty animal that he wouldn't do that to her. Sure, he was an expert with ironwork and could shoe a horse better than anyone, but without having any useful twenty-first century skills, he wouldn't be able to support her. Until he figured something out, he'd have to be content to see her occasionally. Under no circumstances would he mention they might be mates—

You are mates, his bear said, interrupting once more.

It doesn't matter. I have to catch up on one hundred years of technology first.

His bear clawed at him and growled. *Mate!*

Zane shoved his bear back. *Bloody pain in the ass.*

He'd tried to absorb everything about his surroundings, but the computer befuddled him, cell phones made no sense, and quite frankly, cars scared him. They moved just too damned fast. Rye had shown him some of the technology on the fire truck, and he had been amazed. Scientific advances had happened quicker than he could have ever imagined. Hibernating for one hundred years had put him at a real disadvantage. Yes, Cargonia was a bit more advanced in some aspects, but it wasn't a hundred years ahead.

Zane tossed his towel over the shower curtain rod and stepped into his bedroom. As much as he liked to walk around naked like he did back home, he'd been caught in a state of undress once when Mrs. McKinnon had stopped by to give him some leftover pie she'd made. Zane wouldn't make that mistake twice.

No sooner had he stepped into jeans than someone came to the door. Because his body vibrated so hard, he knew it had to be Missy. Did she need his help?

His clothes were lying in a heap on the floor, and sorting through the pile to find a shirt would take too long. Instead, he rushed to answer the door.

When he opened it, her beauty left him speechless. Missy had on a white blouse with black shorts that showed off her shapely legs. Her red hair was piled on top of her head in the same way many of the women of Cargonia wore theirs. His bear panted.

"Hey, come in," he managed to say without stumbling over the words. "I wasn't expecting you."

"I know. I'm sorry. I didn't want to bother you, but it's important." She stepped past him then turned to face him.

Zane made the mistake of inhaling her divine scent, and his bear nearly clawed its way out. "No bother. Did you come to ask for another exhibition of my driving skills?"

She laughed, just as he'd hoped. "Ah, no, but I thought it was sweet that you wanted to impress me. Thankfully, the car wasn't damaged in the demonstration."

"I'm glad." He looked around at his temporary one-bedroom house. He should have taken some time to straighten up, but he'd been spending every minute he wasn't at work learning things. "Give me a minute to pick up these newspapers."

The newspapers were his way of learning about the world around him. Every time he found something useful, he cut out the article and put it in a specific pile. So far, he had piles for sports, politics—which he would never understand in another hundred years—electronic devices, and pop culture. Rye had mentioned he received his news from the television and his computer rather than the newspaper, but since Zane didn't own a computer and had yet to figure out how to turn on the television monitor, he'd have to settle for the written word.

"You don't need to bother," Missy said. "Your place looks lived in. I like that. I see you like to read."

"Yes." That was because it was all he could do. He loved books, but newspapers were cheaper.

"I think I found something of yours," she said, acting a bit uncomfortable.

"Oh really? How about sitting down and you can show me? Do you want anything to drink first?"

"No. I'm good."

It was probably for the best since he only had water and beer. He'd always appreciated fine wine, but when he saw the price of a bottle, he decided beer would have to do.

Not wanting to make Missy more ill at ease, Zane sat across from her on the hard backed dining room chair that he brought over. He smiled, trying to look non-threatening since his size often intimidated people. "You said you found something?"

She pulled a small object from her pocket. When she opened her palm, his heart nearly jumped out of his skin. "I found this in the cave."

Instinctively, he ran a hand over his neck. "I thought I'd lost it forever." This was too good to be true.

She handed him the stone, and a piece of him healed. "When did you find it?"

"I went back a few days after I first met you. I know you said you'd checked, but I thought perhaps with a flashlight I could find your wallet or keys to your car. I was hoping they'd help bring back your memory."

She was so nice. "Only nothing was there but the stone."

"Right. Only the stone."

The leather cord that it was on must have snapped when he shifted into his bear form. He usually took it off before shifting, but he'd been shoved through the portal before he had the chance. "It's a talisman for my Clan."

Missy stilled, looking as if a spirit had walked over her soul. "Then it's true."

He didn't like that she'd froze. "What's true?"

She looked away. "Nothing."

"Missy, something has upset you. Tell me. I promise I won't get mad or laugh, if that's what is bothering you."

Missy might know about shifters, but he wasn't sure it was wise to tell her a lot about this other realm. However, if she ever did end up as his mate, she'd find out eventually.

"Okay, but I'm not sure what to make of it. I wasn't planning on saying anything, but in light of what you just told me, I need to." She explained that Jackson was a bear shifter and was brother to the clan's Beta, Kalan Murdoch. "He told me about a book his dad had." She went on to explain about the origin of the two realms.

Zane hadn't expected that information to come out of her mouth. Here he thought the existence of the second realm was a secret. "He was right."

This time her eyes widened. "How is that even possible?"

"You explained what happened quite well. What don't you understand about it?"

Her face turned a pretty shade of pink. "I'm sorry. It's just that so many things about you don't add up."

"Like what?"

"Why didn't I find your wallet, or any evidence of clothes in the cave? Surely, you didn't walk from this so-called realm naked?"

"My realm is called Cargonia."

"I know. Did you really come through a portal?"

"Yes. I was knocked unconscious and then shoved through, only to land in your Silver Lake cave. I believe I mentioned that before."

She leaned back and let out a breath. "I'm sorry; I'm just trying to wrap my mind around all this."

"What's bothering you?"

"A lot of things, but for starters, why did you say you could drive a car when it is obvious you never have before?"

"I never said I'd driven a car."

Huffing out a breath, she leaned forward. "What are you hiding from me?"

He hadn't meant to be so round about, but she kept twisting his words—or maybe he was the one who was changing them to avoid detection. "Okay, the truth. The reason why I seem so inept at doing everything is because I've been hibernating for one hundred years."

Missy leaned back her head and laughed. "Really now."

While Zane could let her think it was a lie, it would only lead to misunderstandings later. "It's the truth. It was why I asked you what year it was."

"For real?"

"Why do you think a seemingly young man like me doesn't own a cell phone, can't fathom what a computer does, or drive a car? Hell, I haven't figured out how to turn on the monitor."

"Monitor?"

He nodded to it. "The monitor."

"Ah, the television."

"You see? Everything is different here. The men at the station are always talking about some sports game they'd watched or what happened on the news channel. I'm floundering in my own ignorance."

"Why were you asleep for so long?"

"The demon that did this to me had a witch put a curse on me, which was supposed to cause me to sleep forever."

"I won't even comment about the existence of demons. That's really scary. As for the curse, I've never heard of one that lasts forever.

It obviously didn't work because you woke up."

That was because she'd entered the cave and broken the spell. "I know, but I did hibernate for what seemed like forever."

"That does explain why you don't know a lot of the basic things." She placed a hand over her heart and sucked in a breath. "Don't tell me you haven't been eating because you can't turn on the stove."

"The stove I kind of figured out. I got lucky since the icebox is like the one I had on Cargonia only with this one, I don't have to add ice to it."

Missy reached over and picked up a rectangular device that had a ton of buttons on them. She pressed one, and the monitor on the table against the wall sprang to life. Zane jumped at the intrusion. "How did you do that?"

She stood, moved next to him, and bent over. His bear wanted to rejoice. Her delicious scent, coupled with the provocative view of her breasts, nearly short-circuited his brain. Zane had to force himself to focus on the item in her hand.

"See this button with the red circle on it? Press it to turn the TV on then press it again when you want to turn it off. Try it."

Zane pressed the button, and sure enough, the noise quieted. "That's good."

She slipped the slim box from his hands. "To change channels, press this up arrow or down arrow. Eventually, you'll learn where your favorite channels are located."

Zane tried it and like magic, people appeared in his set. "I'm impressed. How about showing me how to use a cell phone then?"

"You're serious?"

This wasn't going as planned. "Yes, I'm serious. I've been hibernating for one hundred years. I've missed out on a few things in all that time."

Missy's brows rose as she pulled out her cell, but she didn't comment, clearly not wanting to address the issue further. "To turn it on, you have to swipe the screen then you either place your finger across this button, or type in a code."

"To prevent others from using it?"

She smiled. "Precisely." She demonstrated and then showed him how to make a call.

What the other designs were for, he had no idea. Calling seemed to be the most important function. "Show me more."

For the next few minutes Missy patiently told him about some other features. "You should join Facebook too if you want to know what's happening in the world.

He'd never heard of this Facebook. "Why is that?"

"It connects people via the computer to people all around the world. You can meet friends."

"I can meet friends by going to McKinnon's Pub."

She laughed. "I meant virtual friends."

Perhaps he wasn't ready for learning so much at one time. "Virtual friends, as in people who don't exist?"

"Kind of. I'm a virtual friend to a lot of people because I don't see them face-to-face, but they are very real."

"I don't see the need."

She took several deep breaths. "Suppose at some point you decide to take up your metal work art business again, or you just want to shoe horses. You need to be able to let people know how they can contact you."

"They'd find me at my shop."

She smiled. "Silver Lake isn't a very big town, so that might work here, but the few people here who would buy from you might not be enough to support you. For the sake of argument, suppose you want more people to learn of your great talent. You'll want to reach people who live farther away."

In his land, people shifted, ran through the woods, and then shifted back if they wanted to see someone. That or they rode a horse. "I suppose you have a point."

"Thank you."

Missy was clearly concerned about him making a good living.

For that reason alone, he might have to buy one of these computers. "Where would I get one of these devices so I can do this Facebook thing? And how much would one cost?"

She sucked in a breath through her teeth. "They can be very expensive. It could take months for you to be able to afford one. However, the library has computers you could use."

She was a treasure trove of information. "Would you be willing to help me figure it out?"

"Sure, if you tell me more about Cargonia."

That was a trade he'd be willing to make. "Deal."

Chapter Twelve

A T FIRST MISSY thought Zane was pulling her leg about not knowing something as simple as how to turn on a television. Zane was such a strong man who seemed capable of doing anything. Had it not been for his profound curiosity about how things worked, she might not have believed him.

As far as volunteering to help teach him how to use the computer, it might be fun. She was no expert either, so perhaps they could learn a few things together. Hopefully, she wouldn't lose her patience. Izzy had told her that when she was in front of the classroom teaching chemistry, their eager faces were enough to give her the patience of Job.

Trying to put herself in his shoes, Missy attempted to imagine what the world might be like one hundred years into the future. Disease might be eradicated, making people virtually immortal; artificial intelligence might have taken over the running of the world; and wars might be a thing of the past—that or the people of Earth would have blown themselves up by then, and the few who remained would be forced to live on far away planets. Oceans would have become a huge resource, not only in terms of supplying the large population with food, but also in helping to feed the farm animals. She literally shuddered at how fast the world could change.

"Is something wrong?" Zane asked, his tone laced with concern.

"I was just thinking about what the Earth might be like in one hundred years from now. I'm not sure I'd want to live then."

He laughed. "Me either. It's a big enough shock to see the changes from the last one hundred years let alone consider what might happen in the next century."

"I hope man will learn from his mistakes, but I doubt it."

Zane nodded. "So where would you like to begin my education?"

Somehow, between the time she'd first walked into his house and now, she was leaning toward believing that he really had come from Cargonia, and that he'd been in hibernation for one hundred years.

Her stomach grumbled, and she planted a hand on her stomach. "Sorry."

Zane glanced over at the kitchen clock. "I hadn't realized we'd talked so much. Are you up for some lunch?"

"I'd love some. Do you cook?"

"Maybe not in the way you think of cooking. I really haven't mastered the stove even though I can turn it on." He laughed. "After I burned myself the first time, I decided I should stick with cooking outside."

"That might work in the short run, but when winter comes, it won't be practical. What do you usually eat for lunch?"

"A steak."

Steaks were better cooked over a fire outside anyway, but it would take a long time to build one and then cook them. "Do you have any eggs?"

"I do."

"Milk?"

He shook his head. "Sorry."

This wasn't going to be easy. "How about coming over to my place? I can teach you some simple meals to prepare."

"I'd like that." Zane stood and headed toward the door.

"Ah, Zane," she said standing. "You might want to consider putting on some shoes and a shirt." Missy was having a hard enough time focusing on the conversation while trying not to stare at his magnificent chest.

"Oh, sure, but just so you know, in my realm I'm usually naked when I'm on my own property or in my home. When I am working, I have to be dressed. As you can imagine, playing around fire with no protection could be dangerous."

She laughed. "You're making that up."

"No. Cargonia is mostly shifters, people of magic, and gods and goddesses. We shifters are not self-conscious about our bodies since we often change into our animal form. For the most part, clothes are merely a hindrance. Right after I came through the portal, I shifted. I think. It was why I didn't have any clothes when I arrived here. They must have disintegrated in the portal."

There had to be a better explanation for why he had no clothes. She might believe someone put a spell on him so that he'd sleep for one hundred years, but she was having a hard time with this whole portal thing.

Maybe Ophelia, Silver Lake's powerful witch, would know about how these worked. She also might be able to shed some light on Zane's claim. As much as Missy didn't want to involve Izzy or her mom, it might be the only way to find her.

Zane Barons was unlike any man she'd ever met, which was probably why he intrigued her. Not only was he kind, he was hot. The innocence he exuded also appealed to her.

A blue spark tripped up her arm, and she immediately placed her hands behind her back. "Can I ask you a question?"

"Isn't that what you've been doing?" He had a bit too much cheer in his voice.

Heat raced up her face. "You say you're a shifter, and Rye confirmed it, but why don't you have a marking on your back?"

"A marking?" He smiled. "Oh, you mean like a paw print? I spotted Rye's when he was changing."

"Yes."

"On Cargonia, only after a man and woman mate does the imprint appear. I guess it's like what happens when you humans wear wedding bands."

"Kind of, I guess." She explained that when a shifter mated with a Wendayan, their stamps blended. "So if I mate with a shifter, my vine will have a paw print underneath it and his will have a vine."

His eyes lightened. "Our worlds are so very similar, yet so very unique."

The fact he didn't have an image of a paw on his back, yet he was a shifter, implied he was telling the truth.

As they walked out to her car, she dangled the car keys, in part to test his theory that he had only lived in this century for about a week. "Do you want to drive?"

His brows furrowed. "Only if you don't mind me crashing your car."

"Then I'll drive. At some point, you'll have to learn even if you won't own a vehicle for a while."

"I'd like that. It would suck if I asked you out on a date, and you had to drive."

"At least my father wouldn't be driving us." Missy smiled in part because of the image of the two of them sitting in the back seat while her dad dropped them off at a restaurant, but also because of his use of the word *suck*. Working at a firehouse would teach him all sorts of words, many unacceptable at times.

They both piled into her car. "Why would your father come along?"

She kept forgetting that he didn't have the same reference points as she did. "Before I turned sixteen, neither my date nor I owned a car, so my dad had to drive us. It was the only way to get anywhere."

"I see. No, I would not like that. I don't mean any disrespect to your father since I've not met him."

"None taken."

When they arrived at her house, Zane stepped out and scanned the small two-bedroom brick home. "You own this?" He sounded impressed.

"Yes. It's a little small, but it's all I can afford."

"I think it's wonderful. I'm lucky the McKinnon's are very generous people and let me stay in their guesthouse, but I don't want to take advantage of their hospitality forever. I'll have to find other accommodations soon."

She hadn't asked if Zane paid rent, but apparently he didn't. Starting a life with no money had to be hard. "Do you earn enough money to buy food?"

"Yes, though I catch most of what I need."

"You hunt?"

He grinned. "Well of course, I am a bear."

One flirty response deserved another. "You're definitely built like one. You're very large...everywhere." The last word she had said under her breath as she remembered back to when she had first seen him naked at the cave.

Zane had obviously caught what she had said since he gave her a sexy wink and grinned. "I like you Missy Berta."

Blushing, Missy smiled and turned toward the kitchen. "Thank you. Come on; your cooking lesson begins."

Missy thought it would be easy to show him what to do, but Zane hovered so close that her hormones went crazy. "The stove is hot, so stand back a little."

"Sorry."

She glanced behind her. "I trust you've used a frying pan before?"

"On a gas stove. The first time I used an electric stove, I almost caught my beard on fire trying to figure out why the flame wasn't shooting up."

Missy laughed. "You poor thing. Electric isn't much different. We'll cook the eggs on the stove, but making bacon is faster and easier in the microwave." She tapped the microwave that was mounted above the stove.

"Is that what that is called? You say it's fast?"

"Very."

He leaned closer. "How does it work?"

It occurred to her that she wasn't really sure. "I think it stimulates the molecules in the food. The food cooks, but the plate doesn't heat, except by the food."

His mouth opened. "I'm stunned."

"I'll show you." Missy placed the bacon on a glass tray then covered it with a paper towel. "It will be ready in just a few minutes. Meanwhile, we'll cook the eggs."

Zane asked to do it in order to learn, so she instructed him while he did the actual stirring. The only part he really needed help with was figuring out which setting to use when cooking the eggs. When the food was ready, they took the meal over to the table.

"You're a fast learner," she said.

"I have a great teacher." His eyes sparkled and pride swelled inside her. Zane dug into the eggs and groaned. "I can't believe I made these. They're really good."

She tried them and thought so too. "Taste the bacon."

He shoved a piece into his mouth. When he closed his eyes and groaned, her thoughts shot to what the man would be like in bed.

Stop it!

He had enough to worry about without having some human witch trying to seduce him. On the other hand, if he'd been asleep for one hundred years, he probably could use a release.

She jumped up. "I forgot the toast."

Zane pushed back his chair. "I'll help. Will you place the bread on the stove burner to brown it? Or just put it in the microwave?"

"You're almost on the right track." Nobody would think of those things unless he truly didn't know. "We use a toaster."

"Why didn't I think of that? A toaster for toast." His brows furrowed. "But you don't call a stove an egger for cooking eggs now do you?"

Zane was so delightful. "Of course not."

"You do know I was only kidding. Toasters were just coming into existence when I left Cargonia."

"Good to know your realm isn't far behind." Missy grabbed two slices of bread. "Just plug in the toaster, drop the bread in the slot, and press this lever. Then we wait."

"This is a far better design than what we had. I had to place the bread in a pan and cooked it over the fire. It did a good job though."

"Assuming you had a fire going." A minute later the toast popped up. "Butter or jam?" she asked.

"Jam, please."

Once she gathered the food, she returned to the table and sat down. After she spread the jam on her toast, Zane did the same. In fact, he once more watched her every move before preparing his toast. She thought that was cute. "How are you doing for money? I don't imagine a janitor makes much."

"Compared to a hundred years ago where I lived, I make a lot more now, but unfortunately, prices have also skyrocketed. But don't worry about me. Rye made sure I was paid a few days early so I could buy some staples. As for clothes, the firehouse has a ton of extra T-shirts, so I was given a few. All's good."

"If nothing else, you could always survive as a bear."

He nodded. "However, I've heard enough about Earth to know you people like to hunt us."

"True. Most of the time the guns come out when bears cause trouble, but not always. There will be those who like to kill for fun."

"I'll be careful."

"That's smart. Be aware that humans often leave food out, and that attracts the bears. The bears show up in people's backyards and scare them. It's out of fear that the humans kill them. It's not for food though. We only hunt deer, moose, rabbit and the like to eat, but not wolves or bears."

"Good to know, but I won't be leaving the shifter compound any time soon, except to go to work."

As much as she wanted to ask Zane a million questions about Cargonia and what his life was like, she'd probably taken up too much of his time already. Missy stood and picked up the plates.

"I'll help," Zane offered.

"You don't have to."

She carried the dishes to the kitchen and placed them in the sink. As soon as Zane set his there, he turned her around. "I can't thank you enough. I don't think anyone on Cargonia would have taken the time to help me the way you have."

His brown eyes turned a beautiful shade of amber, and she wanted to get lost in them. While she couldn't be sure where he came from, she did believe he needed her help to catch up on the last one hundred years. For most of her life, she'd played it safe, but where had that gotten her in the romance category? Nowhere. For once, she wanted to let loose and just enjoy herself. If he moved on in a few months, at least she would have some great memories.

Missy wasn't sure who moved first, but when Zane leaned over, she met him halfway. The moment their lips touched, her blue sparks shot from her body. She hadn't wanted to break the kiss, but she couldn't help it. The flood of hormones actually scared her in their intensity.

Zane said nothing, but his gaze searched her face. "I'm sorry. Shouldn't I have done that?" he asked.

She smiled at his hesitancy. "You definitely should have done that. If you hadn't, I would have."

His eyes widened. "On Cargonia, the women are aggressive sexually, but from what I've learned about humans, the women here are shy."

Her mind shot to a few of her friends who were anything but timid. "You do know that women can vote, right?"

He laughed. "I keep forgetting those things. Please be patient with me if I say or do something stupid."

"I think your ignorance, if that is the right phrase, is cute."

Zane stood up straighter. "Cute? Grrr."

She grinned. "Would charming be a better word?"

"Charming is definitely better." He stroked her cheek, and her inner walls contracted with lust. "Now where were we?"

Missy liked that Zane seemed to want her to take the lead. "I think I was kissing you."

"Is that what happened?" He smiled.

Not giving him a chance to argue, she wrapped her arms around his neck and pressed on the back of his head to bring him down to her level. A second later, she was sitting on the kitchen counter with him closer to eye level. It was only natural for her to open her legs to allow him better access. He groaned, and the kiss intensified. Missy should have been reluctant to let go like this, but she had total faith that if she was scared in any way, he'd stop.

Only she didn't want him to stop. Not now. She lowered her hands to his chest and couldn't help but squeeze his large pectoral muscles. The firmness and size caused more sparks to shoot off her body.

Zane leaned back. "What was that light? Did I shock you?"

Oh, crap. She couldn't remember if he'd said whether Wendayans lived in his world. Even if they did, he might not know what happened when one was excited. Her sparks would seem odd to someone who didn't know what they meant. It was why her mom always warned her about dating someone who wasn't aware of their kind. It might lead to too many questions. "Not in the way you might think. It happens to a Wendayan when he or she is…um…sexually excited."

"Really? I like that. What happens if I do this?" Once more he leaned over and kissed her, but this time he dragged her closer to the edge of the counter so she was plastered against his chest.

Oh, my! Even through her bra and shirt, her nipples tingled. When he dragged his tongue across the seam of her lips, Missy practically melted in his arms. If he wanted fireworks, all he had to do was keep kissing her like that and she'd be glowing blue so brightly, she'd blind him. Her pulse sped up, and the urge to be naked overwhelmed her. Nothing like this had ever happened before, so Missy had to take this as a sign from above that the two of them were meant to be together—at least for now.

She dragged her hands down his corded back, further convincing her that this was the right thing to do. She leaned back and tilted her chin upward to look him in the eye. "Would you like to go someplace more comfortable?"

His lids closed halfway, and his mouth hung open. "I'll do anything you want. You have no idea how hard I'm working not to shift right now. Your scent has changed something inside me." He inhaled and groaned.

"Help me down."

His hands tightened on her waist, and a second later, she was standing inches from his powerful body. "Where would you like to go?"

"To my bedroom?"

"Why was that a question?" Zane stroked her cheek. "Are you having second thoughts?"

Missy chuckled. "No. Never." Or maybe she should have said not since she'd opened her heart and decided to believe him.

"I'm glad, but just so you know, I will stop if you ask me to."

Zane was such a gentleman. "How about just doing what you want? If it's too fast or too much I'll let you know." Goddess, how she loved his lips, his scent, and those sensual eyes. The man was totally divine and had such raw sex appeal that she couldn't stay away. Funny, how her opinion of him had made such a big turn once she realized he'd been telling her the truth all along.

Not wanting to waste any more time talking or thinking about what might be, Missy grabbed his hand and led him down the hall to her bedroom. The moment she stepped inside her room, her doubt surfaced, but only for a moment. Making love with Zane wasn't the issue. It was that she might disappoint him.

She spun to face him. "Just so you know, I'm on the pill, and I had a physical last month."

He stared at her for a moment. "What is the pill? Were you sick?"

Oh, wow. If she ever doubted the concept before that he'd been asleep for one hundred years, that comment cleared it up. "I'm healthy. Being on the pill means I can't get pregnant."

He clasped her shoulders. "I'm so sorry. Nothing can be done?"

His tragic tone had her heart pumping hard. "No, it means I can't get pregnant if we have sex, but once I decide that is something I want, I stop taking the pill, and then I can." She studied him to see if he understood. "Does that make sense?"

"Not really, but right now being this close to you has all the blood going to my lower regions. My brain isn't working all that well."

Missy couldn't help but check the truth of his statement. The bulge in his pants was huge. She didn't know if it was because he was more than a foot taller than her, because he was a bear shifter, or both. She just hoped she could handle something that large.

"Would you like to look at it?" Zane asked, obviously catching her staring at his crotch.

"Sure." She'd like to do a lot more than just look at it though.

Before Missy could ask if she could take his pants off of him, he was out of them and completely naked. The man was a work of art and extremely well endowed.

"May I see you too?" he asked.

Missy couldn't move if she tried. All she could do was stand there, picturing herself running her tongue all over his body. "Sure."

Chapter Thirteen

ZANE HAD NO doubt that he was in way over his head. He might have made love to numerous women on Cargonia, but none had been so delicate and small. Not only did Missy's size trouble him, he worried if the way the Cargonian shifters made love would satisfy her human needs. Talking about what she liked might make her uncomfortable though. Speaking to a shifter during foreplay never went over well.

Missy wet her lips, and his libido shot sky high.

"Would you like help with removing your clothes or would you like to do it yourself?" he asked.

From the way she tilted her head and sucked in her bottom lip, she wanted this seduction to be slow and sexy. "I'd love it if you helped me."

Missy toed off her shoes, helping with the first step. Zane ran his hands down his thighs. "Where should I start? I've never taken clothes off anyone before." That was the truth.

"So women just show up at your doorstep naked?"

"No, but once we decide to have sex, we each undress."

"That doesn't sound very stimulating. I'm guessing the naked body is no big deal to you, since everyone seems to have no problem with their nudity in Cargonia?" Her voice trailed off as if she were disappointed.

"On the contrary, seeing your body is a huge deal to me."

Her face flushed before she flashed him a sly smile. "Thank you.

Just so you know, I've never seen a body like yours in my life—naked or otherwise."

She seemed to be pleased, but he couldn't be sure. "Am I too large?"

Missy held up her hands. "No, but you certainly are big; I'll grant you that. I imagine we have men your size somewhere, but I've never seen anyone like you before." She placed her hands on his chest. "And I like big men. They make me feel small and delicate."

He almost let out a huge sigh of relief. "You are small and delicate, but your size has nothing to do with me wanting to protect you."

"There's no need to protect me."

"But what if I want to?"

She ran a finger down his chest, leaving behind a trail of fire. "I guess you can."

She guessed? He wasn't quite sure what that meant, but as long as she was happy, he was good.

Missy was still wearing two things—a shirt and a pair of shorts. It wouldn't be hard to remove except that her top was held closed with buttons—tiny buttons that would take way too much time to undo, especially with his big fingers. "Would you mind removing your shirt while I help you out of your shorts?"

"Sure." Instead of taking off her shorts, he became mesmerized by her agility to undo the buttons. Seconds later, she slipped the material over her shoulders and let the smooth fabric float to the ground. Then she reached behind her back and released her bra. Slowly, she lowered the straps.

When it dropped to the floor, Zane's breath caught in his throat. "You are perfect."

He'd been so enthralled by her that he hadn't even started to remove her shorts. Fearing his inner bear might show up if he drank her in any more, he picked up Missy and placed her on the bed. Not only was she light, she was incredibly beautiful. His body was demanding that he take her for his mate, but Zane knew better. He had to wait to make sure she was ready to be with him.

Dragging his gaze down her body, he worked hard not to stare at her perky breasts. He had to decide the best way to make love to her. While it might be wiser for her to ride him, he didn't think he could wait that long. Knowing her, Missy would want to tease him for hours.

She needs to be in control, his bear said.

He agreed, but it didn't mean he had to like it. "Would you like to lick it?" Kneeling next to her, he grabbed his cock and pointed it toward her.

She grinned, and his body went wild. "I'd love to."

Drawing up onto her knees, she slipped his member from his grasp and leaned over. Her warm breath cascading over his cock nearly made him regret asking if she wanted to suck on him. His control wasn't that strong. Zane grabbed a handful of her thick curls and tugged hard. The moment her tongue slid up his length, Zane's teeth sharpened and his nails grew.

Control yourself, beast. Zane rarely chastised his inner bear, but when he was near Missy, the animal wanted to burst free, and he couldn't let that happen. This woman was such a powerful elixir, stirring deep desires that he'd never known existed.

When she cupped his balls and tightened her grip on his cock, Zane had to close his eyes and focus on staying in his human form. Because his bear desperately wanted to be in his animal form, Zane feared the human part of him might not be able to stop his bear from shifting.

He leaned back to move out of reach of Missy's tempting mouth. "Enough. I can't wait to return the favor."

His balls had hardened, and the hair on his face and body had thickened. "Please, Missy. Let me taste you."

She fell back on the bed. In his delight at seeing her breasts, he hadn't taken the time to remove her shorts, so he quickly undid the button at her waist and slipped them over her hips. Before he could remove her panties, she hooked her thumbs in the waistband and tugged them off. He might have made another comment about how amazing she was, but her neatly trimmed red curls between her thighs had him at a loss of words. Missy was almost too perfect.

His bear was clawing at him and growling. *Mate, Mate!*

Too much is at stake to take her now.

The demon Raymolt claimed Zane would never wake up because of the curse placed on him. Missy's presence had to be the reason why he'd awoken. Each second he was awake was a gift—and he credited that gift to her.

"What are you waiting for?" she asked as she posed seductively.

Hoping he was capable of taking his time, he crawled on top of her, resting his weight on his elbows. Her long lashes beckoned him, and her red lips called for a kiss. As gently as he could, Zane pressed his lips to hers, putting more weight on her as the seconds passed. Missy's goodness seeped into his soul the longer he kept contact. If he had the willpower, Zane never would have moved, but his bear wanted him to explore more of her.

As he slid downward, her breasts glided against his chest, further exciting him. When his lips were at the right height, he cupped one breast and ran his tongue around the outer edge of her nipple. The tip peaked, and his nails almost turned into claws. He wanted to savor her for hours, but between her moans and small hip movements, he'd be lucky to last another few minutes.

Take her now, his bear demanded.

Not yet. Zane was driven to taste her. The first swipe of his tongue had a bit of cum leaking out of his cock. He closed his eyes as he inhaled her delicious scent, savoring everything about her. The next tug had her moaning and clutching his shoulders, doubling his need to drive into her. He would have too, if she hadn't lifted her hips from obviously enjoying what he was doing. Wanting to add to her pleasure, he slipped a finger into her tiny opening, and she cried out his name.

"Yes, Zane!"

Her mouth opened as he curled his finger inside her, hitting a sensitive spot. Her hold on him tightened, and her body bucked as a huge climax claimed her. Thrilled he'd satisfied her, he continued to lick a few more times before crawling on top of her.

"I hope you're ready, Missy, because I can't last another second."

"Yes. Take me."

The increased pressure of her nails on his shoulders not only felt divine, it was the signal he was looking for to claim her as his own. Mating would come later, but for now just loving her was in their future.

When Missy's lips slightly parted, Zane lost all focus. He lined up his cock, ready to take her with care.

"You're so big," she said.

"I'll go slowly."

"I have something that will help." She reached out, pulled open the drawer next to the bed, and then extracted a tube.

"Toothpaste?"

She chuckled. "No. Better."

A second later, she smoothed some kind of cool gel on his cock, her magic fingers ramping up his libido something fierce. He could now see that the slickness would make entering her easier. But even after she finished slathering it on him, she lingered.

"Enough, woman."

She grinned. "Spoilsport."

Zane hovered over her, ready to slide in. His witch must have decided it was best to hurry because she lowered her hands to his hips and drew him toward her while lifting up. Without hesitation, he slid down the narrow wet channel. Her eyes went wide, and Zane stopped. "Am I hurting you?"

"No. You're so amazing!"

His chest expanded, causing her nipples to press against his body. Hormones soared through him, and he could no longer keep still. With as much constraint as possible, he eased deeper into her. Stars surrounded him, and if sunlight hadn't been pouring in through the window, he'd bet a halo of blue would be vibrating around her. Never had he experienced anything this fantastic in his life. This was where he needed to be. For the briefest of moments he considered thanking Raymolt for sending him to Earth—to Missy.

"This is incredible," he panted. "You have no idea how excited I am right now."

"Me too." Missy lifted her hips higher, meeting each of his thrusts with one of her own. "Oh my goddess, that feels wonderful."

Knowing she was enjoying the experience meant the world to him. He withdrew and plunged into her again, setting off a chain reaction he couldn't stop even if he wanted to. Capturing her lips once more, he delved his tongue into her sweet mouth as he continued to thrust into her. With each foray, his climax built, but he desperately wanted Missy to experience her satisfaction first.

Her beautiful green eyes were closed, and her groans grew louder each time he pummeled into her. He was thrilled her inner walls seemed to accommodate his wide girth so well.

"I'm so close." Zane needed to warn her.

"Me too. Kiss me again."

Her demand heated his blood. The kiss that followed altered him. Never would he be able to look at another woman. Missy was all he wanted.

He thrust into her once more, and when she let out a primordial scream and contracted hard around him, he could no longer keep from coming. Together, their orgasms collided, and Zane swore the world spun. Time seemed to mock him as he held her close, their bodies rejoicing.

With what little energy he had left, he rolled over onto his back and took her with him. Missy placed her cheek on his chest and sighed.

Though it started out with some hesitancy, it sure ended up to be the most amazing event in his life. "Thank you," he said before placing a kiss on her head.

"Any time."

Zane sure hoped she meant it.

Chapter Fourteen

MISSY WAS STILL in awe of what had transpired yesterday. Being with Zane had been the most wonderful thing to happen to her in her whole life. Even he couldn't stop smiling after they'd made love. She could only imagine what a relief it had been for him after one hundred years of celibacy.

She had debated asking him to stay the night, but not only did he have to be up early, so did she. Besides, rushing things never worked. She'd learned from experience that getting her hopes up and moving too fast could ruin a relationship. Zane had enough to deal with. If he thought her needy for affection, he'd run for sure.

The front door to the spa opened, and as soon as her mother walked in she ran her gaze up and down Missy. "You're looking good this morning, sweetie," she said with a knowing smile.

"Thank you." Missy had never been able to keep any kind of secret from her mother. Her mom had a lot of skills as a witch, and being able to understand a person's emotions was just one of her talents.

Hoping her mother would go into the back room to do her usual accounting chores and not ask the reason for her cheery mood, Missy went over to the counter to set out the display items. No surprise, her mom stayed in the main room, her arms crossed over her chest.

"You have a glow about you, Missy, almost as if your aura has been ignited. I'd love to hear all about it," she said with a grin.

Heat raced up her face. Did she really have a sparkle about her?

Was that even possible, or was her mom guessing? "There's not much to tell. I gave Zane some cooking lessons and showed him how to use the cell phone. It was good to feel needed again. That's all."

Mom slung her purse off her shoulder and set it down on the counter. "Why Missy Berta, you slept with him didn't you?"

Missy groaned, wishing she could tell for sure if there was any censure in her voice. "If you must know, yes I did. I'm over thirty. I can do as I wish."

Her mother smiled. "I never said you couldn't. Believe me, I'm happy for you." She leaned against the counter. "Tell me about Zane. I believe you said something about him having had amnesia."

Had she not confided in her mother in that long? "It's a long story."

Her mom looked around. "We haven't opened yet. You know I want to be involved in your life."

As long as she didn't become judgmental, it would be nice to have her opinion. For the next fifteen minutes, Missy detailed their rocky start from the horseback excursion to turning him down for a date. After Jackson approached her with the crazy notion that Cargonia was real, she did a little research on her own and noticed a picture of a man wearing an orange stone around his neck—just like the one she'd found in the cave. "I hoped Anna could get a reading off of it, and she did."

"That's fascinating. Did she think it belonged to Zane?"

"She didn't know, so I thought it best to ask him. Since he doesn't own a phone, I had to go to his house and well, one thing led to another."

"I can tell you're happy, but I also sense something is bothering you."

Her mother could always see through her. "Were you aware another realm existed?" Her mom used to have a lot of contact with Naliana, so maybe she knew.

"I won't say the idea is new to me. Cargonia has been part of the folklore for years. There have been supporters, and there are those who say it's hogwash. If whatever he tells you doesn't seem to contradict anything else that he says, you need to go with your gut."

That was what she did. "At first, I doubted Zane, but now I believe him."

"Good. I know the whole idea of another realm seems to defy logic, but so does what we do. Take yourself for example. Do you understand how you can place your hand on a person and help cure them?"

"No."

"You see? Since magic occurs here then why can't another realm exist?"

"You're right. I think I was afraid to take that leap."

Her mother walked around the counter and drew Missy into a hug. "Listen to your heart. You always see the good in a person, but you're also savvy. If he's lying, you'll be aware of it too."

"I hope so." Missy had a history of being gullible.

Her mother stepped back. "Have you contacted Ophelia yet? She might be able to give you some guidance about how to deal with this paradigm shift."

"I was planning to speak with her as soon as I can find her."

Her mom smiled. "Would you like me to contact her?"

How did her mother and Izzy seem to know the witch's whereabouts yet Missy didn't? She wouldn't be surprised if her mom or sister had a direct mental link with the woman. "I'd like that very much. Thanks."

"I'll let you know if I can set up anything." Her mom disappeared into the back room.

For the next hour, Missy tried to put Zane out of her mind, but she failed miserably. Some things he'd told her bothered her, like how he'd been pushed down a portal against his will. Why would someone want to do him harm? She wanted to learn more about why he ended up here. Missy sighed. She had too many questions and not enough answers. Hopefully Ophelia could help.

About a half hour before closing, her mom stepped from the

back room. "Can you come here for a second?"

"Sure." Teagan was with another customer. She bet this was about Ophelia. "Did you contact her?"

"Yes. Ophelia said she'd meet you by Izzy's old house today."

It was where she often met with the Wendayans. She seemed to like that place because it was secluded. "What time?"

"Five fifteen."

Her nerves surfaced. "I appreciate you asking her."

"No problem. I'll be curious to know what she says."

"Of course, but you know Ophelia. She can talk a lot and say nothing."

Her mom laughed. "Yes, the old lady would make the perfect politician."

"I totally agree."

Instead of being excited at the chance to find some answers, a trickle of dread seeped in. What if when she asked Ophelia about the existence of Cargonia, the old witch said there was only one realm? Who would she believe, Ophelia or Zane? Was it possible he was some con artist looking for a handout?

Missy refused to believe that. When she was with Zane, she was convinced he was sincere. She would have sensed any deception. When she spoke with Ophelia, it might be safer to limit her questions to his curse and his amnesia.

Two women entered the store asking about some aromatherapy. Her mom came out from the back and helped them while Missy piddled around, straightening up the items on the shelves. At a little after five, she said goodbye and headed out. As Missy neared where her sister used to live, her nerves stretched taut. She'd been so certain she wanted to hear the truth, but now that she was close, she wasn't so sure.

Once she parked, Missy waited for Ophelia to show up. When the witch didn't appear, Missy slipped out of her car and walked to the side of the property, where the trees were thickest, hoping to find her.

"Ophelia?" she called.

From behind a tree, she stepped into view. "Hello, Missy. It's nice to see you again."

Ophelia looked the same as when she'd seen her last. In fact, she appeared to be wearing the same long black dress, only this time her white hair was pulled back into a bun instead of hanging loose. "Thank you for seeing me."

Ophelia approached and held out her gnarled hands. Missy placed hers in the witch's grasp and closed her eyes for some privacy.

"What is it you wish to ask me?" the old lady asked.

Her tone sounded different—lower and more forceful—causing Missy to open her eyes. Ophelia released her hands, but her eyes were glazed over. "I met a man," Missy said.

She smiled and looked more like herself. "So this is about love?"

"No. I mean it could be, but that's not why I need your help." She told Ophelia that Zane claimed to have been hibernating for one hundred years. "Have you ever heard of a spell lasting that long?"

"One hundred years, you say?" She shook her head. "I've heard of spells that mimic death, but those will last forever. Unless…" She held up a finger.

"Unless what?"

"Have you ever read the fairy tale *Sleeping Beauty* where a princess fell asleep for one-hundred years and only awakens after her prince kisses her?"

Missy's pulse soared. "Sure."

"Were you nearby?"

"Yes, I was looking for Reishi mushrooms in the caves south of town when he wandered out from the dark recesses. I assure you I didn't kiss him though." That happened much later.

Ophelia stroked her chin. "I have heard that some powerful spells can only be broken by the presence of a mate. A kiss is not necessary."

Missy let out a nervous laugh, not sure whether to be thrilled or not. "What are you saying? That I am his mate?"

"You sound so surprised. You don't think it's possible?"

"No."

"Why is that?"

"Because Zane claims he's from another realm." Dang. She hadn't planned on mentioning that. "He said he's from a place called Cargonia and that some demon had a witch there put a curse on him and then dumped him down a portal to Earth." She couldn't believe she was telling this to her, but Ophelia's expression hadn't changed, so Missy continued. "He said he wasn't even aware he'd been transported to Earth until he awoke to find the world had changed."

"That's quite a story."

Missy's heart sunk. "So there is no such place as Cargonia?"

"I never said anything like that."

"Does that mean there is such a realm?" Missy asked, her voice coming out weak.

"Yes, there is. Now let me see if I can tell what the future holds for your young man." Ophelia closed her eyes and hummed, her expression looking almost pious.

Missy's heart beat hard awaiting the answer. The rational side wanted to know the future because she didn't want to be made a fool of. However, her emotional side wanted to wait for the future events to unfold. The birds seemed to have stopped chirping, and the wind had died down. It was as if the whole world was awaiting her answer.

"I see bloodshed and death," Ophelia said, her voice not even sounding like hers once more.

Missy's heart nearly stopped. "Whose death?"

Ophelia shook her head. It was as if she couldn't answer. "I see a lot of anger and hatred swirling around your young man."

"Zane doesn't hate anyone," she blurted.

"Just be careful." Ophelia opened her eyes and looked around as if someone had been channeling her thoughts.

"Of who? Zane? He'd never hurt me."

"Let your instincts guide you."

What did that mean? Before she could ask, Ophelia turned and seemed to float back toward the forest. As much as Missy wanted to go after her, she didn't want to learn more. Zane was not angry, and he wasn't a danger to anyone. That much she was sure. The old lady had to be wrong.

Or did it mean that those who'd put the curse on Zane could be the angry ones? Now that scenario she liked even less.

THE MOMENT VINEA descended on Silver Lake, intense waves of despair and anger at her sister blasted her, hindering her ability to perform her duties the way she wanted—and it was all Naliana's fault. Hell, it was always Naliana's fault.

The white moon wouldn't be for several days, so Vinea was fairly confident she wouldn't have another run-in with her goddess-of-the-light sister. The last time she was there, however, Naliana had received a special compensation to come to Earth. Why not again?

Right now, Vinea couldn't worry about sibling rivalry. She had an order to follow. If she failed, no telling what Androf would do to her. He claimed he'd ban her from the underworld for good, but Vinea didn't believe him. She'd been too valuable in the past for him to boot her out. Then again, he was a spiteful ass.

Clenching her fists, she glanced around the empty field where she'd almost succeeded in stealing Sam Pompley's powers. If her sister hadn't interfered, Vinea would have regained some of her abilities. As it was, with each day, she was growing weaker. She didn't have long before she'd become useless, and that would mean certain death, or rather emotional death.

Androf had promised that if she succeeded in sending Zane back to Cargonia that some of her powers would be restored. In case she had trouble opening the portal for some reason, he'd even given her a spell to use to fool the gods in Cargonia into believing she had the authority to enter. All she had to do was find the portal and lead him to it.

Simple.

Or not.

As recent as a few months ago, Vinea could have spotted where the air currents wavered. By altering the wavelengths, she would have been able to locate this foreign portal easily. After her sister blasted her with that ray of white light, her abilities to change air in any way were diminishing with each rotation around the sun, but Vinea would not be deterred. She'd find a way.

Zanedar Barons should know where it was. After all, he'd come through the damn thing. Most likely it was in the cave since he landed there.

Vinea inhaled to calm her jittery nerves. She was near those caves now, so it wouldn't hurt to have a quick look before taking some time to hatch her plan. She just might get lucky and find it.

Chapter Fifteen

SOMEONE KNOCKED ON Raymolt's office door and then pushed it open. "Excuse me, sir."

Raymolt spun around then relaxed when he saw it was only one of his minions. "What do you want, Winslod?"

When Raymolt was in the middle of planning some deed against the unsuspecting shifters, he didn't want to be disturbed. Winslod, however, only showed his face when it was important, for which he was often rewarded.

"You told me to let you know if there was any news of Zanedar."

Raymolt straightened. "News?" It had to be close to a hundred years since he'd sent that killing bastard to another realm.

"I've been monitoring Earth's progress, especially around Silver Lake where he landed."

"Get to the point." He had little patience today.

"He's awake."

Raymolt jumped up. "That's not possible. Are you sure?"

The witch had assured him the spell was for eternity. Killing Zanedar would have allowed him to be reunited with his brother, but permanent hibernation would keep him from any such joy.

The little gnome slid something he'd been hiding from behind his back. "I'm not sure how we missed this, but this book explains that the curse can be broken if his mate is near."

He waved a hand. "A mate, you say? That's preposterous. A Cargonian shifter would never be mated with someone from a different realm." Or so he'd been led to believe. Not many shifters from Cargonia had ever visited Earth, so there weren't many opportunities for interaction. Only the gods and goddesses had free reign to go where they pleased.

Winslod set the book on the desk. "You can look at the monitors for yourself. I didn't recognize him at first. His beard is gone, and his hair is cut short."

A mate? Raymolt didn't give a damn what he'd done to his hair. It disturbed him highly that Zanedar would find pleasure in a woman's flesh. "Have they mated yet?"

"I don't believe so. When the white moon appears and she shifts, we'll know for sure if the deed has been done."

"Then I need to do something about him before that happens."

"The portals are not aligned yet, sir."

He was well aware of the timetable. Demons weren't granted the freedom to go to the other realm. The gods of the light believed they'd cause harm. How right they were. But damn, he needed to reach Zanedar. He should have killed the bastard when he had the chance.

His path was clear. There were other ways to get through the portal, but it would cost him—dearly. It didn't matter. It had to be done. A brief smile lifted his lips at the thought of killing Zanedar's mate first just to watch him suffer like Raymolt had when he'd killed Raymolt's brother. This was just the little diversion he craved. It would be fun to put an end to this man once and for all.

"DRIVING IS JUST a matter of putting this gear into drive and pressing gently on the pedal. The hardest part is paying attention to the other cars," Missy said.

Zane swiveled his head. "We're in the middle of an empty parking lot. There are no other cars."

Missy chuckled. "There will be when you're on the road."

"I know. I just said that to stall. I don't want to crash like the last time."

She punched him in the arm. Zane was developing a good sense of humor. "You'll do fine. How about driving the car around the lot one time? Then you can practice backing up and finally parking.

"I'm game. Hold on."

Her car was an automatic, which would allow him to accelerate smoothly. Zane followed the edge of the lot and carefully avoided the three cars parked in the large space. Missy had to admit that Zane was doing a much better job than she'd done when she'd turned sixteen. She recalled clipping the hedge and then scraping the car against the side of the garage. Practicing in her driveway might not have been her father's best decision. Thankfully, Zane had good depth perception.

During the entire perimeter drive, his gaze never wavered from the road. "Good job," she said. "Put the car in park while I rearrange the cones. Learning to park is a must."

As soon as he stopped, she jumped out of the car and set the cones about two car lengths apart. To avoid making him nervous, she stayed outside then motioned for him to parallel park between her preset lines. She'd gone over one time how to accomplish that feat.

With dexterity, Zane backed up halfway between the cones and turned the wheel at the right time. While he almost clipped the front cone, he managed to squeeze in. Missy clapped.

She slid into the idling car. "You were great!"

"Thank you, ma'am, but I don't see how I can ever drive legally. I asked Rye about getting a license, and he said I needed a birth certificate."

Missy opened her mouth and then closed it quickly. "I'm sure there is something we can do."

"I love that you're trying to help me, but I might never fit in your world."

Her heart nearly stopped. "You're giving up and going back to Cargonia?"

Zane reached over and stroked her face. "Even if I could, I'd stay. I like it here despite the obstacles."

"But could you go if you chose to?" Not that she wanted him to. Missy was fond of the quirky man, really fond.

"No, I couldn't—at least not under my own power."

That didn't make a lot of sense. "You said the portal was two-way."

He clamped his hands on the wheel and leaned back. "It's one way for me. I don't have the authority to move between the realms—only gods do." He held up a hand. "There are other ways, but it requires the portals lining up with certain stars and then someone to help find them."

"Oh."

He twisted toward her. "Don't look so bleak. Once I earn enough money, I can buy a horse to get around. I don't need a license for that, do I?"

"No, but it's cold here in winter. It won't be pleasant riding in the snow. I doubt the horse will like it either."

"I'm sure I can handle it."

This was getting worse by the minute. "I know people from the eighteen hundreds survived in the winter because they had to, but it isn't easy. Rye lives near you. Maybe he could give you a lift to work if there's a storm. Or I could pick you up!"

Zane shook his head. "Maybe, but I don't want to live like that. I have to be independent."

"Then be an artist, and shoe horses on the side, like you used to. We can figure out the transportation part later."

He stared at her. "You are good for my soul, Missy, and I appreciate you trying to help, but soon people will start talking about the odd man you're with. I don't want to put you through that."

His words were like daggers. "It won't be like that. Look how well you did driving! I bet no one knows you've never driven before or that you'd never seen a cell phone. I'll help you."

"My dear sweet witch; it's not that easy. In case you haven't noticed, Silver Lake doesn't seem to have an abundance of horses."

Why did he seem determined to throw roadblocks in her way? "You want to give up?"

"Give up? No. Like I said, I can't go back even if I wanted to, but I want to stay. I like you."

She smiled, but her lips wobbled. "I like you too. We'll figure something out. A lot of children are born without a birth certificate and they are allowed to drive."

"Really? How is that possible?"

"I'm not sure, but I can ask Kalan Murdoch to see if he knows."

"Kalan, yes. He lent me some pants and shoes."

"He also works at the sheriff's department. He might have a work around."

"Work around?"

Missy needed to watch her idioms. "A solution."

Zane leaned back in his seat. "I appreciate it, but I'll be fine if he doesn't."

Zane was a stubborn man, but she liked that he wasn't trying to find the easy way out. "We have time. What do you say we call it quits for today and rustle up some dinner?"

"Great. What do you have in mind? My budget is still pretty small."

Zane had pride, and she respected that, but she wasn't asking to be taken out. "We could go to the store and make something at my place."

He grinned. "I like your place."

Images of them naked rose to the surface, as did a few blue sparks. "You might not after I suggest you do all of the cooking."

"Me?" he chuckled.

"I want to see if we can scratch cooking off the list of things you need to learn how to do."

"I used to be a great cook, though my best meal consisted of killing a wild drinlag and roasting it over a fire."

"A drinlag? What's that?"

He stretched his hands about eighteen inches apart. "It's about so long, and when grilled, it has the sweetest meat in the realm."

She chuckled. "I'll stick to chicken."

He shook his head. "If I could, I'd take you to Cargonia if only for one day to show you how nice it is."

"That would be wonderful." Her heart sank. At the thought of visiting, she sucked in a breath. "Did you have a wife back in Cargonia?"

"No! If I had, I'm not sure I could have made love with you."

"If you had a wife, would she still be alive?" Missy hadn't asked if there were any immortals in his realm—or if he was one.

He looked off to the side. "No. I try not to think that my parents, siblings, and all my friends are gone too." Zane scrubbed a hand down his jaw. "I imagine my mother suffered the most wondering what happened to me. My brother was killed only a few days before I was sent down the portal. His death devastated her. When I disappeared, she would have been further traumatized. I hope she learned what happened to me, if only to ease her grief."

Her heart cracked. "I'm sorry."

"For what?" he asked.

"For the pain this has caused."

Zane nodded. "Thanks. Do you remember when we first met I said I got drunk because my best friend had died?"

"Yes." She clamped a hand over her mouth. "Was that your brother?"

"It was. Rork was my best friend. I know it's been over a hundred years since his death, but to me only a few days have passed. Time didn't heal the wound in my heart while I was asleep."

She reached out and clasped his hand. "I'm a good listener if you want to tell me what happened."

Zane stabbed a hand through his hair. "I'm not proud of what I did, but you should know the good as well as the bad about me."

She swallowed. "There are a lot of things I'm not proud of either."

"Is that right? I bet you haven't killed anyone?"

Her nerves jangled. "Of course not."

"Well, I have."

Perhaps there were different laws in his realm or else it was in self-defense. "What did the person do?"

"He killed my brother."

"How horrible. Tell me what happened." Knowing Zane, the death had been justified.

He glanced off to the side. "I'm not exactly sure why Janoc and Rork were fighting that day, but everyone knows that a shifter doesn't stand a chance against a demon."

"A demon? You mentioned him before. Is that like a god from the dark realm?"

"No. Demons aren't gods nor are they as powerful. They aren't immortal either, but they are close to it. Most lived hundreds of years. They thrive on spreading ill will and being evil. The demons live among us on Cargonia and are quite good at covering up their horrible deeds."

They sounded like the Changelings. "Why did this demon pick on your brother?"

His chin trembled. "I'm not sure. All I know is that a few weeks before his death, Rork was having trouble with Janoc because the demon insisted on getting a special deal on some real estate transaction. I wasn't there when the fight started, but when I arrived, Janoc was beating my brother to death. Rork was already on the ground, unable to move, but Janoc wasn't satisfied. He kept pummeling him."

Her stomach churned. "How terrible for you. What did you do?"

"The only thing I could. I attacked Janoc, all the while praying that Rork would pull through. He was a strong bear, but the blows and burns to his upper body were too severe. After I killed Janoc, Rork died in my arms before help could arrive."

Burns? Her stomach churned. Even now, Zane's eyes turned almost black, and a tic formed around his mouth. "If your demons are nearly impossible to kill, how did you kill Janoc?"

"I had my sword with me. It was one I made. It was sharp and made of the strongest steel. Janoc was so focused on killing Rork that I don't think he was even aware I was there. All it took was one huge swing of my sword to his neck and… well, suffice it to say, he died."

It was probably better that he didn't give her the graphic details. "Why didn't your brother shift to heal himself? Or did he?"

"He was too weak to shift. Besides, we can heal ourselves quite well even in our human form."

"I wish I had been there. I might have been able to help."

Zane reached out and cupped her cheek. "My little healer. Yes, I wish you had been there too. You said you heal through magic?"

"Partly, yes."

"We have witches on Cargonia, most of whom are bad, but not Wendayans like you have here, and that is a shame. If I ever need your healing services, I'll be sure to call."

"I'll be there, but I hope you never need that kind of help." She twisted in her seat toward him. "So how did you end up in Silver Lake?"

"After I killed Janoc, I was called into the Clan's council for them to mete out judgment of my crime. When they heard what happened, they did not press charges."

"They shouldn't have. You were trying to save your brother's life."

"Yes, but Janoc's brother didn't see it that way."

She sucked in a breath. "Was he the one to put a spell on you?"

"A witch he hired did. While he never said it, I think he feared that if I had been able to kill his brother, I might be able to kill him too."

"Do you know how this witch put a spell on you? Did she do an incantation, light candles, or sprinkle you with a powder?" Missy had dabbled in spells, but she wasn't as successful as she wanted to be. But she'd never tried any evil ones.

"Not really. Raymolt, Janoc's brother, came to my house with

VELLA DAY

this old witch. Without any warning, he attacked me. I was so preoccupied with trying to stay alive that I didn't pay much attention to what she was doing. I remember her tossing something on me that felt like sand. When that didn't seem to work, she threw pebbles at me, mumbling something about sleeping forever. I was trying to keep the grit out of my eyes when Raymolt struck me so hard I fell to my knees."

"Why didn't you shift and attack him?"

"I tried. That witch must have put some kind of spell on me that prevented me from shifting. Except for when Janoc was beating Rork. I'd never been so frightened and angry in my life."

She wished there was something she could do to comfort him. "How did you end up going through the portal?"

"I couldn't say. I was out cold when it happened. Demons don't have access to portals like the gods. Maybe the witch helped him. All I know is that I heard your voice in my head, and I woke up. How I ended up in my bear form, I don't know, but I think that was what allowed me to survive for so long."

Ophelia's words came back to her about possibly being his mate, but she didn't hear anything in his story that corroborated it. "So the witch put a spell on you for one hundred years?"

"She said it was to last forever."

"I wonder why no one found you in the cave. A hundred years is a long time."

"Maybe people saw me and ran. It would be the smart thing to do."

"Wouldn't they become suspicious after a while?"

He chuckled. "I doubt many would be returning very often."

She smiled. "You're right. I'm just happy you woke up, and foiled that stupid curse."

Zane smiled. "I think it was being around you that did it."

Missy wasn't ready to address that comment or the fact she might be his mate. Her stomach grumbled, and she placed a hand on her belly.

"I think someone needs a home cooked meal," he said.

"I can't think of anything better. Let's hope the store doesn't carry any drinlag."

Zane laughed. "I'm sure you'll get your wish, though if you want to make it in one piece to the store, you'd better drive."

If the cops stopped them for whatever reason, she'd be in a lot of trouble letting him behind the wheel. "I'm determined to find a way for you to get a license."

"Then you'd never get rid of me."

Right now, she had no intention of doing so.

Chapter Sixteen

"M AYBE YOU CAN be a chef!" Missy said, enjoying the lasagna
that Zane had made. Sure, she had to guide him, but not
only had he done a fine job, he'd even added some of his own
touches.

"I had no idea we'd have so many spices in common. My mom
made food like this," Zane said.

"I'm still confused how the realms ended up with similar food.
You don't have a country called Italy do you?"

Zane shook his head. "No, but both gods and goddesses fre-
quently visit your realm—at least they started coming a few hundred
years ago when they realized the humans weren't so bad after all.
They've been known to bring back some of your spices—and share
some of ours."

"That's really cool. Maybe some of our products were really
conceived in your realm." She wondered if Zane ever ran into one of
these gods, might he ask to be transported back to Cargonia. She
shivered at that thought.

"It's possible." When Missy stood and picked up her plate, Zane
pushed back his chair. "I'll help," he said.

She held up a hand. "You cooked, so I'll clean up."

"Hmm. I guess that's fair. In Cargonia, we all help." He stood.
"I'll watch then."

No sooner had she placed all of the dishes in the dishwasher and
was about to clean the pots, when he stepped behind her and

wrapped his arms around her waist.

"You drive me crazy," Zane whispered into her ear.

She dribbled soap on the wet sponge and washed the pot used to cook the lasagna. "What brought that on?" She wasn't looking for a compliment, merely stalling for time to gather her wits about her. Sparks were shooting off her hands, and her body was going wild with need.

Once she rinsed the pot, Zane reached in and set it on the drying rack then turned her around. "Being near you, inhaling your scent, and watching your expressive eyes, has me wanting more. You've invaded my soul, Missy Berta, and I need you more than you can ever imagine."

His whispered words sent spikes of need soaring through her. "I need you too."

Zane grinned then drew her close. The kiss that followed created a connection more intense than ever. It might have been because he'd bared his soul, but she felt joined to Zane in ways she couldn't explain. People always needed her for her healing skills, but only Zane desired her for other things—at least she wanted to believe that was true.

His hands slipped under her shirt, and a second later he broke the kiss to lift the material over her head. He inhaled deeply. "I like your bra."

"Why's that?" Flirting with Zane was easy and fun.

"Because it heightens the anticipation."

She reached in front of her and grabbed his crotch. "Oh, yes! My anticipation is on the rise, too."

He cracked up. "Now I'm glad I was asleep for so long."

"Why's that?"

"I needed to wait until you were born and grew up."

"I'm glad too." Missy dragged a finger down his chest. "You know you look pretty good for someone who is one hundred and thirty-five years old."

"That so?"

"Yes."

"Perhaps you'd like to see if the rest of me will live up to your expectations."

"I'd love that."

Zane certainly wasn't shy. He knew what he wanted, and at this stage in her life, she wanted to give it to him. Her attraction wasn't due to the fact he was different, but rather how appreciative he seemed of anything she did. She also loved his can-do attitude. No hurdle seemed too big for him, and that made him special.

He stepped back and unzipped his pants, but before he could take them off she grabbed his hands. "Let me."

Holding out his arms, his eyes lightened, bordering between light brown and a golden amber hue. He'd already taken off his shoes since he loved to walk around barefoot.

Kneeling down on the small rug in front of the sink, she reached up and slowly tugged on his pants, inching the material over his thighs.

Zane groaned. "Just so you know this is pure torture. My bear is clamoring to get to you."

"He better not emerge. I want a man not a beast."

Zane chuckled. "Then don't take too long down there." He flexed his hands, and when he extended his fingers, his nails had grown.

"I'll be quick." Or maybe not. She wanted to sexually torment him to the point of distraction.

"You better be. I want to return the favor, assuming I can last that long. You do something to me, Missy; something I can't seem to control."

No one had ever said anything like that to her before. She smiled then eased his pants lower. When his cock popped out, she jerked back a little. It seemed larger this close up.

"Touch him," Zane commanded.

She'd do more than that. "How about a lick first?" she asked.

"Okay, but hurry."

Keeping her hands at her sides, she dragged her tongue from balls to tip, loving his earthy scent, or perhaps it should be called his Cargonian scent. When she swiped her tongue across the tip, she moaned from the salty taste of his precum. He wasn't kidding when he said she needed to be quick. Wanting to touch him more fully, she grabbed his shaft and tugged it closer. Drawing him deep into her mouth, she swirled her tongue around and around until he tugged on her hair so hard, she stopped and looked up at him.

Zane's eyes were closed, and he was swaying. It was almost as if he was praying to some god to give him the strength to last longer. Not wanting him to go off like a geyser, she let up on the pressure, licked him once more, and then stood.

His shirt needed to go; it was in the way of her thoroughly enjoying his body. As soon as she slid her hands under his T-shirt, his eyes opened. "If you stopped, you must know how close I am to exploding."

"I had faith you could hold on."

"Not when I'm this close to you." He sucked in a breath when she palmed his pecs.

She smiled then lifted off his shirt. "I love your chest." Only then did she notice his amulet. "You found a leather strap!"

"Actually, Rye found it for me."

"It looks good on you." Missy fingered the burnt orange stone then let go when it began to pulse a different color. "What happened? It looks alive."

Zane lifted it up. "This stone can feel things. When another member of my Clan draws near, the entire stone pulses a light yellow. When a demon comes close, it turns almost completely black. It's our warning system."

"That's amazing. But now the center is red. What does that mean?"

Zane leaned closer. "Red means I want you."

She couldn't tell if that was the truth, but she liked his story. "Then have me."

"If you want to see my stone go crazy, how about taking off that bra."

Missy reached around her back and unhooked it. Wanting Zane to remove it, she lowered her arms.

It didn't take long before he took the hint and pulled down the straps, his eyes glistening. The stone began to pulse a brighter red as the bra fell to her feet. "You are so beautiful."

Zane dropped to his knees, and because he was so tall, she only had to bend over a little to enable him to suck on her tits. The first pull had her clamoring for more. She threaded her fingers in his hair and pressed hard on his scalp. The tension sent sparks flying everywhere. "That feels so good."

"Mmm."

With each twist and turn, heat raced up her body, making her even more desperate. "Please, Zane."

When he dropped back on his haunches, she thought he'd stand and take her, but did he? No. He seemed determined to torment her now, like she had just done to him. After undoing the button at her waistband, he slipped both her shorts and panties down to her ankles. She quickly stepped out of them and kicked them aside.

"I can't wait to taste you," he said with a growl.

The first swipe of his tongue had her gripping the counter with one hand and his head with the other. When he flicked her clit, she nearly came right then. It was too much, too wonderful, and way too addictive. What was it about Zane that had her libido shooting sky high? Was it that they were mates?

He slipped two fingers into her wet opening, and when he wiggled them around, she stood on her tiptoes trying to control her climax. She thought she could last the onslaught of lustful sensations, but the moment he sucked on her sensitive nub again, waves of ecstasy crashed down on her.

Zane looked up and smiled. "Ready for another one?"

She could make love with him for hours and never tire of him. "Yes."

Zane stood and lifted her up. On instinct, she wrapped her legs around his waist and placed her hands behind his neck. With their gazes locked, he stepped them over to the refrigerator and kissed her as he pressed her back against the door. Every sense heightened and reeled. It didn't matter they weren't in a bed. Right now, all she could think of was that she wanted and needed Zane.

ZANE HAD TO work hard not to keep from sinking his teeth into her neck. She was his mate as sure as he was breathing. The how and why Missy was chosen didn't matter. Not that he'd ever return to Cargonia, but if he did, no one would believe his mate was a human or rather a human witch with talents.

Missy opened her mouth, and the moment their tongues touched, flames of desire nearly consumed him. His cock twitched, but he wanted to make sure she was ready before he plunged into her. His need was growing by leaps and bounds as her fingers clawed his back and her legs tightened around his waist. Once he started, he wouldn't be able to stop.

Her groans and huffs had the hair on his arms thickening. When his bones cracked, he was forced to break the kiss. "Get down for a minute," he pleaded.

She lowered her legs, and as much as he loved her breasts pressed against his chest, he believed she'd enjoy him more if he came in from behind. It would make his entry easier. Missy ran her hands up his chest, and he nearly lost it. "I like touching you like this."

"I like it too."

She lowered an arm and latched onto his cock. "And I like this."

He couldn't take much more. Grabbing her by the shoulders, he turned her around and pressed on her back. Instinctively, she palmed the refrigerator door and spread her legs. She actually had the nerve to giggle, knowing full well that he was ready to burst.

More bones cracked at her sassy willingness. *Not now*, he pleaded to his bear. He pressed his chest to her back and cupped her breasts.

His inner bear roared, which made Zane's teeth sharpen and his fur grow even more. He focused on pleasing Missy and not on his needs, but redirecting his thoughts didn't help all that much.

Unfortunately, he could smell her arousal, making it harder to breathe. When he kissed the shell of her ear, his amulet slid down over her shoulder, no doubt having turned completely red. Other than with his family, Zane had never experienced such acceptance before. As sure as he was standing there, he loved Missy Berta, witch extraordinaire. Even if she hadn't been his mate, he would have found her alluring and highly desirable. As much as he wanted to claim her for his own, Missy needed to believe that they belonged together. He owed her that much.

"Zane?" she called, her voice thick with emotion.

"Just trying to calm down a bit."

She reached between her legs and managed to grab half of his cock with her fingertips. When she squeezed his hard shaft, Zane's control shattered. With her sex so close, he slid out of her grasp and right into her wet channel. Even without any lube, he was able to enter easily. The foray took him close to oblivion.

When Missy moaned and thrust her hips back, he clasped her waist and drove right back in. Her blue aura grew until she was completely surrounded in light. As much as he wanted to ask more about that strange phenomenon of sexual excitement, he was too consumed to stop now.

Missy lowered her head, and when she clamped down hard, his world tilted on its axis. She then let out a series of moans and grunts that ended in a scream. It was when her voice reached a crescendo that he spilled his seed into her.

The stars he saw in front of him weren't coming from her. It was almost as if the Cargonian witch had cast another spell, only this time it was to make sure the two of them never parted.

Zane wrapped his arms around her waist and pressed his cheek against hers. "You are so fantastic."

Missy lowered her arms and lifted up a bit. "Ditto."

As soon as he slipped out of her, she scooted over to the kitchen drawer. Once she retrieved a cloth, she wet it and cleaned herself. She then soaked the other end and placed it over his cock. "We Earthlings like to be clean."

He chuckled. "As do we Cargonians."

Missy dropped the towel into the sink and wrapped her arms around his neck. "I like you, Zane Barons."

Lies should never occur between mates. "About that. My full name is Zanedar Barons."

She chuckled. "For real? Zanedar? Is that what I should call you?"

"Have you ever met another Zanedar?"

"No."

"Then Zane is good. I am trying to fit in here."

Missy lifted the amulet from his neck, and her touch made the stone pulse again. "I really like this. It's almost like you're a Wendayan and have sparks. All I have to do is check out the color of the stone to see if you're excited."

He kissed her briefly, unsure whether he could keep from taking her again. "You don't need to look at the stone to know that. I always want you."

"I am curious about one thing," she said. "Why did it flicker when I rubbed it? Do you know why?"

Tell her, his bear demanded.

"Yes."

"Why's that?"

Chapter Seventeen

B EFORE ZANE WOULD tell her what was on his mind, he insisted they dress first. He said it would help keep his mind on what he needed to say, making Missy curious as well as cautious. Zane had already admitted that he'd killed a man; what else could he possibly tell her now that required this much care?

She sat down on the sofa and folded her hands on her lap. "I'm listening."

Zane sat next to her and lifted her hands to his lips. "I'm not sure where to begin since I've never done anything like this before." He looked off to the side. "I wish I could speak with my dad, but I can't."

Unease rolled off him, but she wasn't sure how to help. Because his amulet had returned to its original orange color, this wasn't about sex. "Just tell me. It can't be that bad."

He huffed. "No, it's not bad. At least to me it's not."

The suspense was killing her, and she slipped her hands from his. "Zane, please."

"Okay. When I was asleep in the cave, I told you it was your voice that roused me."

"Well, I thought I heard a noise, so I did yell to see if anyone was there."

"Yes, but I also felt you before I woke up."

Her heart pounded. Ophelia had said that a spell like the one placed on Zane probably could have only been broken by the presence of a mate. Is that what he was trying to tell her? "What do you think it means?"

Please say I'm your mate.

Asking outright might cause more issues between them if it weren't true. Most likely, his mate was long gone, but he wanted her despite them not being fated. Oh, hell. She needed to hear what he had to say before going off the deep end thinking the worst.

"It wasn't just that I awoke because I heard you. My body, as well as my bear kept telling me that you were my mate and I had to wake up."

It was true! "Really, I'm your mate? Are you sure?" Missy was deliriously happy.

"Yes."

She tilted her head, waiting for more of an explanation.

Zane lifted her hand again, and when together they touched the stone, the amulet started to pulse at a rapid pace and then stopped, holding steady with a bright glow.

"My amulet is a part of me, and it recognizes my mate. That is why when you touched it alone, it pulsed. When we touch it together, it glows brightly, showing that we, as fated mates, have found each other."

Missy's gaze remained on the amulet. "Wow. I'm speechless."

He tucked a finger under her chin and gently lifted it until her gaze connected with his. "I'm excited, but how do you feel about all this?" Zane cupped the side of her face and rubbed his thumb across her cheek.

Missy leaned into his touch and smiled. "As soon as I saw you in the cave, I felt this draw between us. It was something I'd never experienced before. I know fated mates exist since I've seen it with my sister and a ton of my friends, but I've never had those kinds of sensations running through me like when I first saw you."

"Well, I was naked, and not to brag, but I am…"

She punched him. "Be serious."

"Fine. Why didn't you say something?" he asked.

"I didn't know what those feeling meant until I consulted one of our witches. Ophelia said the only way a curse that powerful could have been broken was by the presence of a mate. So I was waiting for you to bring it up. After all, shifters seem to know for sure. Wendayans only feel the tug of attraction."

Zane's stone pulsed red just as he leaned down to kiss her. It was the kind of kiss that was deliciously soft and sensual yet so full of passion. "I was so afraid that you would think I was crazy. I mean, there is so much of this world I know little about. You may find it's too much work teaching me all the time."

She smiled. "That's where you're wrong. You are strong, wonderful, and caring. Why in no time at all, those things will become second nature to you. I have complete faith in you. You truly are an amazing man, Zanedar Barons."

He stroked her cheek. "You better watch out. Any more compliments and I'll have to make love with you again. I've heard that women here are more delicate than the Cargonian women."

She didn't want to think about him making love with anyone else, even though she had slept with her share of men looking for Mr. Right. To think, all she had to do was wander into a cave and find him.

"I am a bit sore. How about a rain check?"

His brows furrowed. "Is it raining?"

She laughed. It was one of the many things she adored about him. "A rain check means I'll take you up on your offer later."

Zane scooted closer. "With a few well-placed kisses, perhaps I can convince you to make it sooner rather than later."

She grinned. "You are welcome to try."

RAYMOLT HAD SPENT an interesting if not frustrating week on Earth's realm. For years he'd had his kit ready should he need to come here. Forging a driver's license was as simple as hiring the right person to create it. As for money, Cargonia used the ink and plates similar to those used by the US Mint. It made moving between the realms seamless for the gods, which was why they chose the dollar for their currency. He'd heard of slight problems when the gods visited other countries but that was not his issue today. His goal had been to learn everything he could about Zanedar—his habits and the identity of his mate—and then eliminate both.

Finding his prey had been easy. Before Raymolt had left, Winslod had stayed by the monitors night and day, tracking the werebear. Knowing where the man went on a daily basis was all well and good. It was getting Zanedar alone that was hard. Silver Lake was more crowded than he would have liked. It wasn't like he could walk up to the man and attack him. While no shifter here could take him down, even a demon would be punished by his kind if he caused a stir in another realm.

Those in charge of the demons were constantly warning them about exposing Cargonia's existence to Earth's realm. It was why access to the portals had been restricted, but he'd fooled them. Raymolt had stolen an instrument that helped him detect the portals, and his lineage was just powerful enough to allow him to pass through it.

Today, he would be setting his eyes on his brother's killer for the first time in one hundred years, and he couldn't be happier. Just this morning, he'd learned of this big race that everyone in town liked to attend. Knowing Zanedar, he'd be there. The werebear always did love water and boats. Given his size and werebear stench, the shifter would be easy to find regardless of the crowd size.

He parked his rental on the river's edge far from the others because he wanted to be able to leave should Zanedar spot him.

Once Raymolt learned who was near and dear to him, he would come up with a plan to get Zanedar's mate alone. He was fairly confident that once confronted with the possibility of her death, Zanedar would do as Raymolt asked—engage in a battle. The final victory would be so sweet. He chuckled to himself. He still couldn't decide whether to drive a stake through Zane's heart or just rip it out with his bare hands. Setting him on fire might be more fitting though. Raymolt had always loved fire. It didn't matter really which way Zanedar died. Janoc would finally be able to rest once his killer was tortured and put down. The only negative was that Zanedar would be reunited with his family once and for all, but that was better than letting the werebear live in bliss.

FOR THE LAST six days, Zane had barely kept focused on work. His thoughts had centered around Missy and not on cleaning the firehouse. He had feared that all would be lost once he told her they were mates, but Missy seemed to think he was a great catch. Disappointing her now was not an option. And that meant fitting into this world.

She'd mentioned she'd gone to a library to do research on his world after her friend Jackson Murdoch mentioned Cargonia might be real. If she could find information about his realm, he could only imagine what he could learn about Earth. That was why he'd asked Rye about the library's location. Since then, every day at lunch Zane had studied what they had to offer. The information had been mind-expanding. The books on technology fascinated him the most. The librarian was even kind enough to show him how to find articles on the computer. That alone was worth missing a meal. While he had a long way to go in catching up on a hundred years of progress, he was making great strides, and he was determined to prove to Missy that he was worthy of being her mate.

By the time Saturday rolled around, he was doubly thrilled because the town was having its annual regatta at Turkey Point, a location on a river that ran through the west side of town. Cargonia had many boat races, and he was looking forward to seeing what Silver Lake had to offer in the way of boat construction and talent.

For the last few nights, he'd stayed with Missy at her house, and he'd never been happier. Each time they made love, he believed he was more comfortable with the idea of mating with her. He was ready, but before he made it final, he wanted to make certain she wanted it too. Love swelled his heart to epic proportions, and from the way she liked to rub up against him, she too was having a hard time keeping her hands to herself.

"We don't want to be late," Missy said as she bounced out of the bedroom wearing short shorts, sandals, and a green top that barely reached her waist. His woman looked fucking hot. That was his friend Tanner's favorite expression. He'd say it every time he spotted a nice looking woman, and it described Missy well.

"I'm good."

She laughed. "You forgot a shirt."

"Sorry. I sometimes forget where I am."

Zane ducked into the bedroom. This would be his first official outing with Missy. While he'd met a few of her friends, he was anxious to interact with more of them. Back on Cargonia, he'd had an active social life, and he was looking forward to building a new network of friends with Missy.

When he returned to the living room, she had a picnic basket in hand. "Can you carry this?"

"Absolutely." He lifted it, and it was heavier than before. She must have added a lot more food. "These boat races must be some affair."

"It's the town's beginning of summer highlight. I think you'll be impressed. The river isn't very wide, but that is what makes the event exciting. The participants have to be careful not to run into each other."

"I can't wait." While it galled him a bit that Missy had to drive, he understood his limitations. As soon as she headed toward town, he twisted toward her. "Can you tell me who we might run into?"

"I can't name them all. I know most everyone in Silver Lake. I heal some shifters and Wendayans, but I also work at the store that caters to humans. Because I've been called on to heal some of the locals, there's no telling who we might see."

"I had no idea you knew so many people, so even if you tell me their names, I might not remember them all."

She smiled. "There won't be that many who come by. If they do, I'll introduce you. You'll do fine."

"I just don't want to embarrass you."

When she reached out and rubbed his leg, his bear went wild. *Just a little bit longer*, he told his eager animal.

Zane cleared his throat. "A while back, you mentioned something about Changeling creatures. They sound a lot like our demons, except yours are easier to kill than our nasty beasts. Will they be there?"

Her lips pressed into a thin line. "I don't know. I can't tell one shifter from another. In fact, only shifters can sense another shifter, so I'll have to rely on you to tell me when one is near. Most likely, you won't be able to tell the good from the bad though."

He liked that he had a talent she didn't. "If that's the case, how do you protect yourselves against them?" At least with his amulet, he had some advance warning when a demon came near since the center would turn black.

"We don't. It's partially why I make sure to stay out of trouble. I wouldn't be surprised though if I've healed a few, thinking they were good people."

He didn't like that Missy was so vulnerable.

When they arrived at the event, the area close to the water was so full of cars that Missy had to park a good distance away. It was a partly cloudy day, and the air was dry, making it perfect to sit and watch the festivities. The chirping birds and swaying trees reminded him of his hometown, and a wave of sadness assaulted him.

I live here now, he reminded himself. While he did miss his family and friends, he had Missy, and that was good enough for him.

Zane looked around. "Just to be clear, no one shifts at these things do they?"

Her face paled. "No! Humans can't learn about your kind—I mean shifters."

"Got it."

It would be difficult to get used to refraining from shifting at will or even talking about shifters, but he'd try.

Missy seemed to know where to go, so he followed her. She stepped around a lot of people who'd staked out their areas for watching the festivities.

"Hey, there's Jillian and Brian. Let's sit with them," she said with excitement in her voice.

Zane had no idea who these people were, but they seemed to bring her joy. If he'd met them before, he'd forgotten. He touched her arm and leaned close. "Are they witches like you?"

"Yes. Jillian is a Wendayan and a white tiger shifter. She's a local lawyer in town. Brian is her mate, and he's a bear shifter, but he has a bit of Wendayan in him now too. He's an amazing artist. If you need anything made from wood, Brian is your man."

"Nice." His ego stung a bit. While Zane mostly worked with iron, he was quite good with wood too. Perhaps he needed to make something for Missy and show her what he was capable of.

All along the banks of the river, people were laughing and chatting, as if this was their one chance to relax with their friends. Out of habit, Zane studied the area. In Cargonia, predators lurked everywhere, and he always had to be on his guard.

While the river bent about four hundred feet from where they were sitting, obscuring the water from view, he felt comfortable with her choice of location. He also sensed quite a few shifters, making him more at ease.

"Hey, guys," Missy said to her friends. She placed the blanket on the ground next to them, and they both sat down. "Jillian and Brian, this is Zane."

"Hi, Zane," they said in unison.

"Nice to meet you."

He expected them to ask the usual questions about where he was from, but when they didn't ask him anything, he had to assume Missy had already briefed them. It was just as well. Lying wasn't in his nature.

"Oh, look," Jillian said. "The first race is about to begin."

"We got here just in time then," Missy said.

Zane sat up straighter. "Those boats look just like the ones we have back in—North Carolina." Damn. He'd almost said Cargonia. He had to be more careful.

Missy's eyes widened, clearly worried he'd slip again. "I think they're all over the country."

"I bet you're right."

A signal sounded, and six boats took off. The crowd cheered, though he was pretty sure no one on the water could hear any particular shout. "Is there an entrance fee for the race?" he asked, trying to figure out the motivation for organizing such a massive endeavor. Things related to business always fascinated him.

"Yes. The proceeds are for the animal shelter in town. It's what helps support them."

"That's wonderful."

While the Cargonians were generous people, animals were well taken care of in his realm, which meant there was no need for shelters. Medical help for the shifters in general was limited because they could usually heal themselves. Only shifter orphans needed a lot of care. Too often fires or an animal attack killed their parents. His heart ached remembering a house fire that took the lives of his two good friends, leaving their three-year old daughter alone.

Missy nudged him. "See the orange and red boat?" she asked, pointing to the one with the brightly colored intricately carved bow. "Blair's racing in that one."

"Who's Blair?"

"That's Jackson's sister."

Ah yes, the man who helped convince Missy that Cargonia existed. All these names had his brain scrambled. He should have brought a pen and paper to keep track of her friends.

Putting aside who was who, Zane studied the participants' strokes and how well the teammates worked together, all the while attempting to pick out the winner. All six boats disappeared out of view for a few minutes before returning. When they rounded the corner the first time, they were neck and neck. When they returned, they were not.

"Excuse me," someone said next to him.

As much as he wanted to watch, this woman was probably a friend of Missy's, and he didn't want to be rude. The tall blonde haired woman with black-rimmed glasses squeezed her blanket between where they were seated and another couple a few feet away. Because a two-foot space existed between them and Missy's friends, he tapped her on the shoulder. "Can we move a few feet closer to Jillian and Brian?" He nodded at the blonde.

Missy dragged her gaze from the boats to the woman, but there wasn't any recognition. "Oh, sure."

With a bit of work, they managed to scoot over. Once the newcomer settled next to them, the woman held out her hand to Zane. "Thanks. I'm Vanessa."

"Zane. Nice to meet you." The cheers grew louder as the teams sped toward the finish line, and he returned his attention to the race.

One of the three boats that had been in contention fell back. With a last minute effort, the team wearing the pink shirts pulled ahead and won, and the applause nearly deafened him. Unfortunately, it wasn't Blair's boat, nor was it the one he'd chosen.

When the noise calmed down, Missy glanced over at the woman who was sitting there all by herself. "Are you new around here?" Missy asked.

"Yes. I'm here visiting my folks in the next town over. I'm Vanessa."

Missy held out her hand. "Missy."

Since there was a break in the action, Zane decided to see what food Missy had packed and opened the basket. No sooner had he pulled out the sandwiches than his chest began to hurt. He must have grunted because Missy glanced at him.

Her eyes widened, and she nodded to his amulet, which had turned black in the middle. His gut churned. "I'll be right back," he said.

This was bad. Very bad indeed. If Raymolt were actually here, then Zane's new life as he had come to know it could end. This time there wouldn't be a witch to merely put a spell on him. If he fought Raymolt, he'd surely die.

VINEA, WHO HAD said her name was Vanessa, was pissed. She finally had the perfect opportunity to insinuate herself into Zane's and Missy's lives and what happened? He leaves! From the way his body had stiffened, there could be only one explanation. She too had felt a demon presence. From what little Androf knew of Zane's history, some demon had a spell put on Zane that was supposed to last forever. Now that the werebear had roused, she bet this demon wanted to make sure he didn't have long to enjoy this world.

To think she'd gone to all the trouble of changing her hair color and wearing these disgusting glasses, only to have her plan fall apart. Sure, all she'd had to do was swipe her hand over her head and change the color and length of her hair back again, but it hadn't been fun dressing like a geeky girl. She fancied low cut, sexy outfits—not oversized tops and baggy pants.

Vinea shifted her thoughts to the one person she was trying to hide from—Devon McKinnon—hoping he wasn't here. She could still see his face the first time he'd spotted her in that bar up north. Vinea had gone there in search of eliciting help in taking down Sam Pompley. If it hadn't been for her stupid sister foiling her attempt to steal his powers, Vinea would be a lot more formidable today.

If Devon were here, she had no doubt he'd frown at her, though in all likelihood, he wouldn't even recognize her. The whole purpose of the disguise was to walk about town without being discovered. It would be an understatement to say she wasn't Silver Lake's favorite goddess.

Vinea searched for Zane, wondering what was taking him so long. Had there been some colossal altercation? In truth, if the demon did kill Zane, her job would be over, and she could return to the dark realm victorious.

The problem was that if she left now to find the two of them, Vinea wasn't sure she could explain her sudden departure—especially if she headed in the same direction that Zane went. She didn't need Missy to question her about why she'd insisted on sitting next to complete strangers and then went after one.

Even if she managed to give Missy a good excuse and then ran into Devon, she wasn't sure she could avoid interacting with him. Sure, she'd lied to him about her identity, but she'd had no choice. Stealing Sam Pompley's powers had been her goal.

Devon was a nice guy, but she didn't dig nice guys. Why would she? She wasn't a dark realm goddess for nothing! And therein lay her dilemma. In the hundreds of years of her existence, he was the first and only person to get her motor running. It didn't matter she hadn't even slept with him. If he hadn't been so angry with her, she bet he would have.

Right now, she couldn't let Devon distract her thoughts. She was here to do a job. Forcing her body to cool off, she focused on this demon. Normally, a demon couldn't travel through portals unless he either had special permission or had help. Hopefully, the demon had the ability to return to Cargonia and take Zanedar with him.

As much as she detested the lowly vile demons, she'd do anything necessary to succeed. Failing wasn't an option. Besides, she had to get out of Silver Lake before the white moon appeared. Running into her sister could be deadly, especially if Naliana had the chance to blast her with more light. Then she'd be left in limbo with no place to live.

If she hadn't been immortal, she might have considered taking her own life.

Chapter Eighteen

"WHERE DID ZANE go?" Brian asked. "He looked like he'd seen a ghost."

Missy could hardly say that the center of his amulet had turned black, and it was possible a demon from another realm had come after him. While she trusted both of them completely, she needed to ask Zane first if he minded if these two knew about his history.

"I'm not sure. I wouldn't worry though. He probably saw someone he knew." That was lame, though hopefully they would buy it since Zane worked at the fire station.

Missy picked up one of the sandwiches, and as she took a bite, she noticed the blonde woman looking at her, probably listening to the entire conversation. Missy went over the dialogue in her head, but she hadn't mentioned shifters or demons.

Other than her blanket and water bottle, Vanessa hadn't brought any food whereas Missy had a ton. Wanting to be friendly, she pointed to the picnic basket. "Would you like a sandwich?"

The pretty blonde held up a hand. "I don't want to be a bother."

"No, I brought way too much. You'd be doing us a favor."

Vanessa smiled. "In that case, thanks."

Missy handed her a peanut butter and jelly sandwich. The first time Zane had tasted one, he'd been hooked. "Have you been in town long?" Missy asked.

There was something about her that seemed familiar, but she couldn't put her finger on it.

Vanessa finished chewing. "Only a few days." She nodded to where Zane had gone. "Is Zane your husband?"

"No, we recently met." But in case Vanessa had any idea about putting the moves on him, Missy would have to speak to her about keeping her distance.

Missy sensed Zane before she saw him and glanced up. "Oh, here he is now, just in time for the next race." She forced her voice to hold a lot of cheer.

As the large man strode toward her with his teeth clenched, Missy's heart pounded. That wasn't good. When she checked out Vanessa's reaction, the newcomer was busy finishing her food, not paying attention to Zane. Perhaps she was merely hungry and not after her man.

"So?" Missy asked when he slipped down next to her.

"It might have been a false alarm," he whispered.

Now wasn't the time to discuss it. "The next race is about to begin."

"Good." For the next few minutes, they watched paddleboard races. When two of the contestants fell off their boards, the crowd cheered. While that wasn't a nice reaction, at least the entrants seemed to enjoy the dip on the warm day.

Zane seemed interested in who might win, but every now and then she'd catch him looking around. When the last race finished, he hurriedly packed up. She wanted to ask him what he planned to do and whether he had spotted the demon, but she'd wait until they were alone. She knew he better not consider approaching him on his own. Zane would be killed.

She should suggest he elicit help from Sam Pompley since he might be able to do a little mind control on the creature. Lexi said Sam could make people believe that something was right in front of them when it wasn't. Wouldn't that be great if this demon returned to Cargonia believing Zane was still in hibernation!

"Hey, do you guys want to come over to our place?" Jillian asked, interrupting her thoughts. "We just finished the remodel, and

I'd love to show it off."

"That would be great," Missy said before Zane had the chance to say he'd rather go home. While she couldn't be certain, she doubted the demon would try anything with so many people around.

Zane closed the lid on the picnic basket and stood. Hoping to distract him, she jumped up, stood on her toes, and kissed him. Not only did his eyes turn that beautiful shade of amber she liked, the center of his stone pulsed red. As if he'd forgotten they were in the middle of half the town, he parted her lips and delved into her mouth. For a moment, even Missy forgot where she was.

"Ah, guys," Jillian said with way too much cheer in her voice.

Missy leaned back and licked her lips, wanting to taste all of him. She remained close, sliding her hand up his chest, secretly collecting the amulet on her way and tucking it inside his shirt so no one would notice the pulsing color. Zane grinned but looked away, probably because hair had sprouted on his face. She faced Vanessa, to take her mind off what she and Zane had almost done.

"Nice to meet you, Vanessa," Missy said.

The woman smiled and then stilled, her gaze shooting over Zane's shoulder. "You too. Maybe I'll see you around."

Before Missy could respond, the blonde picked up her blanket and hustled off.

"She's a strange one," Brian said, his gaze following her.

"Perhaps she remembered an appointment." That was lame, but Missy wasn't in the mood to talk about the tall, beautiful woman.

"I guess we'll see you at the house in a few minutes," Jillian said.

"You bet." Because they had parked in different spots, they headed off in opposite directions. As soon as she and Zane climbed into the car, Missy faced him. "Tell me what happened."

"It's nothing you need to be concerned with."

That attitude pissed her off. While people always said Missy was one of the most easygoing people in Silver Lake, if someone was threatening the man she was falling in love with, she wanted to know about it.

Whoa! Had she just admitted that she might love Zane? How was that possible when she'd known him all of a few weeks? She forced her mind back to the problem at hand, refusing to get in an argument with herself about whether it was even possible. Focus.

"How can you say this doesn't affect me? I saw the middle of your amulet turn black. You said that meant a demon was near. Unless I'm mistaken, we don't have any of those in my realm." She held her breath, hoping he wouldn't say those evil beings were everywhere.

"You're right. I thought Raymolt might be here, but when I walked around, I didn't sense him."

"He might have seen you walk toward him and disappeared." She'd seen Naliana float a few inches from the ground. Perhaps Raymolt possessed a similar talent. "Can this Raymolt disappear?"

Zane shook his head. "No."

That was good. "What does he look like?"

"Like any other human. He's maybe six foot five with arms the size of canons. But that's how we see him. When a demon dies— which isn't very often—his real self appears."

She shivered. "Don't tell me he has a red face and horns?"

A small smile lifted his lips. "No, but his skin is more like scales, his head is small, and his legs are stubbier."

"No one has ever mentioned that they've seen a creature like that around here."

He clasped her shoulder. "How about we go to your friends' house and enjoy ourselves? Let's not let the possibility that he's here ruin a good time. We're safe from him for now."

"Okay." Missy started the engine. "Just so you know, I am worried. What do you think about telling a few people who you really are? That way if the demon approaches, they'll know not to try and be a hero."

He shook his head. "If I do tell anyone, it'll be Rye. From what I can tell about the shifters here, they are brave men. If they interfered, they would end up dead. I could never live with that."

She could understand his concern. "As for telling Rye, I wouldn't be surprised if he already knows about you. Jackson Murdoch keeps in touch with him. Knowing that chatterbox, he's already told his Alpha. Rye is probably waiting for you to mention it to him."

"I'll speak to Rye when I think the time is right."

Assuming you're still alive. Missy's stomach tumbled at that thought. Refocusing on getting them out of there, she sat behind a long line of cars waiting to exit. Eventually, the line began to move. "How do you intend to deal with this Raymolt guy? You said demons were hard to kill." Zane was a large man, but she'd bet there were many others in his realm that were equally as big and strong.

"They are, but remember, I was able to kill his brother because I had my sword along with the element of surprise. Unfortunately, I'd look a little funny riding my bike to work having a blade at my side. People would be bound to ask why I was carrying one."

She had to smile at that image. "If you want to be called crazy, that would surely do it. What about a gun? Would that kill a demon?"

"I'm afraid not. Bullets pass through them."

"What are they? Made of air?"

He shrugged. "I don't know. I'm not sure if anyone has ever looked closely at a dead one. The demons found the one I killed and took him away."

"Well, when you kill this one, we can take him to our shifter doctor. He'd be discreet."

"Don't count on having access to a dead one. One reason why the demons are so successful at killing shifters is because the demons are sneaky, preferring subtle ways to draw out their victims. The shifters are often caught off guard."

"Like your brother." Zane winced, and she immediately regretted mentioning that delicate subject.

"Yes, like Rork."

"Can't you shift and take him down? I would think a bear could overpower this creature?"

"You would think. Demons are really fast. A bear doesn't stand a chance against one. Different demons have different talents though. Some can shoot fire from their palms, while others can electrocute you with a touch. The rare few can do both."

"They sound like some of our Wendayans. I bet Jillian's brother could beat one. No one is faster than Dalton." Asking him to help might endanger him though, and she wouldn't want that on her conscience either.

"I don't want to take that chance."

She understood. Five minutes later, she pulled into the grocery store parking lot, wondering if she could enjoy herself tonight, believing this Raymolt fellow wanted Zane.

"Why are we stopping?" Zane asked.

"It's common courtesy to take a gift when you've been invited to a person's house. Since this is like a house warming, I thought I'd pick up a bottle of wine."

"I can see there are a lot of traditions Cargonia could learn from your world."

"I hope you don't plan on going back just to share all the cool things we do," she said. Zane had said he couldn't go back, and she wanted to hold him to it.

"Not on your life."

VINEA WAITED UNTIL the crowd thinned before she went in search of the demon. If he had left the event, he wouldn't have gone far. When she entered the wooded area near the bend in the river, she smelled him, but the scent was faint, implying he'd already left. Damn. The best way to reach this demon would be to hang out around Zane. The demon would show up eventually.

While she was able to disappear and move about at will, she wanted to blend in. Vinea had rented a car and had even booked a room in a hotel the next town over. She had tried to get a room in

Silver Lake, but apparently people came from far and wide to watch these lame races.

She sneered. Some people needed to get a life.

As she neared her car, her body began to vibrate, and not in the same way it had when she'd smelled the demon. No, this sensation was unfortunately familiar. The same thing had happened when she'd run into Devon the first time—and each time thereafter.

Out of the corner of her eye, she spotted the back of someone who looked a lot like him. He was well over six-feet, had military short hair, and broad shoulders that she found all too attractive. Not wanting to take a chance that he'd catch her in town, she rushed to her car. Just as she had her hand on the door, he turned around. His gaze caught hers and she froze. Had he sensed her presence?

Her pulse soared—a ridiculous reaction since no one had ever affected her like that before—not even Androf—a god who held her future in his hands.

Get in the car, quick!

It wasn't like Devon would come running over to see her. Hell, he was probably wondering who she was. While Vinea had been able to change her hair color, as well as alter the style, she hadn't been able to make herself shorter. Not many women were five feet ten inches and thin. Hopefully, her baggy clothes would hide her figure.

She ducked into the car and started the engine. Thankfully, she managed to peel out of there before Devon had the chance to follow. While it was highly improbable he had recognized her, she believed somehow he had.

It might not be the end of the world if he did, but now she would have to be a lot more careful. Well, damn.

Chapter Nineteen

Z ANE FINGERED BRIAN'S lathe. "This is fantastic."

"Surely you've seen one like this before." Brian said. "It's a nice one, but there are more expensive ones on the market."

Zane looked over at Missy. If he had any hope of making something of himself here, he'd need a shop to do his ironwork and woodworking. From what he saw of Brian's work, the two of them could create spectacular things together. Missy said she trusted these two people not to say anything, and he could hope that was true.

"Sure, but not something this nice, and there's a reason why. I think we need to talk."

Jillian grabbed Brian's arm. "It's okay. We know you had amnesia and can't remember some things."

"It's more than that," Zane said. He glanced over at Missy, and she nodded. He'd tell them everything other than how he thought he had sensed Raymolt at the event today.

"Let's go back to the living room," Jillian said. "It's more comfortable there."

For the next twenty minutes, Zane detailed the existence of the two realms and how he was from Cargonia. Both Brian and Jillian peppered him with questions, but they seemed to believe him. Of course, it helped that Missy told them what she knew.

"That's an incredible story," Brian said. "I don't think I would have rebounded as well. Listen, any time you get bored and want to see what new equipment looks like, you're welcome to come up and watch me work. Hell, if you bring your own wood, you can try out my equipment."

"I'd like that." That was more than generous. He told them that he used to be a blacksmith as well as an artist who worked in iron.

"I wish Brian and Zane could work together on a project someday," Missy said. "I bet that would sell."

"Hey, tell me what you need, and maybe we can come up with something," Brian chimed in.

For the first time since he'd sensed the demon, Zane relaxed. Having people accept him for his limitations went a long way to helping him feel more comfortable here. For the rest of the evening they talked about what options Zane had for learning about computers and other technology.

"There is a community college in Silver Lake," Jillian said. "You might want to take a class. One of the secretaries in the office where I work is going to night school there."

He looked at Missy, and she nodded. "Besides paying for it, wouldn't I need some kind of identification?" he asked.

"Most likely. I'd bet that on Cargonia, you wouldn't have had a driver's license or a social security card, did you?" Jillian asked.

"No."

"That does make it more difficult. Let me check to see what's required. There might be some obscure law that deals with people without any papers."

"I'd appreciate you helping in any way."

By the time he finished answering questions, he was ready to get back to Missy's house. Sitting next to her while she shot him sly glances had his animal going wild with need. All three of them probably noticed his amulet pulsing red through his shirt, but thankfully, no one said a word.

"Let me be the first to say the addition is fabulous," Missy said. "With so many extra bedrooms, you'll have room for lots of kids."

"We're working on it," Brian said with a huge grin.

They chatted a bit more about Zane's transition, but he finally said he needed to take Missy home. He had a lot he needed to talk to her about.

Outside, Missy turned to him. "Did you have a good time?"

Zane appreciated how she was always concerned about him. "I had a great time. I especially like Brian. His wood working abilities are outstanding."

She ran a hand down his arm. "I want you to have friends. I can only imagine how hard this is for you. Everything is new, and all the things you're used to are gone."

He opened the driver's side door for her and motioned she scoot in. He then rushed over to his side and took his seat. "I'm fine, really. Cargonia had its good points, but it wasn't perfect by any means. Demons like to target the shifters for no reason, and that made staying alive an everyday challenge."

"What a horrible thought."

"Let's hope our demons never learn what some of your witches are capable of. They might try to take you, though I have no idea how they'd be able to force you to turn against us."

"That's an even worse thought."

Zane should have never brought it up, but it did seem to keep Missy occupied since she didn't ask him again about Raymolt.

Once she pulled into her driveway, he couldn't wait to get her inside. All during their drive home, he debated whether to tell her that he might not survive if Raymolt found him, and he wanted his last few days to be spent with her—his mate.

When they stepped into the house, he decided that telling the truth would be for the best. "We need to talk."

She stilled. "Is it about Raymolt? He is here, isn't he?"

"As I mentioned in the car, I can't be sure, but I think so. The center of my amulet did turn black." He set the picnic basket and blanket on the dining room table then led her over to the couch.

Missy's eyes darkened. "Zane, we need to leave town. I can't lose you."

He grabbed her to his chest and kissed the top of her head. "I have everything to live for. I won't let him kill me."

She leaned back. "What if he doesn't want to kill you, but rather wants to take you back to Cargonia?"

He shook his head. "It's not how demons work. He's here for one and only one reason—to kill me. Now that the witch's spell is broken, he'll need to take things into his own hands. The best thing is never to be alone. He won't attack if I'm in a crowd."

She glanced at the door. "What's to stop him from breaking down the door in the middle of the night and coming after you?"

"Shh. We can't think like that. Right now, I need to be with you every minute I can—just in case the unthinkable happens."

"I'd like that too, but there has to be something we can do."

He shook his head. "Demons have powers us shifters don't."

"My sister can shoot fire from her hand, and do a lot of other things. Maybe she can—"

"Missy, don't."

She huffed out a sigh. "Fine, but you're not painting a very rosy picture. How are you going to stop him then?"

"Try my best?" He didn't want to mislead her, but he wasn't ready to tell her the truth—that his chances of survival were slim at best if the demon managed to get him alone.

Clasping his hand, she lifted his knuckles to her lips. "I love you, Zane, and I agree that if our time is limited, we need to be together in the truest sense. I want to be your mate."

His heart nearly burst. "Oh, Missy, you love me? You aren't just saying that to make me happy, are you?"

"No!"

He hugged her tight then leaned back. "I love you also. Trust me, I've wanted to say that for so long, but since we just met, I didn't want you to think I was only stating it so that you'd help me or anything."

Tears shimmered in her eyes. "No. I'd never think that. You're an honorable man, Zane Barons."

He kissed her hard. When his bear threatened to reveal himself, he broke the kiss. "You've made me a very happy man. Are you sure about this? You aren't doing this because you think I might die, are you?"

"Never." Her chin trembled. "I'll admit that I might have waited, but only a few more days. I want you Zane. And that's the truth."

Happy and fearful at the same time, he untied the strap holding up her top. When he exposed her breasts, his bear could no longer contain himself. Zane shot up from the sofa and moved away as quickly as possible, fearing that if he shifted while holding her he'd hurt her.

No sooner had he lifted off his amulet and placed it on the floor than his bear burst forth and took up what little space was left in the living room.

Missy's eyes opened wide, and she clasped a hand over her mouth. "Zane?"

He swore he heard a giggle in her tone. When he stood to his full height, his head hit the ceiling, forcing him to drop back to all fours. He debated shifting to his human form right away because he needed her so much, but when she stood and held out her hand, he wanted her curiosity to be satisfied. From what he'd been told, when a shifter mated with a human, his bite would allow her to shift. Whether it worked for shifters from his realm, he didn't know, though for her sake, he hoped so. Missy moved closer, and he lowered his head to show he wasn't going to hurt her.

She petted his crown. "You're so soft."

He growled lightly. There were so many things he wanted to tell her and ask her, but this was her time. When Missy walked around him, he plopped his rear down on the floor, allowing her to better study him. She placed her head on his back and frustration bubbled inside him. As much as he wanted to touch her, he feared his claws would harm her. Never before had anyone shown any interest in his bear form.

Missy moved in front of him. "How long do you intend to stay like that?"

Less than five seconds. His bones cracked, and his body spun. His vision dimmed for only a second, and when he returned to his human form, Missy hadn't moved.

"Is this better?" he asked. Zane picked up his amulet from the floor and threaded it over his head.

She glanced down at his erection. "I'll say, though I did enjoy seeing who your other half is."

"My randy bear couldn't handle hearing about us mating and not have a say so in the matter."

She stepped closer, and when she placed a palm on his chest, his bear went wild. Thankfully, he didn't make another appearance. "Does he approve?" she asked.

"Totally." She had no idea how ready he was to mate with her.

MISSY WAS OVERWHELMED, excited, and scared at the same time. She'd seen many shifters in her lifetime, but never one so close. Part of her had wanted him to hold her while he was in his animal form, but she'd never even asked if he would like that. She'd heard a few did not.

While there were so many things she didn't know about Zane, her mom always said that one of the best parts of marriage was learning all of the other person's little quirks. Even now, Dad surprised Mom in the things he said and did.

Reality swept over her. What if she never was able to learn all of Zane's oddities? Or see how he performed under pressure? She wanted children, but would he be around long enough to give them to her?

"Missy?" Zane asked. "Are you having second thoughts?"

"No." She pressed her body to his and inhaled his warm, musky scent. "I want to be with you more than anything, but I'm worried."

He leaned back and lifted her chin. "I want nothing more than to spend the rest of eternity with you, but no one can predict the future. What do you say we start living life now? I'd hate to have to remain in my bear form for the rest of time."

That made her smile. Zane had such a gentle way of coaxing any bad mood out of her. "I guess I should finish undressing, huh?"

His eyes changed to a beautiful amber color. "How about I help?"

"I'd like that."

Just as Zane reached around her back to undo the tie at her waist, she reached up and kissed him. Emotions swamped her. She forced aside the possibility that this could be the last time she made love with him, and instead, embraced the idea that this would be the most amazing night of her life. She'd never been afraid of a shifter's bite nor of changing into an animal. She'd seen it happen enough to know it was a natural thing.

Zane dropped her top on the floor and delved his tongue farther into her mouth, acting as if he wanted to connect with her on the deepest level. Her loved poured out as she ran her hands up his back.

He broke the kiss. "I can't wait any longer. I'm about to go insane if I don't have you."

She wanted him too. Both reached for the zipper on her shorts at the same time, but Missy blocked his hands. "I can do it faster."

"Go."

She kicked off her shoes and was out of her shorts and panties in seconds. Not wanting to wait, she jumped into his arms and wrapped her legs around his waist.

"You're asking for trouble, my little witch."

"You're right about that."

A second later, Zane's lips were upon hers, and bolts of pleasure encompassed her. Blue sparks flew off her arms as his amulet glowed red. Wanting him to suck on her tits, she leaned back. Zane grunted then pounced, drawing first the right breast and then the left into his mouth. "I need my hands to touch you," he said between licks.

He walked them over to the sofa and set her down. "Touch me all you want."

"Oh, I plan to." Zane crawled on top of her and slid down between her thighs. His legs hung over the end of the sofa, but he didn't seem to mind. Zane cupped both of her breasts and kneaded them. "I love these."

"Show me how much." Missy had never been this bold before, but with Zane she had no problem. Exploring the world with him would be such a high.

Pressing on the sides of her tits, he returned to sucking her taut nipple. Sparks turned into a blue glow. Just like his necklace, her orb pulsed with pleasure. His swirling tongue and gentle massage heightened her excitement beyond anything she had ever experienced. Wrapping her legs around his waist, she pulled him upward, signaling she was ready.

Zane took the hint and seated himself into position. He gazed deep into her eyes and then he kissed her hard. She hoped he didn't have any regrets because she surely didn't.

With her arms around his neck, he plunged into her. Heat seared her insides, and bliss consumed her. Missy dropped her head back and willed him to ride her hard, loving every thick inch of him.

Every time he drove into her, his amulet bounced on her shoulder. Zane must have thought it was distracting because he tossed it behind his back. No one was more considerate or kind than this man. His lips met hers again, and his desperation and grunts had her aura growing larger and larger with each second.

He dragged his lips down her chin and across the hollow of her throat. Her heart pounded believing the moment was near for them to fully mate. There would be no turning back now, but never in her life was she surer of anything.

"Now, Zane," she pleaded.

"I love you," he whispered. "Now and forever."

A second later, his sharpened teeth dug into her neck, but it wasn't more than a pinch. What she did feel was an intense swelling of love and overwhelming joy. Her aura surrounded both of them, signaling her acceptance, and with the next thrust, her orgasm swooped in hard and claimed her. She dug her nails into his shoulders and opened her mouth to draw in air. Her vision spun, and for a moment, she thought she might shift right there. It didn't matter the white moon hadn't arrived.

Zane's hot seed filled her, and her blue orb intensified, their cocoon of love holding much hope. His amulet had dropped back over his shoulder onto his chest and was glowing with the brightest shade of red she had ever seen, proving that the mating had joined their souls together forever and that their love bound their hearts for eternity.

She wasn't sure how long he held her. One minute she'd started to doze off, and the next, water was running. Zane came over and cleaned her up.

He then lifted her up in his arms and sat down with her on his lap, holding her close as he rubbed his hand along the outside of her thigh. "I hope I didn't hurt you."

"No, never." She tapped his shoulder. "Can you lean forward for a sec?"

He did. "Did a mark appear?"

On his upper left shoulder blade sat a circle with a bear paw in the middle. But the most amazing part was the green vine running through it. "Yes! I hope it looks like mine."

Missy showed him her back. Zane ran a finger over the marking. "That's incredible. On Cargonia, we don't blend our markings."

He'd said that. She turned back toward him. "That makes our joining all the more special."

"You got that right. That's the correct way to say it, no?"

She laughed, loving everything about this man. "Totally."

Chapter Twenty

THE WHITE MOON was fast approaching, and Vinea didn't want to stay in this realm any longer than necessary. First, she needed to find this demon, and the best way to learn about any newcomer was at McKinnon's Pub and Pool. She could only hope that Devon wouldn't decide to stop in since she wasn't ready to speak with him.

To ensure he didn't recognize her—or anyone else who'd interacted with her—she changed her appearance once more. This time she wore her hair dark and very short. To completely throw people off, she put on a business suit—something she never would have done under normal circumstances—more proof that she was desperate.

Vinea walked into the bar and scoped out the place. It was still early, which suited her fine. What customers were in there, were in the back playing pool. It was too bad her realm didn't have a place like this—a bar where she could learn the popular game. If Androf expected his people to blend into this realm and do his dirty work, he should give them skills—like teach them to shoot pool and play golf.

Whatever. Gods of the dark realm weren't known for thinking of others. It was their shortsightedness that kept the balance of good versus evil in favor of the gods of the light. Perhaps when she returned from this mission victorious, she'd mention it to him.

Sliding onto the bar stool, she waved to the bartender.

"What can I get you?" The name on his tag read Finn.

"Whatever you have on tap."

Finn smiled. "Coming right up."

While she waited for her drink, she rehearsed her story, hoping this Finn person would buy it.

"Here ya go. Do you want to run a tab?" he asked.

While he was cute, and she wouldn't mind a hot diversion from being in this town, she didn't have time. "No, but I do have a question. I hope you can help me."

"I'll try."

"I was supposed to meet with a client yesterday, but my plane was delayed by a day. I was hoping he might have stopped in here. I imagine he'd be upset that I didn't call, but I couldn't find his number." Vinea tossed him her sexiest look.

"What's his name?"

She only knew him by Raymolt, but she could toss out any name. "He's working undercover, but he usually goes by Raymond Jeffers. He's maybe six feet five, has short dark hair, and is rather thick." She patted her stomach, hoping she guessed it correctly.

Finn waved a finger at her. "I did see someone like that. I think he said he was staying at the Silver Lake Motel. You might try asking them there."

"Thanks, sweetie." She tossed back her beer then winked. Vinea then placed a five on the counter. "Keep the change."

Fearing she was already too memorable, she slid off the stool and walked out. Next stop? The hotel. She hadn't thought the demon would be so bold as to stay in one, but if he was like the other demons she'd met, he was arrogant to the point of being stupid. All the better for her.

MISSY INSISTED SHE drop Zane off at the fire station the next day. He'd said that the demon wouldn't attack if a lot of people were around—and the firehouse was never empty.

"Be careful," she said.

Zane leaned over and kissed her. "I promise. But you need to be careful too."

While he had a smile on his face, his words cut deep. "Why?"

"What better way to get to me than through you?"

A tight band squeezed her chest, but she attempted to act unaffected. She didn't need Zane taking a day off just to babysit her. "Then I'll be extra careful."

After Zane kissed her again and slipped out, she waited until he was inside before taking off. Back at the Crystal Winds Spa, she parked in front rather than in the back alley.

Teagan was at the front desk, but the back room was dark. "Hey, Mom's not in yet?"

"She came and left for an early appointment."

Her mind must have scrambled. "I remember her telling me. Thanks." Needing to speak with Ophelia, she called her sister hoping she could help. Thank goodness it was final exam week and Izzy didn't have to be at school today.

"What's up?" Izzy said.

"Mom's out somewhere, and I need to speak with Ophelia again. Is there any way you can ask her for me?"

"I can try to contact her. Are you okay?"

She couldn't hold it in any longer. "Not really."

"Oh, Missy. Why don't you come over and tell me. I'm sure Mom will understand if you come in a little late. Teagan's working today, right?"

"Yes. I'm here now. I'll ask her if she minds. If she doesn't, I'll be right over. You sure I won't be bothering you on your day off?"

"No! I'm happy for the company. It's not like I can go out for a jog or anything."

That made her smile. "Thanks."

Teagan looked up from the counter. "Everything okay?"

"Not really. Can you do me a huge favor?"

"Sure."

"I don't have anyone scheduled for a massage this morning, and I really need to speak with Ophelia. Izzy said she might be able to arrange it, but I wanted to discuss it with her first. Would it be okay to take off for an hour or so, assuming she can meet with me?"

"Of course, but what's wrong?"

"I promise I'll give you every detail once I see Ophelia. The short version is that Zane is in trouble, and we believe a demon came here to Silver Lake to kill him."

Her hand flew to her chest. "That's terrible, but what can Ophelia do?"

"I'm not sure, but I'm hoping she can teach me a spell to use on this demon. He's way more powerful than Zane, and I want to give him a fighting chance."

"Why not ask Sam Pompley to help? He can alter a man's mind."

"There's no telling when the demon will make his move, and I can't ask him to follow him around for the next few weeks, especially if he's on assignment. Besides, even if Sam could alter the demon's mind, we need him gone. I'm hoping some kind of spell will send him back where he came from." Or kill him.

"You might be right. Ophelia is your best bet. I know a lot of spells, but they are only for shifters and witches in this realm."

Missy leaned over and kissed her cheek. "Thanks. I'll try not to be long."

When Missy arrived at her sister's, she knocked and went in. Izzy was on the sofa looking more uncomfortable by the day. "How's Logan doing?"

Izzy placed a hand on her belly. "He's becoming more anxious to meet us."

"I'm sure he is."

Izzy patted the seat next to her. "Tell me what's wrong."

"Zane's in trouble, really big trouble."

She sat up straighter and winced. "What kind of trouble?"

Missy started with the regatta and how Zane jumped up and raced off when his amulet turned black in the middle. "He didn't see this demon Raymolt, but he's pretty sure he's here."

"And you think he plans to kill Zane?"

"Yes." She explained how demons from Cargonia are very powerful. "Rarely does a shifter survive an encounter."

"I guess it's the same with our shifters and humans."

"At least our humans can own guns. Zane doesn't think anything can stop this guy. That's why I need to speak with Ophelia. I'm hoping she can teach me some kind of spell to put on him."

Izzy nodded. "That's smart. I contacted her right after I hung up with you; she said to go back to my old house as soon as you can, and she'll meet you there."

Missy hugged Izzy. "I owe you big time."

"I just want you to be happy."

Wanting to share her one good piece of news, she twisted around and lowered the collar of her shirt. "Can you see it?"

"Is that a paw print over your vine?" Excitement laced her voice.

"Yes."

"Oh, Missy. You don't know how happy this makes me. I didn't think you'd ever find your mate."

Chuckling, she faced her sister again. "If Naliana arranged this, she clearly had to look far and wide."

"I have no idea how she knows who belongs with whom, but all that matters is that you're happy."

"I am."

"You better get going. You don't want to keep Ophelia waiting."

"No." Missy gave her sister one last hug before heading out.

It didn't take long for her to reach Izzy's old house. Like before, Missy parked close to the forested area and eased out of her car. She didn't see Ophelia, but she suspected the old woman liked it that way.

As Missy walked toward the trees, Ophelia appeared. If she didn't know better, she'd say this witch had some goddess blood in her. "Thank you for meeting with me."

"Nonsense, I can always use the company."

Something seemed amiss. Ophelia wasn't this straightforward or friendly. "Thank you."

"It's about your young time traveler, isn't it? He's in trouble."

How did she do that? Witch or no witch, it was spooky how she could read a person's mind. "Yes."

Missy went through the scenario once more, and the old lady listened carefully.

"What do you think I can do?" Ophelia asked. "Surely, I'm too old to fight this demon myself."

Missy wouldn't put anything past Ophelia. "Is there any way you can teach me a spell that would kill him?"

Ophelia slipped her hand in her pocket, pulled out a small burlap sack, and handed it to Missy. "This might help."

VINEA SHOOK HER head. The demon wasn't as smart as he thought he was, unless he had used his real name in the hopes Zane would come looking for him. In that case, Vinea had to admire his resourcefulness.

Once she learned his room number, she took the elevator to the second floor and knocked on the demon's door.

As if he was expecting someone, he opened up right away but then huffed out a breath, implying he had been waiting for Zane. "Yes?"

His haughty chin lift pissed her off. "May I come in?"

"Do I know you?" Once more the arrogance galled her.

"No, but you'll be glad when you do."

He puffed out his chest and rose to his full height. Really? He was trying to intimidate her? Vinea vaporized and moved inside his room before reappearing behind him. She tapped him on the shoulder, forcing the demon to whip around. "How—?"

"Close the door. I'm here about Zanedar."

A flash of something crossed his face, but it was too quick to tell whether it was fear or excitement. "You know where he is?"

"Don't you? What kind of demon are you?"

If he had horns, they'd be sprouting right now. "How dare you talk to me like that? Why I could twist you in two and reduce you to rubble."

She shook her head. "Sit down and stop making promises you can't keep. And that's goddess Vinea to you."

The man actually paled. "My apologies, goddess."

Like she believed that. "I've been sent here to see that Zanedar doesn't remain in this realm. My superiors feel he might be a threat."

"What kind of threat?"

"Does it matter?" This demon was such a dolt.

"I guess not, but I have no intention of sending him back. He killed my brother, and I want him dead."

That wasn't the plan, but she wasn't above improvising. "Fine. You can kill him. As long as he can't talk, I think my gods will be happy."

He huffed out a laugh, acting as if she had no power over him. "How can you help me? I can handle that puny shifter all by myself."

"If that were the case, you would have drawn him out and killed him already."

Raymolt turned toward the window and peered out. "He's never alone."

"Then *we* need to make sure he is."

Raymolt faced her again. "How?"

"I have a plan."

"I'm listening."

VINEA WAS RATHER pleased with the way her discussion with Raymolt had turned out. She detested the weasel, but if he could take down Zanedar as quickly as he claimed, that was all that mattered. She left the hotel and headed north to Maple Avenue, needing to do a little more thinking before executing her plan. She figured by tomorrow, she'd be bragging to Androf about how she managed to finish her task in record time. Because she'd saved his butt and the rest of the gods by keeping the two realms apart, she would demand that he return some of her powers. Of course, she'd never tell them her abilities were disappearing at an alarming rate or that her emotions were getting the best of her. That alone would result in expulsion.

If she thought she'd be successful, Vinea would stay around for the white moon and tell her goody-two-shoes sister she was the bane of Vinea's existence. If it hadn't been for Naliana's cheery attitude all those years ago, Vinea would have been the one in charge of mating. As the older sister, she should have been chosen.

Not paying much attention to where she was going, she found herself at the Silver Lake café. In her realm, a good cup of coffee didn't exist. Given what lay ahead of her, she could use a strong cup of java.

The café was just like she remembered it; only this time there were a mere three customers in there. The last time she'd been, it had been packed.

"Sit anywhere you like," a waitress said as she rushed over to an elderly couple near the window.

Vinea was tired. Having her hatred of all things lessen with each passing day scared her—an emotion she hadn't experienced in hundreds of years. At first, she hadn't thought much about the bolt of light her sister had shot through her, but there was no denying it any longer. It had adversely affected her. Unless she succeeded in her mission, she would be kicked out of the dark realm. Then where would she go? The light realm wouldn't welcome her. That was a given. She might have to try Cargonia, but she doubted those gods would want her either. *Damn you, Naliana.*

She found a seat toward the back and plopped down. With a swipe of a hand, she created some money in order to pay for her coffee. Setting her purse on the seat next to her, she dug her hand inside to retrieve her wallet with the newly acquired cash.

"Vinea?" The deep voice jarred her, sending her heart into overdrive. Shit. Where was her goddess cool when she needed it?

Vinea looked up and debated disappearing. "Devon McKinnon. What the hell are you doing here?" The better question would have been how the hell had he even recognized her?

Chapter Twenty-One

M ISSY WASN'T SURE what to make of the potion Ophelia had handed her. First off, neither she nor Izzy had told her about Zane's recent problem, nor had there been any mention of wanting a spell, so how had Ophelia known what to bring?

Did it really matter? As her mom would say, some things were never meant to be understood. Missy suspected that Ophelia would always remain one of those mysteries.

Once she said goodbye to the old lady, Missy shoved the pouch filled with some potion into her pocket and slipped back into her car. On the drive back to the spa, she repeated the curse Ophelia made her learn, even though she wasn't sure it would work. Ophelia wouldn't say for sure whether it could kill a demon from Cargonia. She just said to try it. Missy had no problem with trying as long as she didn't fail. Zane's life was on the line—and maybe hers too.

She slapped the wheel. The more she dwelled on Zane's situation, the more upset she became. If the great Ophelia wasn't sure she could help, then what could Missy do? Ask Rye to keep Zane at the fire station twenty-four seven? Or let him stay in the safe room at McKinnon and Associates? If she thought Zane would go for it, she would. The problem was that she doubted the demon would tire of waiting around and just leave.

"Are you all right?" a deep voice said suddenly entering her head.

Missy jerked, and the front wheel hit the berm. Heart pounding hard, she managed to straighten the car and return it to the pavement. "Yes," she said. Crap, she was talking to herself.

"Missy, it's Zane. I can feel your pain. What's wrong?"

It took a second for her to realize he was sending his thoughts to her. Sure, people who had mated were capable of telepathy, but she hadn't thought she and Zane could ever achieve something like that. After all, he wasn't the typical shifter.

"I'm fine, really. I was just thinking about the demon, that's all."

"Okay, but if you need me, I'll be there."

"You need to stay put," she warned.

"Stop worrying about me. I'll be fine."

How could he say that? They both knew the demon was here to kill him. *"If you say so."*

It was unsettling to speak with Zane in her head. She liked talking to him face to face better so she could see the expression in his eyes.

"Missy, don't be like that. I'm scared too. Okay? I'm working hard to remain upbeat. What will help is to let me do all the worrying."

Zane was right. He shouldn't have to worry about her too. *"I'll try,"* she telepathed.

When she arrived at the spa, her hands were still shaking. Both her mom and Teagan were busy with customers, so Missy checked the inventory to see what needed to be ordered, but her mind wasn't on work. She didn't need to be psychic to know the next few days would be bad. While Missy really wanted to be with Zane, he was safer staying at work.

As soon as her mom's customer left, she motioned Missy into the break room where her mother poured them some coffee. "Tell me how your meeting went with Ophelia."

Izzy must have told her. "I'm not really sure. For you to understand everything, I need to start at the beginning." She mentioned the regatta and how Zane thought he sensed the demon and how he reacted. From there she went straight through to the mating. With each remembrance her excitement built.

"Oh, Missy, you should have told me you two had mated,

though I did sense something was different about you." She smiled.

Missy sighed. "I figured you could tell. You can see why I needed to meet with Ophelia."

"Yes and Zane sounds like a wonderful match."

"He is." Missy could almost feel Zane biting her on the neck once more, and her body reacted accordingly.

"*Mate, you are being a bad girl. I am trying to work; behave.*"

Hearing Zane's voice in her head startled her once more. She wasn't used to having telepathy. "*Sorry, hon, but just thinking about you gets me hot. I will try to behave. Love you.*"

"*Love you too, beautiful.*" She could almost hear him chuckle.

When she realized she'd been grinning, heat raced up her face.

Her mom cleared her throat. "I'm so happy for you. I can see why you're worried about this demon. You think that when he finds Zane alone, he'll kill him, which was why you needed Ophelia for the magic spell, right?"

"Yes."

Her mom sipped her coffee. "I wish I had a solution. I know if anything ever happened to your father, I'd be lost."

That wasn't helping, but Missy wasn't going to lose Zane. "We just have to be careful."

Mom placed a hand over hers. "Careful yes, but make sure you enjoy your young man as much as you can."

That implied she too believed their time together might be short. Her heart burned. "I plan to."

No sooner had her mom returned to the front than Teagan rushed into the back room. Her face was drawn. Oh, shit. Missy jumped up from the table. "What is it?"

"I had a premonition." Teagan grabbed the back of the chair.

While Teagan's visions weren't always bad, from the way she was shaking, this one had been. "Sit down and tell me."

Teagan pulled out a chair. "I really don't know what it means, but I saw ashes."

That didn't make sense. "As in a fire? Or do the ashes represent the firehouse and hence Zane?"

"I can't tell. I sense tremendous pain, and then everything turns brown."

"Brown?"

She shrugged. "I'm stumped. All I know is that you have to be really careful at all times."

Missy sat across from her and clasped both of Teagan's hands. "I promise. I'll warn Zane too."

The bell above the front door chimed, and Teagan inhaled then bit down on her bottom lip. "I better get back to work. I can't dwell on what might be."

"I'm right behind you."

As hard as she tried to concentrate on work, Missy kept going over Teagan's warning. While her visions were rarely clear and often misleading, they were accurate. The problem was that the warning wasn't necessary. Missy understood all too well what was at stake.

Eventually, five o'clock rolled around, and her mom and Teagan left. Missy said she'd stay to lock up because Zane wasn't off work until six, and she'd insisted on picking him up. Because she didn't want the demon to think she was alone either, she locked the front door, turned off the lights in the store, and went into the back. With an hour to spare, she booted up the computer to research demons, trying to find out if they had vulnerabilities. Could they die by fire or some other method?

Unfortunately, the only thing she could find were myths, and no two articles made the same claim. Hoping to take her mind off the terrible situation, she changed tactics and researched new herbal remedies.

At six, she shut down and left. Even though she'd just mentally spoken with Zane, as soon as he stepped out of the station, relief poured through her.

He climbed into the car. "Want to catch a bite to eat?" he asked.

"I hope that doesn't mean you plan to hunt for something?" Zane was catching on to some of the modern lingo, but she could never be sure. "I have some chicken at home I can prepare. It'll be faster and easier."

Zane burst out laughing. "No, I didn't mean *catch* in that sense. I heard some of the guys at the fire station ask each other to go for food that way." He sighed. "I thought a restaurant might be more crowded. We'd be safer with more people around us."

Despite the heat, chills raced up her body. "How long will you have to hide in plain sight?" she asked.

"Until it's over."

"I STILL DON'T understand, Vinea. Why did you target Sam?" Devon asked.

The man was dense. She had the feeling that if she avoided answering him, he'd never leave. "Because I wanted his powers."

His jaw tightened. "It was bad enough that you lied to me, but stealing a man's magic is just wrong. Doesn't that bother you?"

That was rich. "No. As for stealing being bad, tell that to my parents and sister. They stole my powers and then kicked me out of the light realm."

"You probably deserved it. Even if you didn't, it doesn't give you the right to take what belongs to someone else."

There was no use talking to a man with such strict morals. "Look, I gotta go. Just forget you saw me okay?"

He reached out and grabbed her hand. While Vinea could have evaporated, she didn't need the exposure.

"Listen, I didn't mean to come down so hard on you." He looked around. "How about we go someplace more *private*?"

Where had that change of heart come from? It didn't really matter. As much as she hated to admit it, her body was going wild with desire, something that should never happened around a mere mortal. "Where do you have in mind?"

"How about we drive over to the lake? No one goes there during the day."

If he wanted a dalliance, she could get into it. Besides, the big takedown wouldn't happen until tomorrow. Vinea pulled a five out of her wallet and dropped it on the table. "Let's go."

As if he'd forgotten all about her evil past, Devon placed a hand on her back and led her outside. If he weren't so straight-laced, she'd think he was trying to con her. Who was she kidding? Even if he weren't so uptight, he wouldn't be able to fool her—no one could.

Even though Vinea believed Devon wouldn't try to pull some stupid stunt, she glanced around, hoping Sam Pompley wasn't there. She'd failed to take his powers, but the fact she went at him with a crystal knife was enough to build distrust in a person—or would it be more accurate to say everlasting hate?

"Hop in," Devon said.

She liked his tricked out truck. "Nice ride."

"Thanks."

She slid in. "I've never been to the lake," she said. It was too close to where James lived—and Naliana on occasion.

"You'll like it."

It only took ten minutes to reach it. During that time, she asked about his work as a way to take the focus off her, but once he started talking, she realized she was interested in his life. He came across as someone who was angry, a little bitter, and very driven. She was pretty sure she'd had a hand in the angry and bitter parts, after what she had done. Vinea didn't want to think about why that bothered her now.

"You know," he said. "You and I aren't all that different."

Vinea refrained from laughing. "Oh, really? Why do you say that?"

"I told you that Connor was asked to run McKinnon and Associates after my dad retired, but were you aware that he's my younger brother?"

An uncharacteristic twinge pinched her heart. "So you understand what it's like to be passed up?"

"Totally." Devon stopped the car. "The lake is right past those trees."

He jumped out, came around to her side, and opened the door. No one had ever treated her with that kind of respect, and she didn't like it one bit. Being beholden to anyone wasn't her style.

Devon led the way. He kept his pace slow, probably because he could tell walking in heels on the soft dirt was difficult. When they approached the lake, a spear of delight shot through her—a highly unwelcomed emotion. For a goddess of the dark realm, it could be quite dangerous.

Vinea worked hard to push those new feelings aside. She did not want to care about Devon. Her heart was black, and she was just fine with that. She would fight it and win.

"Come over to the water," Devon said. "It's so clear you can almost see the bottom."

Vinea stepped over and peered down, not liking her reflection. Now that she no longer had to hide from Devon and his family, she swiped a hand over her face. A second later, her auburn hair appeared, and the dark rimmed glasses disappeared.

The dress and shoes were way too uncomfortable, so she imagined a cute pair of shorts and a turquoise halter top, and her new outfit appeared.

Devon jumped back. "Whoa! How did you do that?" He held up a hand. "Never mind. I don't even want to know, though you didn't have to go to all that trouble for me."

She hadn't been thinking of him. Before she could explain, Devon kicked off his shoes and then dropped his trousers. "I can't wait to get in the water. Get undressed."

"You want to go for a swim?" she asked. Here she thought they'd make out first then move on to have some hot, sweaty sex.

"I wanted to cool down first. Seeing you has my libido jacked up again." He lifted off his shirt and moved closer.

She didn't believe it until she spotted his huge erection. "Nice cock."

"You can try it out after we take a dip. Come on."

"No thanks. You go ahead."

As if he thought she needed convincing, he cupped her face and kissed her. Her body exploded with need, and she pushed him away, hating her emotional reaction.

"Why did you stop?" he asked. "It's what you want, right?"

"Yes, no…" She couldn't come up with a good response.

"You're going in whether you like it or not." His cheerful demeanor turned dark. At least that response she understood.

She'd had enough of his he-man attitude. "I am not."

Devon dunked his shoulder and plowed into her, taking both of them into the water, and while Vinea fought and kicked, he overpowered her. She called on her ability to throw his sorry ass twenty feet, but that power had evaporated. Water surrounded her and she couldn't breathe. If she'd been in the dark realm, it wouldn't have been a problem, but on Earth it was.

Vinea had never been swimming in her life. When her head hit something hard, pain ricocheted through her. She had no idea how long she could hold her breath, so the only thing to do was to disappear. But when she tried to change form, nothing happened, shooting her pulse into overdrive. She couldn't breathe. Devon was trying to drown her, but she couldn't let that happen. It didn't matter she was immortal. Her stomach churned, and a tight band squeezed her chest. How had she misjudged him?

Even though her eyes were closed, a strong light appeared in front of her. Then it was as if she were floating, and an amazing sense of warmth filled her. Something good seemed to be trying to root out the evil in her body, and she couldn't let that happen.

As hard as she tried to make her muscles move to fight him off, nothing worked. *Androf, I'm sorry I failed you.*

A rush of water flew past her face, and the next thing she knew, Devon was dumping her on the hard ground. Vinea sucked in a large breath and coughed. When she opened her eyes, he was leaning over her, smiling.

"You bastard. You nearly killed me." She rose to her feet. Still shaky, she punched him in the chest, but he didn't budge.

"I did it to save you," he said with such smugness, she wanted to hit him harder.

"Save me from what?" The man was crazy. He placed a hand on her back, but she jerked away. "Don't touch me."

"How do you feel? Did the quartz thaw out that cold, black heart of yours?" Devon cocked a brow and looked way too satisfied.

"I feel like I nearly drowned." Vinea wouldn't tell him about the white light and the feeling of being loved.

She stepped away from him. One of her shoes was missing. With a sweep of her hand, she was immediately clothed in another pair of shorts, a dry T-shirt, and new sandals. Thank goddess, she hadn't lost that power.

As much as she wanted to yell and scream at him for attempting to kill her, she couldn't drag her eyes off his body. "I don't know what game you're playing, but I don't appreciate it. You're a dick."

Devon grabbed his crotch. "I admit I have one, but I guess you're not interested anymore."

"Fuck you."

"Listen, Vinea, I was hoping the rose quartz would draw out your evil."

She laughed in his face. "You're a fool. That's only for Changelings, not for goddesses." Or so she hoped.

He tossed her a charming smile, but she could tell it was fake. Deep down, Devon McKinnon hated her, only he was too polite to say so.

"It was worth a try," he said. "I really did like you, you know, until you basically screwed over my friends." His lips twisted into a sneer.

So now the true Devon McKinnon appeared. "Yeah, well that's who I am. I'm just bad to the bone." Something sharp pressed on her heart, but she pushed aside the anxiety.

"Then I suggest you go home and never come back. Leave me and my Clan alone. Understood?"

"Loud and clear." Vinea had to get out of there, and it wasn't because Devon told her to go. Something was happening to her body that she couldn't let him see. She just hoped like hell that her inability to disappear when Devon had held her underwater had been due to the fact she was submerged, and not because her powers were finally gone. Vinea twisted away and strode off. A second later, she was back inside her car.

Phew. That was close.

Vinea leaned back against the seat, confused for the first time in her life. When Devon had held her down against that stone, she'd felt things she hadn't experienced since she was a goddess of the light. She slammed her hand against the wheel. No way would she let that quartz affect her permanently.

Then inspiration struck. There was only one thing to do to counter anything that stupid stone might have accomplished. She needed to kill Zanedar. That would put her back in the good graces of Androf and restore her powers.

Chapter Twenty-Two

M ISSY WAS SORTING the cash at the register when Teagan walked out from the back room of the spa with Mrs. Andrews. Seeing how her face glowed, Teagan must have given her a facial.

"I'll see you next week," her cousin said.

"You bet." The older lady dug her hand in her purse and slipped Teagan some cash. "Thank you."

As soon as the door closed, Teagan bounced up to the counter. "I'm heading over to the Silver Lake Café. Do you want me to pick you up something for lunch?"

She knew what Teagan was doing—protecting her. Since someone needed to man the store, she had no problem letting her bring something back. "Sure. That would be great." She gave Teagan her order and then stepped into the break room where her mother was pouring some coffee.

"How's it going?" her mom asked.

She wasn't sure what she was referring to. Given they hadn't had a chance to chat yet this morning, Missy figured she was asking about Zane. "Okay. We're on a wait and see time frame. So far the demon hasn't made his move."

"That has to be scary."

"It is more than scary. I'm sick to my stomach all the time. I know I've only known Zane for a short while, but I love him." Her mother had just opened her mouth to respond when Missy's cell rang. She held up a finger. "Let me take this and then I'll tell you how we plan to handle the demon." She held the cell up to her ear. "Hello?"

"Missy, it's Izzy."

"Izzy?" She could barely hear her sister. "What's wrong?" Mom leaned forward and her shoulders tensed.

"I'm sick. Really sick. I think I have the flu. It must be going around."

A ton of questions shot to mind, but it would be better to go see Izzy, especially since a well-placed hand could help. "I'll be right over." She glanced up at her mom. "Izzy's sick."

"Go. I'll hold down the fort."

"No! Don't come." Izzy's voice grew stronger.

That made no sense. "Why?"

"I need that broth you made for Anna. Can you still get those mushrooms?"

The ginger and mushroom broth had helped her friend. Driving over to Izzy's would take time, and the cave was at least twenty minutes away. "Okay, but by the time I drive there, find the mushrooms and get to your house, it could be an hour." Hopefully, Izzy would be okay until then.

"I'll rest, I promise."

"Do you want me to call your midwife?" The baby could be in distress, causing Izzy's flu-like symptoms.

"No. I've called Rye. He'll be here soon."

Rye would get help if he thought her situation was dire. "Okay, but drink lots of fluids and rest."

"I will. And thank you."

Missy disconnected. Her Mom stood next to her. "You heard everything?" Missy asked.

"Yes. You need to go." Her mother looked ten years older. "As soon as Teagan returns, I'll check on Izzy. Don't worry. I won't let anything happen to her."

"Good. Let me get my bag. There are crystals in there that

should help."

Once she retrieved the bag and handed it to her mom, Missy rushed out to the front of the store and left. Her hands shook so hard, it took her a few tries to unlock her car door. Her mind was trying to understand how Izzy could appear so healthy one minute and be so sick the next, especially when she was never ill. She was a strong witch. The only thing Missy could think of was that the baby must be in trouble.

Crap. Missy should have asked why she didn't shift, but perhaps Izzy worried it would hurt the unborn child. Others shifted late in their pregnancy without any problems, but she might not want to take any chances—or else she wasn't telling her something. Missy's stomach churned at that thought.

Once she opened her car door, she jumped in and then locked it. *"Zane, I have to run to the caves to get some mushrooms. Izzy is sick,"* she telepathed as she started the engine.

"I can come with you if you want." While he sounded calm, she sensed his internal radar was going crazy.

He'd be safer at the station. *"I'm good. I won't be long. I'll let you know when I get back."*

"Be careful." The hesitation in his voice confirmed he was seriously debating racing after her, but he really needed to stay put.

"I will."

No sooner had she pulled out onto the road than Zane's words popped in her head about the demon trying to get to him through her. Given it was possible, she wouldn't step foot out of her car if anything looked suspicious. She would have to find something else to help her sister.

Missy kept a keen eye on the traffic. Once she left the main part of the town, not a single car was behind her. By the time she arrived at the path leading to the caves, her nerves had calmed down considerably. Thankfully, the base of the path was empty. At least the demon wasn't waiting there to kidnap her.

After scanning the area to make sure no one was skulking about,

Missy slipped out of her car, locked the door, and rushed up the path. Between Izzy's illness and that damned demon, her stomach was in knots, and her heart was beating way faster than it should. She inhaled to help her focus, but it didn't do much good.

Throughout her short hike, the only sounds came from the wind and the animals scurrying about. By the time she reached her destination, Missy was ready to find those mushrooms and return to her sister's house pronto.

Because time was of the essence, she didn't spend time searching for any fungi that existed outside of the cave. Instead, she headed straight inside. Missy clearly remembered where she had found them the last time, so it shouldn't take her long.

As she traveled deeper into the cave, it wasn't surprising that the image of Zane popped into her head. After all, this was where it had begun for them.

She quickly found a patch of the mushrooms and had picked almost a dozen when a noise outside startled her. Thoughts of the demon coming sent her heart into overdrive. Voices sounded, and she relaxed a little. It was probably hikers wanting to explore the caves.

She snipped a few more and quickly returned to the entrance, ready to let someone else have some privacy. Sunlight streamed in, and as she reached out her hand to block the rays from blinding her, yellow sparks skittered across the opening. She'd never seen that phenomenon before.

Needing to leave now, she stepped into the opening. Before she could lift her leg again, what felt like a bolt of electricity shot through her, tossing her backward with such force that she landed on her butt. When her head banged against the ground, the mushrooms went tumbling. Oh, no.

Dazed and in pain, Missy lay there, stunned and disoriented. She couldn't fathom what had happened. Her bones ached, and her head pounded.

Had it been the demon?

"Well, well. Sorry I had to put a force field in front of the cave, but I couldn't chance you breaking out and interfering." The sun backlit her captor, blinding Missy. All she could tell was the voice belonged to a woman.

"Who are you?" Her voice cracked.

"I didn't mean for you to be hurt. Don't you remember me? I'm Vanessa, the woman who sat next to you at the regatta."

Missy shifted to the side, and Vanessa's face became clearer. The woman Missy gave a sandwich to had blonde hair; this woman was auburn.

The woman moved closer, providing Missy with a better angle. She was the same height, but because Missy's vision was still blurry, she couldn't make out her features very well. "I can't really see you."

"That's okay. You don't need to. By the way, my real name is Vinea. Perhaps now you remember me?"

Vinea? That name sounded so familiar. When the pounding in her head subsided a bit, realization slammed into her, and her throat nearly closed up. "You're the woman who tried to steal my cousin's powers."

"Give the lady a prize."

Missy rose to her feet and swayed. She stopped moving until she regained her balance. This woman wouldn't get away with this.

"Missy, are you hurt?" Zane's voice nearly cracked, but his message came in loud and clear.

"I'm okay, but some woman who says her name is Vinea has me trapped in the cave with some sort of spell."

"I'll be right there."

Her fists clenched. *"No. It has to be a trap."* She didn't see any demon, but why else would this woman try to keep her captive?

"What do you want?" she asked Vinea, trying to sound as strong as possible.

"I'm just buying time."

Buying time probably meant she was waiting for Raymolt. It didn't surprise her that this goddess of the dark would hook up with him. Being from two different realms must not matter. *"Don't come,"* she warned Zane.

"You are my mate. Hold on. I'm on my way."

"No!" Damn, she hadn't meant for that to escape. *"Don't come, Zane. The demon will be here."*

Only he didn't answer her.

"My, my," Vinea said, pacing in front of the cave entrance. "Don't tell me you've mated with Zane already? The expression on your face says it all. You're in love. How sweet."

Missy stood taller, hating this woman. "Yes, and he'll be here soon to take care of you."

The goddess laughed. "How can a shifter harm me? I have infinite power."

Her chest caved from the pain. *"Zane, it's a trap. She wants you to come."*

While Missy could feel the waves of anxiety seep deep into her soul, he wasn't answering. Didn't he sense she was in extreme emotional pain? Missy returned her focus to this woman and painted on her most confident face. "Don't underestimate him. He's from a different realm."

Vinea laughed again. "What makes you think Cargonia is any different from here? A shifter is a shifter. I know for a fact that he doesn't possess any magical talents like many of your shifters here do. Even though you've mated, I don't think his ability to heal will help him win a fight." She cackled.

Defending Zane might cause more harm, but she couldn't help it. "Don't be so sure."

"Just sit back down and wait. Then you'll get to watch him die."

Her heart nearly stopped. If Missy recalled correctly, Vinea had tried and failed to take Sam's powers, so she wasn't all that powerful. Zane should be able to stop her—unless the demon showed up.

Missy paced the cave. She'd been in there enough times to know there was no other exit. Damn. There had to be something she could do. As soon as Vinea disappeared from view, Missy edged closer to the entryway. Not wanting to touch the electric field, she tossed a rock at the entrance. Sparks shot everywhere, and the rock bounced back off the air. That wasn't good.

Vinea couldn't have known she'd be coming up here to collect the fungi, so how had she had time to set up this force field? Missy checked the entrance for wires or perhaps a battery. If she understood how the force field was created, she might be able to shut it off—or not. Crap! Where was MacGyver when she needed him?

Vinea reappeared again. "By the way, you don't need to worry about your sick sister. She's okay. I was the one who called you and pretended I was her."

Missy froze. "That's not possible."

Vinea smiled then tilted her head, a pout forming on her lips. "Missy, it's Izzy. I'm sick, really sick."

Oh my goddess. She sounded exactly like her. Anger ripped through her at being duped. The only positive was that Izzy wasn't ill. That meant when her mom arrived at Izzy's house and found out she hadn't called, she would send help.

Most likely she'd contact Rye, but even if he rounded up ten men, some of them would be killed if they came to rescue her, and Missy didn't want that.

From the horror of it all, her legs gave way, and she dropped to the hard ground, tears streaming down her cheeks. Why was this mad woman doing this? "What do you want from Zane? He never did anything to you," she choked out.

"He's from Cargonia, and that's all that matters. We can't have knowledge leaked of its existence. The last thing we need is for their gods to interfere in our realm. No telling what dire events will occur."

That made no sense, but Missy didn't think anything she said would help. Acid accumulated in her stomach while she waited for the demon to appear, causing her body to weaken.

As if she'd conjured him up, heavy footsteps sounded outside, and adrenaline slammed through her. A large man appeared at the cave's entrance. Had he been here the whole time? Was he the one Vinea had been speaking with before?

"What's keeping him?" he asked Vinea.

"He'll be here," she said with such arrogance Missy wanted to smack her.

The man peered in at her and then faced Vinea. "Is that Zanedar's mate?"

Missy's heart almost stopped. This must be Raymolt. Only he would call Zane by his full name. She contemplated moving deeper into the cave to hide from view, but he'd find her eventually. There was no way out.

The only positive was that when Zane showed up—and he would—she could see him one more time.

Missy rose to her feet. "Yes, I am. Are you Raymolt?"

The demon stilled. "I see you've heard of me."

That she had. "What do you want?"

"I want to finish something that happened a hundred years ago."

Chills raced up her spine as she lifted her chin. A man like this demon would detest weakness. "I wish you luck, because you'll need it."

The beefy man with the short brown hair laughed then glanced over at Vinea. "She's cute. I will have fun with her once I kill her mate." Raymolt spit on the dirt. He then stilled. "He's coming."

Her heart dropped to her stomach. Missy couldn't breathe. She was so focused on warning Zane that she rushed to the entrance, forgetting about the electric current. When her hand hit the barrier, the current burned her palm, and the jolt once more threw her backward.

Vinea shook her head. "Why do you keep doing that? Won't you ever learn?"

"Run Zane, run!"

"I can't. I won't. This needs to end."

Zane must not have seen Raymolt step out of view behind a few bushes, because her mate rushed toward Vinea who was standing guard in front of the entrance.

She blocked his path. "Well, well, we meet again," she said. "Don't try to get in the cave to save your mate. I've erected a force field."

"Step aside," Zane commanded. Even in the face of death, he wouldn't stand down, and her love for him grew.

Missy pushed herself up onto her feet. All of a sudden, Raymolt charged up the path, and her throat tightened. "Zane! Raymolt is right behind—"

Before she could finish her sentence, Raymolt smashed a large bolder on top of Zane's head. Pain raced through her, almost as if he'd hit her. She tried to scream, but nothing came out. *"No!"* she silently wailed. *"Get up Zane."*

As if he needed to hear her in his head, Zane rose to his knees. Blood dripped down the side of his face, and Missy cried out. Raymolt watched and smiled, clearly waiting for Zane to make his move.

He stood and faced Raymolt. "I see it's time to settle old scores," Zane said with acid lacing his tone.

"Settle a score indeed. You deserve to die."

Raymolt's features contorted as he once more lifted the rock. Zane ducked his head and charged, knocking the demon to the ground. Missy wanted to cheer, but drawing attention to herself might distract her mate.

Raymolt brought the rock down on Zane's back and her mate grunted. She closed her eyes, willing him to be all right. *"Please, Zane."*

Raymolt lifted the rock again, but before he could make contact, Zane rolled to the side and jumped up. A few seconds later, he shifted into his bear form. At least now he towered over the demon.

Raymolt laughed. He dropped the boulder at his feet and held out his palm. As if she were watching her sister perform her feats of magic, flames shot out of Raymolt's hand, setting Zane's flank on fire. Her mate dropped and rolled, extinguishing the flame, but clearly Raymolt intended Zane's death to be prolonged and painful.

"Ready to die yet, bear?"

Raymolt used both palms this time to light Zane's face. He screeched as the stench of burnt flesh filled the air. Putting out the fire with his paws, he dropped down onto all fours, his back sagging.

Raymolt laughed. "I can do this all day long."

Zane growled then moved out of her view, forcing her to step closer to the electric field. Raymolt ran behind Zane's bear, lifted his arms around his neck, and held on tight. Sparks shooting out from Raymolt's arms encircled Zane.

"Zane, you can't die. You can't."

Zane grabbed his attacker's arms, and while it seemed as if he'd dug his claws into the demon, Raymolt didn't cry out. He just kept squeezing until Zane's bear collapsed. Raymolt pulled out a large ancient looking knife with some sort of serrated edge. Was this how Zane would die? With a slash to his throat?

Missy couldn't live without him. Before she could even think, she rushed out of the cave, completely forgetting about the force field. Only this time, nothing happened. No sparks, no shock. She was free! She ran directly at Raymolt, and her sudden impact was sufficient to cause him to drop the knife.

He whipped around and shot a lethal glare at Vinea. "Why did you let her out?" he spit out as he charged the goddess, leaving Zane huddled on the ground. Stunned, Missy just stood there.

Vinea's eyes widened, and she held out her hands. "I...I didn't."

The demon spun around toward Missy. "It doesn't matter. You're next to die." Raymolt looked at where he dropped the knife.

Her muscles froze, and her breath caught in her throat. The urge to run kicked in, but there was no way she'd leave Zane.

Out of options, she stuck her hand in her pocket and pulled out the potion Ophelia had given her. After seeing the demon's abilities, she doubted it would do anything, but she had to try.

What was that curse Ophelia had taught her? *The seed of the earth will...* Oh, shit. She couldn't remember.

Oh, no. He strode forward, picked up the knife, and faced her, his eyes sparkling, as if he would relish killing her. With trembling hands, she opened the drawstring on the burlap pouch. "Don't come any closer."

That sounded weak, but she didn't know what else to say. She glanced over at Zane, who wasn't moving, and her will to live almost disappeared. He was lying on his back now and while she couldn't see his chest rise, she refused to believe he was gone. If he were, wouldn't her heart stop too?

Raymolt laughed. "You gonna stop me with your bag of tricks, little girl?"

The man slowly stepped closer. For Zane and his brother, she had to do something. Missy emptied the powder in her palm and rushed toward him. Knowing she was going to die, her last wish was to cause him some pain.

She first cast out a wave of calming energy toward the beast, and while he stopped advancing toward her, his eyes still held seething hatred.

When she was within three feet of him, she threw the powder in his face then stepped back, waiting for him to kill her. She quickly recited the rest of the spell, but the words came out so soft, she barely heard them.

"What the—" the demon cried, clawing his face.

Vinea looked between the two of them. She too seemed paralyzed and in shock. His skin turned red, and his hands blistered. Raymolt dropped to his knees, his screams of agony so horrifying that she dropped the cloth sack containing the remainder of the power. Some had landed on her arm and she brushed it away. Why hadn't it burned her?

The demon's eyes turned black, and as he crumpled to the ground, smoke lifted off his body as he turned to ash. Missy just stared. How was that even possible? He'd just evaporated. All that was left was a heap of ashes. Just like Teagan had predicted.

Vinea stepped back. "Who the hell are you?" she said, fear coloring her tone.

Missy wanted to say she wasn't anyone, but even those words wouldn't come out. Every muscle seemed to have frozen.

Vinea looked over at Zane, whose arm jerked. He was alive. Missy's muscles finally shot to action, and as she rushed over to him, Vinea managed to block her path.

"He's mine," Vinea said, her lips in a sneer.

"What are you talking about?"

"I have to make sure he dies." Vinea shoved Missy so hard that she tumbled on her already sore butt, scraping her elbows and banging her head again.

Pain shot through her, and her vision blurred. Missy had to stop her. She didn't care if Vinea was some goddess. Zane couldn't die.

"Missy, I'm sor—" Zane telepathed.

"No!" She tried to rise, but immediately lost her balance and fell back down.

A knife appeared in Vinea's hand and she raised it above Zane. Missy rose to her feet and stumbled toward her. "No. Please don't kill him."

Chapter Twenty-Three

A S IF SOMEONE commanded her from above, Vinea dropped the knife and turned toward Missy, her body shaking. "I can't do it. Why can't I kill him?" Vinea looked at her hands and then back at Zane. "I am so sorry."

Missy sent out more calming thoughts. "That's good, Vinea. Now step back." Missy edged closer. She didn't trust her not to change her mind.

"But he's supposed to die. He has to. I can't go back a failure." Her eyes widened, and an ugly scowl marred her face. "What is happening to me?"

Missy had no idea what Vinea was talking about, but the woman seemed to have lost it. As long as the goddess moved away from Zane, Missy would be content. "No, he doesn't need to die, and you're anything but a failure."

Vinea's skin paled. Before Missy could reach Zane, the goddess turned around and ran down the path. Seconds later, she vanished.

Stunned, Missy kicked the dropped knife out of the way and ran to Zane. His amulet lay on the dirt, the leather strap broken. She picked it up and rushed over to him.

"Zane, can you hear me?" He didn't respond. His eyes were open and unfocused. *"Can you hear me, Zane? You need to wake up,"* she telepathed, hoping to reach him that way.

When he didn't move a muscle, Missy choked out a cry and dropped to her knees. With her hand on his head, she placed her face on his bear's chest.

Please Naliana or anyone up there who can hear me. Help me. Please. He can't die.

Even as she said the words, she knew he was gone, and the grief staggered her. Her vision turned black and pain tore through her body. The world spun, and it was as if her whole body exploded. When her vision returned, she was lying next to Zane. Only the hand on his face—or rather the paw—was covered in fur.

It took a few seconds for Missy to realize that she'd shifted. Only how was that possible? It wasn't the white moon yet. While she should be reveling in the experience, her agony over Zane's demise only made the shift more painful.

"Zane, I love you," she telepathed.

She returned her head to his chest. A minute later, sheer determination to save him made her sit up. Missy might not have powers like her sister, but she was a healer dammit. If anyone could help Zane, she could. Unfortunately, she was in her bear form and didn't have any candles, crystals, or potions with her. However, she did have her thoughts. Closing her eyes, she telepathed all of her love into healing him.

Using the rest of her energy, she rubbed her muzzle against Zane's face, careful not to press too hard. She placed her hand over the burnt fur, sending her magic through him. Where Raymolt had hit him with the rock on top of his head, a slow trickle of blood oozed out.

Missy stilled. Pumping blood meant Zane was still alive. *"Zane?"* As much as she wanted to shake him, she had to be careful. *"I love you. Please wake up."* She pressed the amulet against his throat, hoping it carried some recuperative powers. It flickered. Yes! As she held it close, the burnt orange glowed more brightly, giving her hope he'd live.

Shouts sounded far away, one of which sounded very much like Rye. Not wanting to leave Zane or shift back, she huddled as close as she could. Needing them to find her, she roared. The sound came out tinny and light, but it was her first attempt.

"This way," one of them shouted. "The caves are over here."

Thirty seconds later, four men appeared: Rye, Kalan, Connor, and Devon.

Kalan had clothes in his hands. They must have guessed Zane might shift and be in need of them.

"There they are," Rye called. He placed a hand on her back. "Missy, is that you?"

She roared and then bobbed her head.

"He's going to be okay," Rye assured her.

That was what she used to say, even if she didn't know for sure, but it always seemed to help soothe the loved ones.

Rye peeled off his shirt. "If you want to shift, you can put this on." He handed it to Kalan. "Put it in the cave for her."

Missy glanced around and spotted her tattered shorts and ripped top. The strap on one of her sandals had broken, but they were probably wearable. As much as she didn't want to leave Zane, even for a few minutes, she'd be able to help him more if she were in her human form. Lumbering over to the cave, she waited for Kalan to leave before concentrating on returning to her human form.

Izzy had told her that all she had to do was concentrate on being human, so Missy pictured herself standing in front of the mirror. Then everything happened in reverse, only faster this time. Her vision however took longer to restore than she'd hoped. When she tried to walk, she must have leaned too far to the right and fell to her knees. "Ow."

Missy remained still for another minute until she was positive she could make it out of the cave. Not needing any of the men to see her naked, she quickly pulled on Rye's shirt, which thankfully covered her butt but not much more. She gingerly stepped out of the cave and slipped on her sandals.

When she looked over, Zane had returned to his human form. Had he woken up and shifted? If he had, he was unconscious now. Someone had placed a T-shirt over his chest and the pair of pants over his hips most likely on the off chance they came across someone. The four men lifted him up and carried him down the path. Missy trotted after them, holding her shirttail close to her body, praying Zane would be all right.

ZANE'S BODY ACHED as he struggled to open his eyes. A strong scent entered his brain, but he couldn't figure out what it was or identify where he was. The image of Raymolt kicking his younger brother surfaced, and then the face of an angel appeared.

"Zane, you need to wake up," the soft voice pleaded. Someone lifted his head and placed something small and uncomfortable underneath it. Immediately, a sense of calm enveloped him. He wanted to fall back asleep and stay that way for a long time, but a hand stroked his chest and then his face. He had to see what was bringing him such pleasure.

"Open your eyes," said the voice in his head. *"I'm here, waiting for you."*

It was a woman. A very sweet woman, but one who seemed so far away. He wanted to please her, to be with her, to see her face. His leg twitched and then his fingers. Images floated in his head, but he wasn't able to put them in order—Raymolt, the ground, a woman, and then pain. Lots of pain.

What felt like sand landed on his chest, and Zane sneezed. His eyelids finally worked, and he opened them. And there she was: the most beautiful redheaded woman in the world. With a smile on her face, she hovered over him.

"Welcome back."

Zane wet his lips, not sure he could talk. This was déjà vu all over again. "Missy?"

Her eyes sparkled. "Don't tell me you've forgotten who I am already?"

"No." Just for a few bad moments. He looked around, noticing he was back in her bedroom. "How did I survive? What happened to

Raymolt and that woman?"

"I'll answer your questions later. Right now you need to rest."

Zane pushed up on his elbows, but Missy planted a hand on his chest. He lay back down. "I can't rest until you clear up a few things for me."

"Why don't you shift? You'll heal faster."

"I thought I told you I can do it myself, though I'll admit my bear is faster. Remember, shifters on Cargonia are built differently.

She smiled. "I know one part that's definitely not the same."

"Oh, yeah? What's that?" He reached toward her breast.

She swatted away his hand. "I'll show you later. Right now you need to keep quiet." Missy sighed and placed a hand on his forehead. "Your fever broke about an hour ago, but that doesn't mean you're out of the woods."

"I am out of the woods. I'm in your house!"

She chuckled. "Sorry. I keep forgetting." She explained what that phrase meant.

He raised his hand to his neck. When his fingers grasped his amulet his eyes widened. "You found it?"

"Yes. It broke when you shifted, but I retrieved it off the ground. I placed it on your chest and when the center flickered, my hopes soared."

"But why didn't the leather thong break?"

She smiled. "It did, but Rye found me a replacement."

He must have been asleep for a while. "I'll have to thank him."

"What do you remember about what happened?" she asked.

She must have forgotten about her warning for him to rest. "I remember shifting and fighting Raymolt. After that, things are a blur. Care to fill in the details?"

"I'm not sure where to begin."

"Start with who was the woman? She said she was Vanessa. I vaguely remember the face."

"We sat next to her at the regatta." Missy told him about the fake phone call from Vanessa aka Vinea. That led to a ten-minute story about how she was a goddess from the dark realm who'd lost some of her powers along the way. It was why she'd come to Silver Lake some time ago—to steal Sam's powers. She posed as Vanessa probably to find out about him.

"Who's Sam again?"

Missy waved a hand. "He's my cousin, and he can manipulate minds."

"I'd like to meet him," Zane said. Witches, or rather Wendayans, were a novel concept to him.

"That can be arranged. Anyway, after Vinea called pretending to be Izzy, I rushed to the cave where she trapped me with an electric force field."

"I remember her telling me that. How did you escape?" Zane wouldn't be surprised if her magic could cancel the electricity. Rye had told him about Kip Landon, a witch who could have short-circuited the electric flow.

"I think Vinea just wasn't able to keep the force field intact. When I saw you'd been injured, maybe even fatally, all I could think of was getting to you."

He clasped her hand and lifted her knuckles to his lips. "You are the best thing that has ever happened to me."

She smiled. "Ditto."

His head hurt, and his thoughts were still not clear, but he wanted to know more. "Why didn't Raymolt kill me?"

"Because I killed him first."

That was outrageous. "How?"

Missy glanced away then returned her gaze to him. "I previously met with Ophelia; she's a very powerful witch here in Silver Lake, one who has been around a long time. I had asked her for a potion that would stop him, but I had no idea that it would disintegrate him."

"Disintegrate?"

Missy went into detail about her ordeal, and how when she threw the powder on him and said a spell, he literally turned into ashes. She also explained that Vinea had been ready to kill Zane, but then changed her mind.

"Why?"

"I don't know. She ran off before I could ask her."

"Then what happened?" Zane could guess, but he liked talking to her.

"I ran to you. When I thought you had died, I was so distraught that I shifted into my bear form."

He studied her. "I thought you told me that humans could only shift for the first time on the white moon."

"I know. I think my intense fear of losing you caused the shift."

Now it was his turn to look off to the side. "You were stretched out next to me, weren't you?"

"Yes."

He smiled. "You are such a beautiful bear."

She sat up straighter. "How do you know? You never opened your eyes."

"I didn't need to. You're my mate, and I was able to see you in my mind."

She leaned closer. "If you say so."

He sobered. "Just so you know; it was your heat that kept me going. I felt your life, and my body responded." He reached out and squeezed her hand. "You are an amazing woman, Missy Berta. I love you."

A pretty pink blush rushed up her face. "I love you too, and I couldn't bear it if you left me." She winked. "No pun intended."

Zane chuckled then sobered. "Without your help, I'd be dead." Zane had never needed a woman's help before, but perhaps that was why she had been destined to be his fated mate. He raised his arms. "I could use a hug."

She smiled. "I could use one as well."

The moment Missy snuggled against him, the world seemed to right itself. He could finally put his brother's death to rest and start living his life. Zane didn't have to look to know his amulet was glowing red.

"Did I mention that I love you?" he asked.

She chuckled. "Perhaps a time or two, but a girl never gets tired of hearing it."

"Then I guess I'll have to tell you everyday."

She lifted her head and kissed him, softly at first and then with more passion. Missy sat up. "We shouldn't do anything. You need to gain your strength back."

"I might not be up for running a marathon or fighting a demon, but I always have enough energy to make love to you."

Missy lifted his red amulet. "If I'm to believe this stone, you want to, but are you ready?"

He placed her hand on his very hard cock. "Does that answer your question?"

"Mostly." She turned his head to the side. "Your cut has healed I see—as well as your burns."

"I'm good as new." He'd mostly healed, but he wanted Missy to believe he was one hundred percent.

"How about we take it slow, and if you tire, we'll stop?" she asked.

Zane sat up, his energy gaining strength by the minute. Thinking about being with his mate again seemed to heal him from the inside out. "It's a deal."

Chapter Twenty-Four

W HEN MISSY HAD been trapped in the cave, she'd truly believed that her time with Zane had come to an end. To be here with him now was the greatest gift she could imagine, and she wanted to enjoy every single second of it.

"I guess I'm a little overdressed." Not wanting Zane to tire, she slipped off the bed and stood a few feet from him. Keeping her gaze on his face, she kicked off her shoes.

"I'm healing faster by the second," Zane said.

"Good. By the time I'm done, you should be back to normal."

"I can't wait."

Missy lifted her T-shirt over her head and tossed him her shirt. When he moved the material to his face and inhaled, he closed his eyes and groaned. "My bear just woke up."

She loved how he always made her feel so special. "I'm hoping to wake up more than just your bear."

Zane laughed, and the sound brought intense joy. Encouraged by his sudden new health, she unzipped her shorts then turned around. Bending over, she wiggled her rear and slowly eased the shorts over her hips.

"I can't take it any longer. Come here."

"No. Be patient."

"I almost died. Or rather I might have died before you brought me back to life. I have to touch you."

Missy wanted to touch him too, but the experience would be

heightened if he could last a little bit longer. She turned around and waggled a finger at him. "Stay right there. You'll get all you want in a moment."

Zane tossed her what he probably thought was his most wickedly angry face. All she could do was laugh.

"It's not funny. I'm in agony," he said as he grabbed his hard shaft and pumped his fist up and down.

"Don't you dare come. That's my job."

He let go. "Then hurry up."

What an infuriating man. Missy stepped out of her shorts and then crawled onto the bed. "Since you're so anxious, how about helping me out of the rest of my clothes?"

"I'm glad you've come to your senses."

As if he'd never had a run in with the demon, he dragged her to the mattress and climbed on top of her. His scent had already invaded her soul, and she couldn't wait to be with him again. This time, it would be the start of a new life.

"The first thing that needs to come off is this bra," he said with a smile. Zane reached behind her, looking for the clasp. "What the—"

"This one is different from the others. It's an easy-off bra. Just slip it over my head."

"You're trying to drive me crazy."

"I am."

Zane climbed off her and helped lift the tight material over her breasts, his amulet pulsing bright.

"How about I ride you for a change?" She licked her lips, wanting to entice him more.

"I'd like that."

Because it would be easier if she took off her panties instead of having Zane contort his body to get them off, she removed them then tossed her undies on the floor. Thankfully, he was already naked. Straddling him, she pounced on his lips, savoring his sweetness. This was the man she loved, the man who was everything to her. Zane, or rather Zanedar Barons, was all goodness and power.

Missy had no doubt that if he set his mind to it, he could conquer anything.

He delved his tongue into her mouth and she dueled for position. Each thrust and parry sent her reeling, her blue sparks shooting off in every direction. Needing to feel the tug of his lips on her breasts, she lifted up and put her left nipple against his mouth. Zane sucked on it and groaned.

"You are so beautiful," he telepathed, as he swirled his tongue around one peak while he massaged the other. She wiggled her hips, sliding her slick sex across his cock. When he turned to the other breast, he clasped her hips and pressed her downward. The added friction had her aura pulsing an intense blue. Whether it was that she'd almost lost him or that her need to be with her mate was just so strong, Missy wasn't certain. What she had no doubt about was that she had to have him now.

"I need you inside me," she panted. Zane released her, allowing her to rise to her knees. Reaching between her legs, she grabbed his big cock and aimed it at her entrance. Because she was so turned on, when she dropped down, she encompassed almost all of him.

"Holy fuck!" he muttered.

His eyes had lightened so much they were practically gold. Zane once more clamped down on her hips and rose up, impaling her fully. Stretched to the max, she leaned over and kissed him. The man was such a beast.

With their lips locked, they made love to the fullest. The first few thrusts were slow and easy, but once they began their exploration, they both went wild. She grabbed his head and kissed him harder. Missy wanted him so deep inside her until they became one. Time lost all meaning as her glow grew.

Needing air, she broke the kiss. Before she could return to the wonders of his lips, Zane slid his mouth down to her neck. The thought of him biting her sharpened her teeth and caused her own scalp to itch. It took her a second to realize her bear was trying to escape, and she couldn't let that happen.

On the next thrust, Zane dug his teeth into her neck, and Missy did the same to him. The divine sensation caused her blue aura to encompass both of them and pushed her over her climactic cliff. Bolts of pleasure pierced her body, and she soared higher than she ever had in her life.

As Zane's hot seed exploded inside her, his body shot off blue sparks too, confirming they truly had joined, and Missy couldn't be any happier.

She closed her eyes and imagined she was speeding back through a portal to his world to see what life had been like in his time. He wrapped his arms around her, and held her tight, making her feel cherished and protected.

Both of them must have fallen asleep because when Zane jerked, she awoke. When Missy opened her eyes, he smiled.

"Hi there, beautiful," Zane said.

Missy chuckled. "Hi yourself, handsome. I think we need to clean up." Actually, it was a little too late for that.

She slipped off him and rushed to the bathroom. After grabbing a washcloth, she cleaned herself then returned to Zane. Once he was clean, she tossed the cloth into the bathroom sink then crawled back into bed. Truly content, she fell asleep in his arms.

LIGHT STREAMED THROUGH the window, waking her up. When she opened her eyes, Zane as looking at her with a smile on his face. "Did you sleep?" she asked.

"Better than ever."

"I think we should stay in bed all day. You can call in sick," she suggested.

"As much as I would like nothing more than to make love with you all day long, I have a lot of catching up to do and a lot of money to make. You don't want a slacker on your hands, do you?"

Zane was anything but a slacker. "No."

He tapped her butt. "Then let me up. It's past eight."

"You can't go back to work. You almost died."

"I'm good."

"Are you sure you're ready?"

Zane laughed. "Sweetheart, I was born ready."

Her cell rang, and while Missy really didn't want to get up, she did. Zane seemed eager to get back on his feet anyway.

Naked, she rushed to the living room and picked up her phone off the dining room table. "Hello?"

"Missy, this is Anna's mom, Merry."

The anguish in the woman's heart caused her to grab the top of the chair. "What's wrong?"

"Anna is in labor, and Dalton is freaking out. He took her to the hospital, and the doctor said she's due any minute."

That was earlier than planned. "We'll be right over. Thank you for calling."

As soon as she hung up, she realized she should have asked Anna's mom who else she'd notified. Not knowing if she'd contacted Izzy or Teagan, she called both and told them the good news. They said they'd meet her there.

"Who was that?" Zane asked. For a large man, he sure could sneak up on her.

"Anna's in labor. I need to go to the hospital."

"Let me get dressed," he said. "I'll come with you."

She loved that he was willing to be with her and her friend. "I thought you had to go to work."

"It can wait. I want to support you."

"You are the best."

Missy dressed quickly and in less than fifteen minutes they'd arrived at the hospital. In the waiting room, Missy spotted Anna's mom and rushed up to her. "How is she?"

"I don't know. Dalton is in there with her. He said as soon as the baby is born, he'll let us know."

Elana and Kalan were there also. A few minutes later, Teagan, Kip, Rye, and Izzy charged in. A minute after that Mom and Dad

VELLA DAY

arrived. Needless to say, the waiting room was rather crowded.

Mom came up to them and held out her hand. "Hello, you must be Zane."

Missy should have introduced them.

"Yes, I am. Nice to finally meet you."

"I'm glad to see you've recovered."

"I have, thanks to Missy."

Her mom hugged her and then Zane. "I'm so happy for you two. How's Anna?"

Before she could even answer, a beaming Dalton rushed in. "Baby Tanya has arrived. She's six pounds three ounces and is twenty inches long. Anna is just glowing."

They all surrounded him and gave him their congratulations. "When can we see her?" Elana asked.

"In a few minutes."

The room exploded with cheer, and soon the conversation turned to Izzy, who was the next to deliver. Not that Missy was jealous, but she'd always dreamed of having a large family. For years, she'd been resigned to the fact that at her age it just wasn't going to happen. Now that she'd found Zane, the possibility of a family was more real.

One by one they visited with Anna. Because it was clear she needed her rest, Missy told her friend that they'd be over in a few days to see how she was doing. Not wanting to upset her, Missy didn't bring up the trouble Zane had with Vinea and the demon. Later, when her friend was feeling better, she'd tell her the whole story.

"You up for a run?" Zane asked as soon as they slipped into the car.

"You nearly died two days ago, not to mention you have been unconscious most of the time since. You don't need to be running."

"I beg to differ. I should be in my bear form to finish the healing process."

"You said you don't need your bear to heal."

"I don't, but he does a better job."

"Okay, but no running full out."

"Ah, so this is how it's going to be? You're going to boss me around?" He winked.

Missy laughed. "Hardly. I imagine if you play your cards right, you can get me to do anything you want."

"If there is one thing I'm good at, it's playing cards. In my day, we didn't have much to do at night, so we often played poker."

"I'll keep that in mind." She wasn't sure if he really understood what she meant, but that was part of Zane's charm.

The best place to run free was close to Silver Lake. The land was flat, which meant it wouldn't tax Zane. Missy wasn't positive he was one hundred percent, though after the amazing lovemaking session, she didn't know why she doubted him.

Once they reached the lake, they quickly undressed and stashed their clothes on top of the boulders nearby. Missy then lifted off his amulet and tucked it under his clothes. "We can't lose this again."

Zane smiled. "No."

Just seeing his naked body again had her wanting to slam him against the rock and do him right there.

"Why don't you?" he asked with way too much cheer in his voice.

"Why don't I what?"

"Did you forget I can hear your thoughts when they are about me?"

Heat raced up her face. "I guess I need to be more careful."

Zane approached her and pressed her lightly against the cool rock slab. "I'm always willing."

"I know." She glanced to the sky. "The moon isn't quite full. Do you think this will work?" She didn't know why she was so unsure of herself. After all, she had shifted once.

"I don't see why not, but just in case, close your eyes." Missy did as he suggested. "I want you to picture your head on my chest."

"Like when you were injured and we were lying side by side?"

"Yes." She could see where he was going with this. "I don't feel anxious anymore. Thank you."

He grabbed her hand. "Open your eyes."

"Now what?"

"Run with me, clearing your head of all bad thoughts. Embrace the wonders of being a bear."

Missy didn't have time to think before he took off, practically dragging her along next to him. He let go seconds before he shifted, and a trickle of fear seeped in that she wouldn't be able shift at will.

Then a strong ache nearly crushed her as her bones cracked, and her vision turned black.

"Relax," said Zane's voice in her head. *"I'm here."*

Knowing she wasn't alone helped ease the transition from human to bear. A few seconds later, she was on all fours.

Zane stopped, stood on two feet, and roared. Had she been in her human form, she would have laughed.

"Come on," he telepathed.

As she lumbered after him, all of her anxieties disappeared. When she'd shifted the last time, she'd only moved a few feet. Now she had the chance to run.

The sun had just set, and the air was cooling off. Once more, Zane stopped in the middle of a large field and rolled on his back. Wanting to play, she jumped on top of him. Being considerably smaller than Zane, it was easy to rub against him without doing any harm. In turn, Zane was even gentler. Missy's bear scooted up his body and rubbed her nose against his. Even in their bear forms, her loved poured out of her.

Some squirrels ran past them, and Missy decided Zane had enough excitement for one day.

"Want to go for a swim?" she telepathed.

"Human or bear? Either way works for me."

While the shifters thought nothing of nudity, it would take her a while to get used to it. However, what better way to begin than by swimming with Zane?

Human. Race you to the lake in my bear form, she telepathed.

Once she rolled off him, Zane headed straight for the water. When he was less than ten feet away, he shifted into his human form. Without breaking stride, he dove into the lake.

There was no turning back now. Concentrating on her human form, she changed with little effort this time. While her bones cracked and her vision blurred somewhat, the pain was far less. She looked around to make sure no one was there and then joined Zane. Life with him was going to be such an adventure.

The End

Don't forget to sign up for my newsletter to receive three free books, as well as up-to-date information on my stories. If you prefer to only receive notices regarding my releases, follow me on BookBub.
http://smarturl.it/o4cz93?IQid=MLite
bookbub.com/authors/vella-day

I hoped you enjoyed Missy and Zane's story. Up next is Vinea and Devon's story—MELTING HER WOLF'S HEART.
Here's the first chapter.

Chapter One

V INEA SUMMER'S BEST friend, EmmaLee Donovan, leaned
forward and rested her elbows on her knees. Her dark blonde
hair hung down over her face, but it failed to block the circles under
her eyes. "You've got to go back to Silver Lake, Vinea, or the guilt
will eat you alive."

Vinea jumped off the bed in her efficiency apartment and paced.
"And leave you?"

Not only was EmmaLee her best friend, she might be her only
one. Vinea wouldn't feel as guilty about leaving if EmmaLee's
boyfriend didn't use her as a punching bag. That kind of violence cut
Vinea to the core.

To think six months ago she'd never experienced compassion on
any level. Now guilt and the desire to make amends were her
constant companions. Ever since Devon McKinnon held her down
under water against the pink quartz, she'd changed, erasing the
goddess of the dark realm forever. In its place was a down-and-out
waitress, taking orders from demanding people then smiling about it.
No wonder her boss, Androf, god of the dark, told her killing her
wasn't enough of a punishment for her failures. To him, developing
a conscience was worse than death. Well, the laugh was on him. She
might be staying in a dump, but at least she'd stopped hurting
people.

EmmaLee stood and hugged her. "You have to go back and
make things right. It hurts me to see you like this."

"You're right. I do need to set some things straight, but so do you."

Her friend waved a dismissive hand. "Slater doesn't mean it when he hits me. He just drinks too much sometimes, that's all. He's real sorry afterward."

In the past, Vinea wouldn't have thought a thing about such violence, but not anymore. "He's no good for you. Trust me, I know bad when I see it."

EmmaLee returned to her chair and crossed her arms. They'd had this discussion many times. "Slater's a good man at heart." She looked up at her. "At least he's nothing like those evil beings you were with."

Her sweet friend was so naïve to the ways of the world, and in some ways that was a good thing. "That's not saying much. They are gods after all. But just because Slater is a mere moral doesn't mean he can't hurt others as much as gods can."

EmmaLee and she were an unlikely pair, but it was her friend's love and belief in the supernatural that had bonded them in the first place. Vinea could still remember the look of awe on her face when EmmaLee had caught her changing her clothes with a wave of her hand. Instead of freaking out, EmmaLee wanted to know more. Desperate to talk to someone about all the changes Vinea had been experiencing, she told her everything.

Vinea stabbed a hand through her hair. "You're right. I hurt Devon badly, and I need to explain to him why."

"From what you said, you hurt a lot more people than him."

Vinea laughed. "You're not going to let me forget are you?"

EmmaLee jumped up again and rushed over. "I'm sorry. I didn't mean to bring up the bad memories."

"It's okay. I was a bad person back then; a real bad person. When I was a goddess in the dark realm, I thought nothing of doing unspeakable acts. It's hard for me to even believe I was that person."

Her friend hugged her again. "What can I do to help?"

Vinea didn't deserve her friendship. "Stay away from Slater."

ONCE EMMALEE LEFT with the promise of leaving the SOB, Vinea changed into some warmer clothes. Billard might not be very far from Silver Lake, but the Tennessee mountains were a lot colder than north Georgia. Now that she was living in the human world, she had to deal with these temperature changes.

Before Vinea left, she called her boss at the diner and explained that she needed some time off.

"How long will you be gone?" Warren asked. Thankfully, he sounded more concerned than pissed.

"I'm not sure." How long did it take someone to right a lot of wrongs? A week? A month? Or would it take a lifetime? "To be fair to the girls, maybe you should just replace me."

"I'm sorry to hear that, Vinea, but I lost Carol because so many waitresses needed a break. Poor girl had a breakdown after working double shifts for a month. If you come back sooner than planned, stop in. I might be able to squeeze you into the rotation."

Vinea smiled. "I appreciate it."

What a change Warren was from Androf. One was kind and accommodating and the other pure evil. While it sickened her to leave EmmaLee and the rest of the staff at Billard Eatery, it could take weeks if not months to do what she needed to.

Because she didn't have a car, she figured no one would be harmed if she teleported to Silver Lake. She still did possess a few of her goddess talents.

Picturing her destination, she disappeared from Billard and reappeared across the street from McKinnon and Associates in Silver Lake, Tennessee. Darn. Her aim was a little off. Even though she'd pictured the front entrance, she landed a hundred feet away. It seemed the longer she resided on earth, the more erratic her talents became. At least she hadn't appeared in a crowd of people. That would have caused all sorts of problems.

Vinea inhaled, ready to confront her past. The outcome might not turn out to be what she hoped, but she had to try. A lot depended on whether Devon would even be here. From what he'd told her, he only came to Silver Lake when his brother needed an extra hand. Most of the time, he worked in Pittsburgh. Either she'd have to visit him there once she learned his address, or she'd have to wait in Silver Lake until he returned.

Stop procrastinating!

As she crossed the street, she surveyed the cars in the lot. Tucked behind a larger vehicle was a white truck like the kind Devon drove. Vinea crossed her fingers, hoping this truck was his.

Once at the front door, she rang the bell. A lot could happen in six months, but she hoped Lexi still manned the desk. Vinea might have lied to Devon repeatedly, but at least she hadn't tried to steal his powers—like she had from Sam Pompley—Lexi's mate. While she hadn't harmed Lexi, she doubted the woman harbored any positive thoughts toward her. More than anything, she wanted to help Sam's mate in some way to show her that she was no longer an evil goddess.

"May I help you?" came the voice through the intercom.

Vinea looked up at the camera. Didn't Lexi recognize her? "Hey, Lexi. It's me, Vinea. Is Devon around?" Good. That sounded a lot calmer than she felt.

"Vinea? What the hell? You have some nerve to just—"

Her voice became muffled as if she'd placed a hand over the microphone. Vinea strained to hear what a deep voice in the background was saying. The words *interfere* and *Devon* were all she could make out.

"Vinea? Give me a minute. I'll check." Her tone, while professional, was loaded with controlled anger. She didn't blame Lexi one bit for being upset. Actually, Vinea deserved a lot more, along with a quick disconnect.

While she waited, she pictured her last encounter with Devon, and chills raced up her spine. Sure it was cold out, but this was more than a reaction to winter. It was sexual in nature—a feeling she had yet to fully understand.

A possible explanation was that only part of their last interaction had been bad—the part where he'd almost drowned her—but the part where he was naked had been oh so good.

The intercom crackled and Lexi's voice came through. "Devon is in an important meeting and can't be disturbed." She sounded triumphant.

"Can't or won't?" That came out snarky but tough shit she was trying to make amends here and couldn't even get past the door. She expected some hostility but she had hoped curiosity about her being there might have gotten her passed the door.

A disgusted huff came over the mic. "Does it really matter? Leave, you're not wanted here." With that the intercom went silent.

That didn't go well. It didn't matter. She didn't need an open door to get inside. Once she made certain no one was watching, she disappeared. Too bad when she reappeared, she was in Connor's office though she swore she'd pictured where Devon worked. Whoops.

Connor looked up. To his credit, he managed to school his features. "Vinea?" He shoved back his chair and stood. "What the hell are you doing here? Haven't you done enough damage?" So much for not showing his emotions.

Her stomach churned at the censure. Sure, she deserved it, but being the recipient of such distain still hurt. "I'll admit I lied a few times." *And stole, and...*

"You did a lot more than that. You tried to ruin Sam, not to mention Devon."

Devon? "I might not have been honest with him, but I never tried to hurt him."

"You hurt him just the same." Connor stepped toward the door and held it open. "Just get out."

"I think I'll go the same way I came."

With a nod, she disappeared. This time, her aim was better and she appeared in the correct office, not that she expected the reception to go any better.

Devon's head was down, and it was as if he wasn't aware she was there. Her body, however, was going crazy with spikes of sexual need. He looked so fucking hot. Sure, he had more lines around his eyes, and he had lost weight, but he still looked good.

"Devon." Her throat nearly closed up at saying his name.

He didn't look up. "I told Lexi not to let you in." His words came out harsher than she had hoped.

A snarky remark shot to her lips, but she stopped herself. Now wasn't the time for the old Vinea to surface. "She didn't let me in. I just kind of appeared." When he didn't look up, she continued. "I came to apologize."

"Apology accepted. Now go away."

Damn, but this was harder than she thought. "When you dipped me in the water, the pink quartz cleansed me."

He finally looked up, but his eyes held distrust. "Is that so? Is that why you held Missy captive in a cave while you lured Zane to his death? And that was after you were cleansed."

The words wouldn't form. "Zane died?"

When she left him, he was merely unconscious. Surely his bear would have healed him.

"No. He survived, but you thought about killing him. Why?"

Her quick comebacks seemed to have disappeared with the cleansing. "It took a while for that to work. Like I told you that day six months ago, the pink quartz works well on Changelings. Maybe I was so evil that it took longer, but eventually all my bad thoughts disappeared. I swear."

Something in her voice must have resonated with him, because his features softened. "I'm happy for you then. I suppose you came here for my help?"

"No! I want to help you."

He leaned back and laughed. "You? Help me? Unless you can infiltrate the Changeling's headquarters and take them all out, I don't see how you can be of service."

She stood up straighter. "I don't kill anymore."

"Oh, really? Well that's good to know. What about stealing and lying?"

"No." It was better to keep her answers short. "Listen, can we grab a cup of coffee or something. We really need to talk."

A knock sounded on his door and Kip Landon stuck his head in. "Oh, sorry. I didn't know you had company." His eyes narrowed slightly before returning his focus back to Devon. "Rye wanted to let you know the meeting's about to begin."

Devon pushed back his chair. "Get the hell out, Vinea. You can leave the same way you came."

The hatred rolled off him. Each wave cut her deeply, but it was what she deserved. She'd hurt him more than she realized. With that she disappeared.

It didn't mean she was gone however. She had to find a way for Devon to see how much her heart and soul had changed. That meant this journey was going to take a lot longer.

PACK WARS (Paranormal)
Training Their Mate (book 1)
Claiming Their Mate (book 2)
Rescuing Their Virgin Mate (book 3)
Box Set (books 1-3)
Loving Their Vixen Mate (book 4)
Fighting For Their Mate (book 5)
Enticing Their Mate (book 6)

MONTANA PROMISES (Full length contemporary)
Promises of Mercy (book 1)
Foundations For Three (book 2)
Montana Fire (book 3)
Hart To Hart (book 4)
Burning Seduction (book 5)
Montana Promises Box Set (books 1-3)

ROCK HARD, MONTANA (contemporary novellas)
Montana Desire (book 1)
Awakening Passions (book 2)

HIDDEN HILLS SHIFTERS (Paranormal)
An Unexpected Diversion (book 1) – FREE
Bare Instincts (book 2)
Shifting Destinies (book 3)
Embracing Fate (book 4)
Promises Unbroken (book 5)

SOUTHERN SHIFTERS KINDLE WORLDS
Bear 'N Dirty

WERES & WITCHES OF SILVER LAKE
A Magical Shift (book 1)
Catching Her Bear (book 2)
A Surge of Magic (book 3)
The Bear's Forbidden Wolf (book 4)
Her Reluctant Bear (book 5)
Freeing His Tiger (book 6)
Protecting His Wolf (book 7)
Waking Her Bear (book 8)

Author Bio

Want 3 FREE books? Sign up for my newsletter.

COPY AND PASTE INTO YOUR BROWSER:
http://smarturl.it/o4cz93?IQid=MLite

Check out my latest interview on You Tube:
youtube.com/watch?v=sQo5pyyVMDI

Not only do I love to read, write, and dream, I'm an extrovert. I enjoy being around people and am always trying to understand what makes them tick. Not only must my books have a happily ever after, I need characters I can relate to. My men are wonderful, dynamic, smart, strong, and the best lovers in the world (of course).

I believe I am the luckiest woman. I do what I love and I have a wonderful, supportive husband, who happens to be hot!

Fun facts about me

(1) I'm a math nerd who loves spreadsheets. Give me numbers and I'll find a pattern.
(2) I just moved to Costa Rica and live on the beach!
(3) I also like to exercise. Yes, I know I'm odd.

I love hearing from readers either on FB or via email (hint, hint).

Social Media Sites

Website:

www.velladay.com

FB:

www.facebook.com/vella.day.90

Twitter:

@velladay4

Gmail:

velladayauthor@gmail.com